# ANSWERS

### *to*

# LUCKY

Also by Howard Owen

*Littlejohn*
*Fat Lightning*

# ANSWERS

## *to*

# LUCKY

*Howard Owen*

HOWARD OWEN

HarperCollins*Publishers*

HarperCollins books may be purchased for educational, business, or sales promotional use. For information please write: Special Markets Department, HarperCollins Publishers, Inc., 10 East 53rd Street, New York, NY 10022.

FIRST EDITION

*Designed by Nina Gaskin*

---

**Library of Congress Cataloging-in-Publication Data**

Owen, Howard
    Answers to Lucky / Howard Owen.—1st ed.
        p.    cm.
    ISBN 0-06-017312-2
    I. TITLE.
    PS3565.W552A82        1996
    813'.54—dc20                                                95-42528

---

96 97 98 99 00  ❖/HC  10 9 8 7 6 5 4 3 2 1

To E. F. and Van,
who gave fatherhood a good name

Lucky is freezing.

The cold seems to be seeping out of the open pit in front of him. His back hurts from bracing against it.

The hands of his family members on both sides feel warm, but Lucky welcomes the cold, or at least some form of discomfort, as only proper.

To his left, he sees several men and women with notepads and a variety of cameras, all in a row and looking like the advance guard of some strange army, held at bay by two grim-faced deputies. The preacher's leaden words are punctuated by mechanical whirs and clicks.

It is all that keeps this from being just another country burial, another grave to be filled on a nameless, cheerless little rise above a turbid river, where almost all the tombstones share a single, terse, Calvinist word: SWEATT.

Lucky stares out at the water, recently exposed by a windstorm that blew the last leaves off the sycamores, as the mourners mumble through "Shall We Gather at the River?" Then it's over. Lucky and the rest struggle out of folding chairs sinking into the mushy ground. A few distant cousins and old acquaintances speak, but they are more articulate with cakes and pies and casseroles than words.

With nothing else to do or say, the family gets into the black funeral-home limousine and leaves. Lucky sees, at the edge of his vision, men with shovels move in like buzzards as the first drop of rain hits the windshield.

Going back, past long-closed country stores and fields gone to broom straw and sandspurs, they come upon a house. It is typical of its time and place: one story, tin roof, asbestos siding, screened front porch with cast-iron glider, yard given to nut grass and sand.

They stop beside it while an oncoming school bus yields eight children of elementary-school age. Six of them go down a rutted road to the left, headed for another farmhouse a quarter-mile away. The other two, both boys, cross in front of the bus, hell-bent for the house beside the road.

Lucky follows them with his eyes. They are perhaps eight years old. Both have schoolbooks with them, and one is carrying a scarred, child-sized football tucked under his arm. They are oblivious to the drizzle now falling. Even before they reach the house, the one with the ball has taken it into his right hand and thrown it high in the air. The other boy drops his books, circles once, and catches it as it descends just shy of the porch, then throws it back up into the gray sky.

They are close enough in size that a passerby can't tell which is older. They are brown-haired and fearless-looking, two peas in a pod, as Genie would say.

The bus moves forward and so does the funeral procession. The boys stop their impromptu game, the one with the ball brushing his hair out of his face as he stares for the briefest instant directly at Lucky. Then he turns and throws the ball to his brother and they resume playing.

Lucky looks back as they pass, and he sees an older man step from a toolshed next to the house. The boys run toward him, fast enough to outrun raindrops.

For the first time all day, Lucky Sweatt cries.

★★★ **1** ★★★

Lucky was upside-down under the sink, trying to keep from calling a plumber, when the phone rang. He could tell, without even concentrating, that Barbara was talking to his father. Something about the too-cheerful lilt in her voice. She was a sweet-natured woman, but in a low-key way. When he could hear the sugar dripping on the linoleum tile, he knew she was trying too hard.

"Just a minute," she said. "I'll get him."

She leaned under. Lucky could see her past the bend in the drainpipe. She didn't look cheerful.

"It's him," she said softly.

Tommy Sweatt and Lucky talked about twice a year, counting the trip Lucky and his family made down to Port Campbell over Christmas. Usually, at some point during the summer, Genie would put Tommy on the phone when she called. Lucky could tell that his mother practically had to drag him out of the La-Z-Boy to get him on the line.

"When you going to come see us?" Tommy would bellow in his Foghorn Leghorn voice, Lucky knowing damn well that it had been his father's turn to visit for twelve years. When he'd tell him that, it would usually put an end to that particular avenue of conversation, and Lucky and Tommy weren't good at sustaining a lengthy chat about the Braves or the Redskins or Carolina basketball, or anything else either one of them had any interest in. Before long, Lucky could practically see Tommy waving to Genie to take the phone back, which she would finally do. Lucky and his father had little to say to each other in person, and the phone just seemed to make it worse.

So, when Lucky learned that Tommy Sweatt himself was on the phone, that he had actually dialed the eleven numbers that separated them as effectively as an ocean, he knew he had to leave the inner workings of the garbage disposal for another time.

"What's the matter?" he asked by way of greeting. He saw Barbara shake her head and leave the room, exasperated at either him or Tommy or both.

"What's the matter is, Tom Ed needs you," Tommy said.

Sometimes, Lucky thought, the old man could make a dog laugh.

"He wants me to be his lieutenant governor?"

"He needs family with him now," Tommy said. "He needs somebody that's smart and can talk and all. And that Jackson boy had to drop out. Gallstones."

Jackie Jackson had been in high school with Tom Ed and Lucky. Tom Ed still played golf and poker with him, and he'd been his campaign driver every election he'd ever entered. Tom Ed saw him as a combination friend and good-luck charm; he hadn't ever lost an election, and Jackie Jackson had always been his driver. Besides, Jackie knew every place that served good barbecue in the whole state of North Carolina, and he claimed to know two that could make lemon pie better than most people's mothers could. And Tom Ed felt that he could trust him.

"He needs a driver."

"He needs family," Tommy said again, louder. "He's about to catch that damn Cameron. He don't need to be worrying about hiring somebody outside at this point in time."

Tommy had a knack for latching on to the worst buzz phrases. Even Tom Ed had been heard to say that if Tommy used "politically correct" once more, he was going to come out in favor of the ACLU.

"Why didn't he call me himself? He's got my number."

"He asked me to," Tommy said. "He said he was scared if he

asked you, you'd just think he was trying to take advantage. On account of the loan and all."

You shouldn't ever underestimate Tommy Sweatt, Lucky thought. He was the one that taught Tom Ed about knowing when to call in your favors. Do 'em like nothing could please you more, he'd tell the boys when they weren't old enough to know what the hell he was talking about, but then remember who you done 'em for and make sure they know that you know when the right time comes.

When Barbara and Lucky first decided they wanted to open a bed-and-breakfast in a part of Virginia where bedding strangers in your home was a sign of need, they spent nine months of weekends and weeknights searching from Roanoke to Bristol. Finally, in December, ten years before, they had come across the old Foster house in Willow Cove. The heirs were asking $195,000 for a place with eight bedrooms that could be made into twelve, oil heat, and termites. But it was on Route 11, which wrapped itself like a vine around the newer I-81 all down the valley. You could see it from the interstate. And by then they'd lived in the area long enough to know a lot of cheap construction help.

What the bank wanted was $60,000 down, and they only had $25,000 plus the $5,000 or so profit they figured they could get if they sold their brick rancher. One day Lucky came home and found Barbara crying for the first time in years. There was nothing to do except go see Tom Ed.

Lucky knew beforehand what would happen. He'd spill his guts to Tom Ed, then have to listen while his brother did the dance about Kyle's and Kevin's educations and taking care of Tommy and Genie. Finally, if he did it all right, Tom Ed would make him a loan, get teary-eyed doing it, like nothing in his life so far had given him as much pleasure as loaning Lucky $30,000—on Tom Ed's terms, of course. Hell, it could have been worse, Lucky thought. He could have let me crawl around and then told me he just didn't have it to spare.

It had taken Lucky and Barbara most of the past ten years to pay Tom Ed back, but now the Willow Inn had to turn guests away. Lucky knew it was Barbara's dream come true, that and the kids, and he had to occasionally admit that it was his, too, clogged toilets and leaky roof notwithstanding.

Lucky also knew that you don't just let somebody make your dream come true and then not be there when they want a little extra interest on the loan. Tommy knew exactly what he was doing; there wasn't any way out.

"Let me talk to Barbara. I'll call you back in an hour."

"Don't call me. Call him. He needs you, son. It's a shame the way you shut yourself off from him."

Lucky told him to give his love to Genie. Tommy grunted and hung up.

Barbara threw a fit, as Lucky figured she would, but it was the end of the big tourist season. The last of the mountain fall color was going fast, and they'd be fortunate to rent two rooms a day until the Romantic Winter Getaway crowd started drifting in during late December.

Lucky knew that Barbara wasn't bitching about the hard work. The way he figured it, she and the kids could probably run the place without him ever lifting a finger.

He talked about obligation, but Barbara wasn't buying.

"You just want to get into Mr. Peabody's Wayback Machine," she said. "You think you can change everything and make it come out right."

He laughed her off, even while he thought, Maybe not right. Maybe just not wrong forever.

And there was the outside chance that Tom Ed was doing more than just cashing in a chip.

Lucky got Tom Ed's number at the Sheraton in Raleigh from Lucinda, his wife, who answered the phone back in Port Campbell.

"Anything you want me to tell him?" he asked her when she came back with the number.

"Yes. Tell him to send me a picture. I can't remember what he looks like."

When Lucky got through to Tom Ed's room, a voice on the other line yelled, "What?!"

"Tom Ed Sweatt, please."

"Goddamn, he's busy. Call back later."

"Tell him it's his brother."

Lucky could hear the man shout something about "your damn brother, for Chrissake," and Tom Ed came on the phone.

"Harry's a little excited," Tom Ed said, laughing. "How ya doin', Bo?"

Tom Ed called everybody "Bo," even some women, partly because he still wasn't good at names, even after all the campaigning. He had a knack, though, for making you think he knew your name.

"I hear you need a driver."

Tom Ed sighed, exaggeratedly, it seemed to Lucky. "I told that old son of a bitch not to tell you that," he said finally.

"But you do need a driver."

"I need somebody to talk to, somebody who won't tell the *Charlotte Observer* every damn time I go to the bathroom," he said.

"I don't know anybody at the *Charlotte Observer.*"

"Then you're hired," Tom Ed laughed. "The pay's bad, but the hours are long. I tell you what, though, Bo, we gonna have some fun. We gonna thow some rats out of the barn!"

When Tom Ed talked like that, Lucky felt like he was talking to the old man, but he knew that it was just Tom Ed picking up what was best about Tommy Sweatt, the loud, likable, irrepressible presence, and making it part of "the whole package."

"So when can you be here?"

"Tuesday, I think."

"Damn, that's three days. Sure you can't get here sooner, Bo? All right; Tuesday then. Harry! Where we at on Tuesday?"

Harry sounded irritated.

"We're gonna be in Pinecrest," Tom Ed said. "We goin' to a pig pickin'."

"See you there," he told Tom Ed, who was already talking to Harry about something else and didn't acknowledge his good-bye.

Lucky first heard of Dr. Nate Crowell and the Reverend Gary Thorne on Tuesday morning, on the radio, before he'd even stopped at Hardee's for breakfast on the way out of Willow Cove.

Dr. Crowell worked at a clinic in Charlotte that performed abortions. He'd made a small mistake and then a big one.

After his clinic had been attacked by antiabortionists, led by the Reverend Thorne, he'd gotten himself quoted in the *Charlotte Observer* as calling the protestors "misinformed Nazis." So they started picketing his house. They'd been picketing it for four weeks, the newscaster said. A neighbor told the police that the protestors had left for six days, then apparently had come back with a vengeance before dawn that Tuesday.

What happened next was up for debate. Dr. Crowell, trying to leave his driveway to go to work, either (a) gunned the engine and willfully plowed into a group of picketers, or (b) panicked when set upon by lunatics with signs and was just trying to escape in his car.

Either way, the Reverend Gary Thorne, founder and leader of the Church of the Rock's twenty thousand members, lay dead in Dr. Crowell's driveway, crushed under the right-front wheel of Dr. Crowell's Acura Legend.

Lucky picked up the story in bits and pieces as he drove down out of the brilliant color of the mountains, crossing the Blue Ridge Parkway and descending into the North Carolina Piedmont, where the leaves were still holding back their best hues.

The Reverend Gary Thorne and the Church of the Rock were based in Gastonia, twenty miles west of Charlotte, and the late minister had claimed two dozen other churches around the state, plus a Sunday morning gospel hour that was carried by five TV stations. He was, Lucky gathered, a man who felt that he had Inside Information and was therefore not much inclined toward compromise.

The church's members, Lucky would discover by watching the six o'clock news, were also fond of picketing bookstores that sold any of the dozens of titles the church deemed unfit. They spent tens of thousands of dollars opposing politicians they didn't agree with. And they saved their most lethal venom for what they called the "right-to-deathers."

A neighbor said Dr. Crowell was the gentlest man in the world, then a spokesman for the Church of the Rock vowed that "the

Reverend Gary Thorne, who died that babies might live," would not perish in vain.

Lucky also learned, on his drive to Pinecrest, that this was the second time in two days that the Reverend Thorne and his church had made news in Charlotte and North Carolina. The day before, the now-late reverend had endorsed Tom Ed Sweatt for governor.

Lucky got to the Pinecrest Inn just after one o'clock. His stiff leg almost betrayed him when he stepped out of the car into the sand that had piled up next to the curb and that gave under his weight. A sign on the marquee out front said, WELCOME TOM ED SWEATT.

A clerk showed Lucky to the Sweatt for Governor suite. The door was open; the room looked as if a hurricane had hit it. You could have walked across to where Tom Ed was sitting, his back to the door, without ever touching anything but paper. There were newspapers and computer printouts and handbills and various other paper products all over the place.·

Tom Ed sat in one of the chairs at a table overlooking a pool that hadn't been drained yet and was covered by a film of pine straw. He seemed to be giving an interview to a young woman who scribbled away in a notepad. A tape recorder was on the table between them.

Lucky hadn't seen his brother since Christmas. They usually crossed paths uneasily once or twice a year, but it occurred to Lucky that he hadn't really looked at Tom Ed for a while. A few years had slipped away somewhere.

When they were little boys, people couldn't tell them apart. Watching Tom Ed now, though, in those few seconds before he got into the middle of everything and could still just watch, the differences were what struck Lucky.

Back then, Lucky could walk into their room, see Tom Ed, and think he was looking at himself in a mirror. But now there were the frown wrinkles that the campaign posters and TV makeup people hid. There was the extra weight. Christ, he must weigh at least 230, Lucky thought, reflexively sucking in his somewhat inferior beer gut. When Tom Ed was in high school and college and later when he played pro ball, he had possessed a kind of Larry Bird thick-legged white-boy athleticism that was almost invisible now. And there was the hair, a slick, graying pompadour that seemed to claim every last ounce of what boy there still was in Tom Ed, and almost sent Lucky out the door and back to Willow Cove.

Lucky looked at Tom Ed's three-piece Armani sharkskin suit and then at his own Levi's, work shirt, and corduroy jacket, and the contrast was pretty much complete. Lucky felt, right then, like some poor-relation cousin or nephew, ten years younger, fifty pounds lighter, walking with a slight limp, the kind who looked up rich relatives to borrow money from.

There were two other people in the room.

One was a dark-complected, thin man who appeared to be in his late twenties or early thirties. He was smoking a cigarette and talking on the phone at what seemed to be the top of his voice. Lucky recognized the voice.

The other one was about the same age, blond and a little over-weight. He was talking to a fax machine.

"C'mon, you bastard, send," he'd growl at the machine, which did nothing. "They were supposed to have sent that shit forty-five minutes ago."

Nobody saw Lucky until Tom Ed got up to get a Coke.

"Hey, here he is!" he said, coming up in a hurry while the other two men turned to stare. He grabbed Lucky and gave him the kind of hug that he was prone to give county commissioners and legis-lators and preachers all over the state.

"Good to see you, Bo. I need some family here."

He introduced Lucky to the dark one, who had just slammed the phone down and was Harry Mavredes, and to the blond, who was Barry Maxwell.

"The M&M twins, Harry and Barry," Tom Ed more or less roared as they shifted their feet, begrudging these seconds they could have spent yelling at somebody over the phone, Lucky sus-pected. "My heart and brains."

After spending twelve days in the company of Harry Mavredes

and Barry Maxwell, Lucky would come to realize that neither one of them would have given the other a cup of water if he had been on fire, for all the talk about "Harry and Barry, the M&M twins." When it was all over, they both disappeared, and Lucky never heard a word from either one of them again.

Harry was the campaign manager; Barry was in charge of media relations. Lucky soon realized that Tom Ed wasn't lying when he said they were the heart and brains of the operation, but he sometimes would wonder whom all the effort was really for.

Tom Ed let the reporter ask him a few more questions, then he got up suddenly, as if he were late to be somewhere.

"Let's hit it," he said. "We got a pig pickin' to go to." Harry and Barry both reached for their coats. They actually had an hour and a half before they made their appearance at Axel Sprague's, it turned out, but Tom Ed confided later that he just didn't like newspaper reporters. "I'm more a TV kind of guy," he said and grinned.

Axel Sprague was the meanest, most powerful man in the state legislature, Tom Ed said, and he was determined that, if he didn't have his endorsement, at least he wasn't going to have his curse.

"Hurt your leg?" Harry Mavredes asked Lucky when they were walking to the van. It was the first thing he'd said to him yet in a normal speaking voice.

Lucky wondered if he wouldn't have to mash Harry's mouth at some point.

★★★ **2** ★★★

Tommy Wayne Sweatt and Eugenia Canfield Balcom were married in 1945, two months after the war ended. They told everybody they'd been married for four months, which was how long they figured Genie had been pregnant.

Nobody believed it would last. The usual relationship of Balcoms to Sweatts in Scots County was that Sweatts would come to Balcoms because they had cut someone and needed a lawyer or they had to have an extra month's grace on their feed bill.

Chief among those who didn't believe it would last, didn't even believe it was there to begin with, was Dorothy Canfield Balcom, Genie's mother.

The surprise twins were born on Valentine's Day, 1946. When Tommy found out he had two boys, he left the waiting room without a word, and no one except his brother Felton and whoever else was frequenting the river-rat bars saw him for two days. Genie's mother and brothers begged her to get a divorce, claiming desertion. Her brother James said Tommy was guilty of "conduct becoming a Sweatt." But Genie wouldn't budge.

Tommy came back to the hospital on a Friday, with bloodshot eyes and various foreign matter in his hair. Dorothy Balcom was sleeping outside Genie's room. His footsteps woke her up; she knew who it was before she even opened her eyes.

Felton had come with him, but he hung back a bit. Tommy's

brother was on his way to doing time in Central Prison, but he was a little hesitant about going any farther toward the short, wiry woman standing between them and Genie's door.

She called Tommy a white trash son of a bitch and then told him, "You have taken a life that could have been grand and reduced it to low comedy."

Tommy, his sense of proprietorship outweighing his fear of the woman Genie would never even let him meet when they were dating, tried to step around her and into his wife's room. Dorothy Balcom, barely five feet tall, grabbed him and spun him around toward her.

"I'll make you a deal," she said. "You leave this place and never come back, and I will see that you get one hundred dollars a month for the rest of your sorry life. I'll get Franklin Junior to draw up the papers this very day. But if you stay, I promise you that neither you nor Eugenia nor those two babies will ever get a cent of Balcom money."

If the Balcoms had had more money, or been freer with it, Tommy might have gotten a ride with Felton on the next out-of-state truck run he made and never been heard from in Port Campbell or Scots County again. Maybe he just didn't believe Dorothy Balcom would deny forever her only daughter. Or maybe Tommy just felt young and lucky. Perhaps he thought he could do better than a $100 a month pension.

"Go to hell, old lady, I want to see my young-uns," he told her, looking down and trying to return hate for hate. He would remember, all the rest of his life, how her eyes, at that instant, turned coal black, as black as the mourning clothes she was still wearing for her late husband. When she grabbed his arm, he pushed her away, and she fell back onto the couch beside her daughter's door.

She started to get up and come at her new son-in-law again, but she stopped. Maybe he got the look in his eye that the Sweatts were supposed to get right before they cut somebody. Maybe she thought she'd wait for a day when Tommy was drunk and Genie was tired of poverty and would come back on her own, begging forgiveness.

The noise woke Genie, and she was ready when Tommy peeked into the room.

"I knew you'd come back," she said. "Come here."

She told him not to worry, that she wasn't going to give him up, "no matter what Momma says. It's just you and me and the boys, Tommy."

Tommy sat there, still smelling of a two-day drunk, holding Genie's hand and trying to paint some kind of word picture that would reassure her, make her think that her life was going to be something besides a hardscrabble road.

She told Tommy that their boys didn't have any names yet. "You better think of something," she said. "I don't have any intentions of naming them after any of the Balcoms, so you might want to give it some thought."

That's when Tommy knew that she wasn't going to blame him, that she wasn't going to look back at that big house on Arsenal Hill with a stone in her heart twenty years later. That's when he swore to himself that he was going to somehow, by God, raise two boys who would make Balcoms look like the small-town clerks that he always said they were.

In the years that followed, whenever Tom Ed or Lucky would pop up to the infield, or get a B minus, or skip Sunday School, or do any of dozens of things that fell below Tommy's standards, he'd take one or both of them off to one side and ask, "You want them Balcoms to hear you're acting like trash? You want to make 'em laugh at us?"

After the war, with opportunity hanging up there fat like a harvest moon all of a sudden, there were plenty of people like Tommy Sweatt. Tired of being not good enough, vowing to outdo all the doctors' and lawyers' sons, determined that one day they'd pay back the little girls with new dresses who giggled at them when they walked past with patched overalls and a lunch bag smelling of fatback.

A lot of people felt that Tommy lacked focus, that he couldn't stick with any one thing for more than a month at a time. But from the time Lucky was old enough to remember until the day his father had him arrested, Tommy seldom woke his sons without telling them, "Do something today to make 'em all want to be Sweatts."

As soon as Tommy knew that Genie planned to stand by him, no matter what her mother did, he started trying to ensure that his sons would be special, the way no Sweatt ever had been before. It was a sign of the ordinary nature of Sweatts up to that time that about half of the five hundred or so in and around Port Campbell spelled their name with one "t" because it was easier than repeatedly telling people it had two.

The first thing Tommy did was seek out Dr. Squires, who had delivered the twins and most of the Sweatts before them, a lot of them for free or for produce. Since the Squireses and the Balcoms lived two doors apart up on the Hill, Dr. Squires had no love for Sweatts in general or Tommy in particular.

"Doc," Tommy said, "I want you to help me name 'em."

Dr. Squires, like most doctors around Port Campbell, had been honored by having a few babies named after him. But that wasn't what Tommy had in mind.

"I want them boys to be the strongest and smartest ones there ever was," he said. "I done named the first one Jack Dempsey Sweatt, 'cause he's the toughest boxer there ever was, except Joe Louis, and I ain't naming him after no nigger.

"But what I need to know from you, Doc, is, who's the smartest man there ever was? That's who I aim to name the other one after."

When Dr. Squires determined that Tommy couldn't be more serious, he thought about it for a few seconds. He thought of Leonardo da Vinci and then Albert Einstein, but he knew that some human being, probably doomed to work in a sawmill or drive a bread truck in a small Southern town, would be wearing the next words he uttered for his entire life. So he said Thomas Edison.

"How you spell that?"

The doctor took out his pen and tore a piece of paper off the sheet attached to his clipboard. He wrote out the name.

"Thanks, Doc," Tommy said. "Yeah, that's the stuff. And he can be Tommy, just like me."

"God forbid," Dr. Squires muttered under his breath while Tommy marched down the hall to tell Genie the good news.

Thomas Edison Sweatt. They called him Tom Ed right from the start. Lucky was twenty minutes younger. They called him Jack until the second grade.

They were just another couple of Carolina towheads. Nobody but Genie could tell them apart for several years. Even Tommy couldn't tell who was who sometimes; he made Genie stop dressing them alike so he would know.

They both had green eyes and were taller than most of their friends. In Genie's snapshot collection, Tom Ed is the one looking straight into the camera, as if he's about to go up and shake hands and introduce himself to it. Lucky, who was then Jack, looks as if he's not so sure of himself; his head is down a little in spite of Tommy yelling for him to quit being so bashful.

But hardly anyone outside their family noticed any difference at all. To the world, they were two peas in a pod.

Tommy went out and bought a baseball and put it in their crib almost as soon as they got home from the hospital. Years later, when he heard that Mickey Mantle's father had done the same thing in Oklahoma fifteen years earlier, he was more sure than ever that he was on the right track. When Tom Ed was eleven months old, he raised a welt on his brother's head by hitting him with the ball, and Tommy just told Jack to hit him right back. He wanted boys that were tough enough to make all the Balcoms in the world back down, he told Genie when she protested.

By the time the twins were five years old, Tommy was taking them out behind their cinder-block, tin-roofed house every day from March to November and teaching them the one sport he'd had any exposure to as a boy: baseball. He bought them kids' bats, and he started out pitching underhand, as slowly as he could, from not more than twenty feet away. He never used rubber balls, though. He said they were for sissies. He never seemed prouder than he did the day Jack took a mighty swing, his eyes shut tight, caught the ball flush on the fat part of the bat, and loosened one of Tommy's front teeth.

Before they even started school, Tommy was already telling them how much better they were than the other children. By the time they started first grade, he had them firmly believing it. They were big for their age, and there were two of them. They'd hear adults say they were "natural leaders." They were the ones who got picked first in games at recess, the ones who got chosen for the best parts in the church and school plays.

"Boys," Tommy would tell them over and over, "you got to get up every day mad at the world 'cause somebody's ahead of you. Don't nobody deserve to be ahead of my boys."

When either one of them seemed to hesitate at the plate, because perhaps Tommy was throwing a little harder than he had before—and by now, he was pitching overhand from forty feet back—he'd throw one right at the reluctant batter. Sometimes, he'd hit one of them with the ball, and that one would come home with a perfect little tattoo of the baseball's stitching.

"C'mon back up there," he'd bark out while one of the twins rubbed his arm and the other pumped his fist nervously into his glove in the field, out beyond the clothesline. "You got to get mad at the ball."

When they were barely home from the hospital, Tommy told Genie that he was depending on her for "the book part." Tommy had dropped out of school before he was fifteen, but he knew that the Balcoms and the other Arsenal Hill types went all the way through college, so by God his boys were going to be educated. They could both read by the time they started first grade, although Tom Ed seemed not to catch on quite as quickly as his brother did. But no one else starting first grade at Mingo Elementary could read at all.

The day Jack became Lucky, they came home from school and found Tommy on a stepladder next to the carport where he kept a Ford that was the same age as they were. They were in the second grade, and they were allowed to walk the half mile or so from school to home, always facing what little traffic there was on Mingo Road. Tommy wanted them to be independent. Genie threw a fit at first, because it was just one year after a drunken teenager had run over Randy Jessup, who was in the twins' grade and lived less than two miles away.

But Tommy held his ground.

"The Lord ain't goin' to let nothing happen to my boys," he told her. Tommy only went to church with his wife and sons about once a month, but he seemed to believe that God smiled on "my boys" anyway. Genie finally gave in. She got tired, sometimes, of always being the only possible voice of reason, always being the cause of sulks on the twins' part. Tommy would let them do just about anything if he thought it would make them tougher. For a while, he appeared to convince himself that the twins really were charmed, that nothing bad could ever happen to them. Either that, or he was willing to take the risk.

"Go on, then," Genie had said, "but if I ever catch either one of you playing in that road or walking with your back to traffic, you'll be riding that school bus the rest of your life."

On that October day, the boys took exaggerated looks left and right, then crossed Mingo Road to the house, and that's when they saw Tommy. He had his arms raised, and his hands were on a plank no more than eight inches across. One end was resting on the roof of the carport; the other was held up by the roof of the chicken coop almost ten feet away. Tom Ed and Jack looked at each other, silently asking, "What now?"

"C'm'ere, you boys!" he yelled to them across the driveway. "Got something I want to show you."

"Oh, no," Jack said, catching on before Tom Ed did. Jack was lagging a few feet behind by the time they got to the side of the carport, where Tommy was waiting.

"We're gonna play a game," he told them. By this time neither of the twins ever expected any of Tommy's games to be much fun. The last one he'd devised for them, they had to throw a baseball to each other, advancing one step each after every throw, until one of them couldn't move his glove fast enough to catch the ball before it hit him. This game promised to be even less fun than that.

He made them get up on the ladder, one at a time. Jack could see Tom Ed's legs shaking up above him. Then they were on the carport roof, three times their height off the ground, Jack biting his lip to keep from crying. Tommy might beat them if they cried.

"This here game," he told them from below, "is about not being a scairdy cat. This here is what is goin' to make you tough as nails."

Jack wondered where their mother was, then remembered it was her day to go into Port Campbell for groceries. He knew she wouldn't let Tommy get away with this, no matter how much hell he raised.

"Okay, Tom Ed," he said. "You first. C'm'ere to the edge of this here board. Now, the purpose of this game is to see how fast you can get across to that chicken-house roof, slide down that there piece of tin, and run back around here to me. Fastest one gets a big old Nehi grape drink from the store."

They looked across to the other side of the chicken house. Tommy had stood a section of tin he'd salvaged from the previous chicken coop, which had blown down the winter before, next to the far side of the present one, making a kind of crude slide. Just going across that eight-inch plank from the carport to the chicken house wouldn't be enough, Jack could see. They would have to slide down the other side, too.

The boys looked down at the top of Tommy's head, and Jack could see for the first time the bald spot shining through his dark-red hair. They could hear the chickens, clucking in disapproval of this interruption in their afternoon routine. A stray poplar leaf blew toward Jack's face and he ducked. He knew there was no way on God's earth that he could get across that board.

"Let Jack have it," Tom Ed said, meaning that Nehi. Jack was just opening his mouth to offer the prize to his brother.

"Let Jack have it!? Are you just goin' to let somebody take your Nehi from you because you ain't tough enough to fight for it? I declare, I'm goin' to have to buy you a dress."

Jack could see Tom Ed's right hand shaking. The wind picked up, and it was making their eyes start to tear.

"Is my baby starting to cry?" Tommy yelled up. "You my sweet little baby girl?"

Tom Ed and Jack worshiped the ground their father walked on. They didn't know anything except pleasing Tommy Sweatt. But they loved each other, too. And this, they knew, was too much.

Jack balled his fists and yelled down at Tommy, "You stop that. You stop it right now!"

It looked as if Tommy was about to laugh, but it never got as far as his eyes.

"Well, then, I reckon you want to go first," he said.

Jack didn't say anything. He wasn't at all sure the board would hold him, and it was bowed somewhat in the middle.

"Do I have two babies up there?" Tommy said, and his disappointment almost made Jack sick. "I don't think you all are safe walking clear down to the school by yourselves anymore. I better start walking you all there myself."

Jack looked over at Tom Ed, who still looked like he wanted to cry. Jack did, too. They had always done everything together; there wasn't one thing they hadn't both taken on, even if it meant letting Tommy put boxing gloves on them so they could "whale the tar" out of each other. Now, Jack felt as if he were leaving his brother behind, but he couldn't stand to not measure up in their father's eyes. It would be years before Tom Ed found out he had a slight case of vertigo. Jack wondered later how his brother was even able to get up on the roof to start with. He asked Tom Ed about that day once, years later, and Tom Ed just gave him a quizzical look and said he didn't remember much about it.

Jack put one foot on the board, testing it with his right shoe.

"I'm counting," Tommy said below. "One . . . two . . . three . . ."

Jack closed his eyes for a quick prayer, but the only words he could think of were "Help, Jesus." He opened them again and put the other foot on the board. Once he started, he knew he could only go forward, away from his brother and toward the other side.

Almost forty years later, when Jack had long since become Lucky, he was on the roof of the inn at Willow Cove when some combination of that same dry-leaf smell and the way Chris was looking up at him made him so weak he had to sit down for a second and silently curse Tommy Sweatt.

Jack almost made it across. But he was wearing brown leather school shoes, slick as glass, and he slipped not two feet from the other side. When he fell, he hit the side of that almost-new chicken coop headfirst, just missing the solid oak post that held the roof up. He tore the door off its hinges and was knocked unconscious.

Tom Ed thought his brother must surely be dead. He came down the ladder as fast as he could and saw blood oozing from Jack's seemingly lifeless head.

Tommy just said, "Lord have mercy."

Tommy wanted Tom Ed to go to the Clarks next door, because they had a phone, but Tom Ed wouldn't leave his brother's side, so Tommy had to run over himself. When he and Ernest Clark got back, Tom Ed was squatting beside his fallen brother and wouldn't even let Tommy touch Jack.

Tommy rode along with Jack in the ambulance. Ernest Clark had to hold Tom Ed back with both arms to keep him from going, too. Tom Ed was there for Genie to hug when she got back from shopping.

Jack regained consciousness halfway to Arsenal Hill Hospital. Dr. Squires, who had delivered him, looked him over and then put eight stitches in his forehead and another couple in his lip.

When the doctor heard Tommy's version of what happened ("We was messin' around with this old plank. I never had no idea he'd try to walk across it"), he told Jack, "Son, you're lucky to be alive," thus naming the second of Tommy and Genie Sweatt's twins.

By this time, Genie had reached the hospital. She'd called Felton, the closest thing to family she had anymore outside her own house, and he came along with her and Tom Ed.

Tommy and Jack were walking down the corridor, headed out, when Genie, Felton, and Tom Ed met them, and Tommy started telling how brave Jack had been when they were putting in the stitches, even though the boy had howled like a banshee. Jack especially wanted his uncle Felton to know what a tough character he had been. Felton stood six foot four, two inches taller than even Tommy, and still had the hardscrabble mean look that most people in Scots County associated with Sweatts. He brought the boys hard candy and Sun Drops, and he never smiled.

"Uncle Felton," Jack told him, right before he stopped being Jack, "I'm lucky to be alive."

By the time Felton had finished telling everybody what Jack said, the boy was Lucky to almost everyone except his mother and his teachers. Eventually, even Genie gave up.

Tommy told his own version of the story so often that even he believed it. Since neither of the boys contradicted their father, Genie had no choice but to believe it, too. Tom Ed didn't talk about that day for a long time, always changing the subject when his father brought it up. Lucky wondered, sometimes, if he was the only person alive who truly remembered everything. In the years that followed, he wondered if things might have been different if he'd stayed Jack, wondered if letting yourself be named Lucky might have been daring the fates.

★★★ **3** ★★★

The barbecue was the stringy, vinegary kind that Tom Ed and Lucky and just about everyone else east of Interstate 85 in North Carolina had grown up on, meant to be consumed with slaw and hush puppies. There were only Pepsis to drink, because Axel Sprague was a teetotaler and because he owned a couple of Pepsi-Cola distributorships, but the old boys kept going to their cars, where they could improve their paper-cup soft drinks with some Early Times. There were no women present.

Tom Ed made a speech, mostly about lower taxes and prayer in schools. He asked the blessing, and he asked forgiveness for "poor misguided souls that slay our unborn," invoking a special request to "welcome into Your waiting arms a warrior fallen in Your work, the Reverend Gary Thorne," and there were several "amens."

The host, Axel Sprague himself, was a pinched-faced old Baptist deacon who looked as if he'd have been more comfortable behind a mule. He had been in the state legislature for twenty years, elected again and again as Plain Ol' Axel Sprague, and it was the great fear of his district's electee to the House of Representatives that the old man would decide one day that he could do the conservative cause more good in Washington than in Raleigh. Sprague had been a Democrat, but when his party got too liberal, he turned Republican and got the same voters who'd backed him as a Democrat.

"Axel Sprague," Tom Ed said on the way back, waving at tipsy fellow Republicans weaving toward their cars or urinating alongside the county road, "is a man of the people. Hell, he *is* the people."

"Unfortunately," muttered Barry Maxwell.

Tom Ed snorted.

"You all think you're so smart," he said. "That old man says the word, and we're halfway there. I don't care what his breath smells like."

Lucky hadn't really considered what helping the Tom Ed for Governor campaign would entail. He soon saw, in his brother's eyes at least, that it would all come down to who worked harder, Tom Ed Sweatt or the Democratic candidate, Knox Cameron, who was the mayor of Greensboro.

Tom Ed had given Lucky the keys on the way back to the Chevy van leaving Axel Sprague's barbecue, and he gave him the itinerary. It was four o'clock, and they had two more stops to make, one at a textile mill where the day shift got off at five, in Wardlow, then at a mixer for University of North Carolina alumni in Sanford.

He laid it on thick at Wardlow, promising fire and brimstone for liberals everywhere. At the UNC mixer, he laid it on thin, shaking hands, stressing the tax issues, and telling the obligatory N.C. State joke.

"You all hear about what the boy from State said to his ex-wife right after they got divorced?" Pause. "He said, 'Does this mean we can't be brother and sister no more?'"

They ate it up, just like the State graduates would when he told a shopworn Carolina joke: "How many UNC boys does it take to change a tire? Takes two. One to watch the car, and one to call Daddy."

They got back to the Pinecrest Inn at eight-fifteen. After dinner, Lucky found out that he would be rooming with Sam Bender, who was in charge of what Tom Ed called the care and feeding of the print media. Sam was a nice enough guy who told Lucky some funny stories and didn't snore too much.

Lucky, hurt a little, wondered to himself why his brother didn't offer to share his suite with the two queen-sized beds.

Sam seemed to read his mind.

"Tom Ed," he said with a wink as they heard the footsteps retreating down the hall, "needs his privacy."

Sam filled Lucky in some on Dr. Nate Crowell before they went to sleep. The doctor had been charged with murder. Five witnesses said he speeded up just before he hit the Reverend Thorne. Dr. Crowell said he just panicked.

"They picketed his house for a solid month before it happened. His wife said she was afraid to go grocery shopping. Called him a baby killer. Harassed his mother, for God's sake. He claims he panicked. Hope he's got a good lawyer. Those people are like piranha, just mindless, rip your flesh apart without even thinking about it."

"But this Thorne guy backed Tom Ed?"

Sam laughed in the dark. Lucky could see his cigarette glowing across the room. "Yeah, and Tom Ed'll back him, too. He'll be there for his funeral, call for the wrath of God and all that."

Lucky was painfully aware that this stranger knew the 1992 Tom Ed Sweatt better than he did.

"Is Tom Ed opposed to abortions?"

Sam's response indicated that Lucky might as well have asked if mules could speak French.

"Tom Ed," he said, crunching an ice cube, "is against losing votes."


The next day, they made five stops before noon, Lucky trying to read the directions and trying not to listen to Tom Ed, who never could understand road maps.

Sam woke Lucky at five-thirty and told him they'd be on the road by six-thirty, probably have 7-Eleven coffee and doughnuts for breakfast. Lucky thought at first he was kidding, but when they got down to Tom Ed's room, the door was cracked, Harry and Barry were already inside, and the candidate himself was on the phone, talking to somebody who obviously hadn't done something he was supposed to have done.

"I don't give a shit, Sandy," he said. "That sounds like a personal problem. Just get it done."

It would amaze Lucky, over the next few days, the kind of abuse people would endure from Tom Ed.

"All ready?" he asked. He saw Lucky and looked momentarily surprised, as if he'd forgotten that his brother was there. "Let's hit it, Bo. Let's do some politicking. Let's sell 'em some Tom Ed Sweatt."

Tom Ed never seemed to get tired. He would catch a twenty-minute nap between stops, wipe the sleep from his eyes as Lucky parked the van next to some school or mill or municipal building, and hit the ground running.

The plan was to have lunch at Tommy and Genie's, in the house they were renting in Westlake, where two campaign workers had already moved Lucky's car. The itinerary said twelve-thirty, and Harry and Barry ran a tight ship. Lucky and Tom Ed deposited the M&M twins, Sam, and two other workers at the Holiday Inn just outside Port Campbell at 12:20. They were ten minutes from Westlake.

"Remember, we got to be at the CottonCrest plant at three," Barry reminded Tom Ed, who just grunted as Lucky drove off.

Tom Ed rang the doorbell, and Lucky remembered a story Genie had told him when his parents first moved out of the house in which the twins had grown up. It was before anybody had ever heard about shrink-swell soil, and Tom Ed had bought them a huge house, custom-designed, near to the lake. It was a bargain, because the builder needed Tom Ed's favor, but it was still the kind of house that nobody named Sweatt could have afforded before then.

They'd been there for about a week, Genie said, when they were eating dinner one night in the big dining room. Suddenly, a bell rang.

They checked the front door, checked the back door, checked the phone, but they couldn't find the source of the ringing.

Over the next few weeks, it happened several times, always when they were eating dinner. Finally, they told Tom Ed about it, thinking that perhaps the house was haunted, although it seemed rather new to have ghosts already.

Tom Ed checked the floor plans at his office, but he couldn't solve the mystery either. Finally, he contacted the bankrupt builder. The builder, Tom Ed found out, had a fondness for gadgets. He thought the people who bought his house might have a maid, and that they might like to summon her without actually having to yell across the dining room and into the kitchen. So, he installed a buzzer under the carpet, right where Tommy's big left foot landed when he hunkered down to dinner.

It wasn't one of Tom Ed's all-time favorite stories, harking back too much to butterbeans-and-fatback days on Mingo Road, but Genie and Tommy told it over and over. Until Tom Ed finally had an electrician come out and disconnect the buzzer, Tommy never tired of surreptitiously pushing it whenever a first-time guest was in the general vicinity of the door, asking the visitor if he would answer it, then collapsing in contagious laughter when the confused guest looked out on an empty front porch.

Nobody could tell a funny story better than Tommy Sweatt, wheezing in laughter that did not beg other laughter but rather advertised such merriment that the listener was eager to join in. And nobody laughed harder at someone else's jokes. If a coworker or a neighbor heard a funny story, he rushed to tell it to Tommy, just for the enjoyment of watching his big face redden and crinkle, just to hear the breathless wheeze of his seemingly heartfelt laughter.

Even after Lucky and Tom Ed had come to understand totally the grim-faced, teeth-gritting, combustible Tommy Sweatt who lived permanently behind this temporary good nature, they would tell him jokes to see his approving laughter. The contrast made it all the sweeter.

By 1992, "river rat" wasn't much of a pejorative term anymore, even in Scots County. But any number of Sweatts had, in their time, cut people, killed people, gone to prison rather than bear that term unchallenged.

Lucky's knowledge of the way Tommy grew up came mostly from his uncle Felton.

Felton was three years older than Tommy, born in 1922. There were ten children who lived, and Felton and Tommy were the youngest. Tommy said that Felton used to keep his older brothers and sisters from picking on him.

The Sweatts lived south of Port Campbell, in Purcells. Purcells wasn't so much a town as a condition, about eight hundred people living down a dead-end road that descended from a state highway to the river. Purcells's raison d'etre was a mill that once lured desperate people there and then closed. Lucky remembered it as an area of small tobacco farms, a place where the water tasted bad and the smell from the big hog farms farther down the river would knock a buzzard off a fence post.

Tommy and Genie and the boys used to go there every other Sunday. Tom Ed and Lucky both hated it. They'd usually wind up getting in a fight with their mean-spirited, freckle-plagued first cousins, who were mostly older. If the twins were grossly outnumbered, they would run off and hide in the woods. Tommy would beat them if he found out that their cousins, no matter what the number or size, were intimidating them. The key, Tommy felt, was to make the boys more afraid of him than anything else.

After Lucky got sick, they didn't go to Purcells as much, and they didn't go back at all after their grandfather died and their grandmother went to live with Felton after he got out of prison.

Felton resembled Tommy, but the big difference, what cost Felton a large piece of his life, was that Felton, in the vernacular of Purcells, "didn't take any shit." Tommy could charm his way out of a tight spot, get everybody caught up in some outrageous story, get them laughing at some joke, and they were his. Felton preferred to just hit trouble upside the head.

Where Felton and Tommy grew up, you either stayed upset a lot or you just gave up. One thing that even Lucky would concede: Tommy Sweatt didn't give up.

What usually upset Felton was disrespect. He could doubtless have lived his entire life in poverty and been happy as long as nobody tried to rub his nose in it.

What bothered Tommy was not having things.

As a boy, Tommy would throw away the sweet potato he'd been given for lunch because he didn't want his classmates to know the Sweatts could only afford meat once a day. Felton would sit in the school yard eating his "old, cold 'tater" and dare anybody to say anything, or even laugh.

They both were over six feet tall before they were fourteen, and they'd both dropped out of school by the time they were fifteen and big enough to drive a truck, which was how you got out of Purcells. Tommy told everyone he got through the tenth grade, but his sister Ivy told the twins he never finished the seventh, that they had to keep holding him back because he missed so much school working in tobacco. The Sweatts expected boys to work first, go to school second.

By the time he got his draft notice in 1943, Tommy had already fractured his leg in a wreck. He was driving a chicken truck up from a farm in Clarendon and ran head-on into a man who Tommy said veered across the center line. The man died instantly, so Tommy's side of the story was the only side. The break didn't heal properly, so Tommy was 4-F for the war and got to meet Eugenia Canfield Balcom at a dance when he should have been at some army post getting ready to go fight the Germans or the Japanese. Nobody ever accused him, to his face, of being a slacker.

Genie was first charmed by Tommy Sweatt's infectious good humor and handsome face, which had permitted him to be more than one Arsenal Hill girl's secret beau, the one she didn't dare introduce to her parents. But then, when she scratched the surface, Genie was touched by what she saw underneath, a nose pressed against the windowpane of what she had always taken for granted: upper-middle-class life in a bypassed Southern town.

Later, on occasion, she would reflect that she had not counted on the depth of Tommy Sweatt's need. Alone in their bedroom at night, he would tell her his secret fears, the imagined laughter behind his back, the fear of those who know poverty is only in remission. One time, after he was passed over for a job that he was sure would be his, he cried, and Genie imagined the big man's wracking sobs were a flood that had been dammed up for decades.

Tommy was known to be short with Genie, and he had betrayed her in ways small and not so small. But Genie knew two things: She knew she loved him, and she knew that he knew where the line was drawn. She let Tommy be loud, and sometimes crude, but there was never a moment in Eugenia Balcom Sweatt's married life, after the birth of the twins, when she couldn't let Tommy know, with just a look that she might have stolen from her mother as an unintended wedding gift, that he had gone far enough. If this look had been disrespected even once, Genie and Tommy both knew that the thread that bound them, strong as a spider's web and just as fragile, would be broken.

Felton wound up in an infantry unit that was part of the D–Day invasion. He never talked about killing anybody, on either side of the Atlantic, but he did show the twins his medals once.

Tommy was one of the few men in Scots County who didn't somehow cash in on the war afterward. Even Felton went to trade school and learned how to be a carpenter. But Tommy wasn't a veteran, and he didn't have enough education or money to take advantage of the first boom times in almost twenty years.

He tried truck farming, plumbing, sales, whatever offered him more than what he was doing at the time. It was generally accepted that he didn't have a lot of patience.

As a truck driver, he would charm the workers wherever he made his deliveries into doing most of the work while he told them jokes and stories, sitting on the back of the truck drinking an RC Cola.

Tommy was prone to exaggerate. He often told Tom Ed and Lucky what a great athlete he had been, how he threw the baseball so hard that the catcher had to stuff a rag in his mitt to cushion the blow. When he would tell these stories in front of his older brothers and sisters, the boys could see them smiling and shaking their heads. By the time they were in the fifth grade, Tom Ed and Lucky both knew they shouldn't believe most of Tommy's stories, but he told them so well that they wanted to hear them anyhow, preferring his entertaining lies and temporary good nature to the dull truth of their day-to-day existence.

The truth, according to Felton, who never lied, was that neither he nor Tommy ever had time as boys to play much of anything.

Not long after Jack became Lucky, Felton finally did what his family was afraid he'd do some day: He killed a man.

His name was Blackie Chavis, and he was from Bramble Station, a place even more destitute than Purcells. Everybody has to have somebody to hate, so the people in Purcells and Bramble Station, two miles apart on the railroad line, hated each other.

Blackie Chavis and Felton had fought before, and Felton tried to stay away from him. But one Saturday night, in an old wooden shack down by the Campbell River, a yellow-line club with blacks on one side and whites on the other dancing separately to the same rhythm and blues band, Blackie came across Felton urinating beside the dirt parking lot and asked him if he was "one of them river-rat Sweatts from Purcells."

Felton was drunk, because it was Saturday night. He didn't even zip up, just turned around in midstream and hit Blackie Chavis hard in the mouth, knocking him into a mud puddle.

Felton had another beer, then went back to his rented house in Purcells. He was getting out of the car when he heard something. Before Blackie Chavis had time to hit him with the baseball bat he had raised over his head with both hands, Felton had sunk a five-inch blade between his ribs. He stabbed him two more times to be sure.

That was Felton's testimony. A man named Alton Bullock, who was with Blackie Chavis, said they were just arguing when Felton pulled the knife and killed Blackie. Felton said he ran down the road to where someone had a phone and he could call the police, and that Alton Bullock must have taken the bat and thrown it in the river.

The Arsenal Hill judge who listened to all the impassioned and conflicting testimony figured he couldn't go wrong by putting another river rat from Purcells in prison for a while. He gave Felton five years, and Felton served most of it.

Tommy went to the trial, and the most unforgettable thing he saw didn't even occur in the courtroom where Felton's case was being heard. A young man from the Hill was being tried at the same time, in another courtroom. Tommy would drift over there, during breaks, and he became almost as interested in this second trial as he was in his brother's. It was pretty obvious to him that the well-heeled young man from Arsenal Hill had gone down to Frenchtown and shot and killed a black man for no good reason, just stuck his father's borrowed gun out the window and fired into a crowd. He told the judge he hadn't meant to hurt anybody.

The same day Felton got five years for killing Blackie Chavis, Tommy read in the paper that the young man from Arsenal Hill had been convicted of second-degree manslaughter. Three days later, the judge gave him a five-year suspended sentence and, according to the *Port Campbell Post,* "a stern warning."

Tommy told the boys this story more often than a less-skilled storyteller could have gotten away with. He always ended the story with the same moral:

"If you're rich, you don't have to fight nobody. You just tell somebody else that needs to do you a favor, 'take care of this son of a bitch for me,' and he does."

Tommy was not so much appalled by the abuse of power as he was envious of the abusers.

Felton got out of prison in 1958. One day in the summer of 1959, Tommy was reading the paper.

"I'll be damned," he blurted out, and Genie tried to shush him. "I wonder if this is the same Alton Bullock that helped send Felton away."

An Alton Bullock from Bramble Station had been shot to death outside his home. There were no witnesses. Tommy liked to take things and make them into stories that grew with the telling, but this was one story the twins didn't hear again. Nobody was ever known to ask Felton about Alton Bullock.

In the summer of 1953, Tommy had finally found somewhere he could stick, landing a job as a foreman at the lumber mill at McNeil. Everybody knew this wasn't what he thought he'd be. Somehow, Tommy Sweatt always believed he was going to be rich, but after running up half-a-dozen dead ends over the years—a plan to raise Christmas trees, a scheme to open a chinchilla ranch, a pyramid deal that almost landed him in jail and his family in the oft-referred-to poorhouse—he altered his dreams, or rather, transferred them. He became all the more determined that the next generation would put the Sweatts over the top. It all depended, as he had been telling the twins over and over from the time they were four years old, on them.

Having finally conceded that this was as far as he was going, Tommy actually did a better job at the lumber mill than anyone expected. In a few years, he was the head foreman, proud of the way Mr. Lawrence, the owner, would let him use a cottage at White Oak Beach for a week every summer.

Tom Ed and Lucky hated the way Tommy would exaggerate his importance, telling people that he and Mr. Lawrence were "just like that." They saw that their father didn't dislike rich people; he disliked not being rich himself.

When the Sweatts would leave Mr. Lawrence's cottage at the beach after their week every summer, Tommy would make them mop the floors and dust everywhere. He was proud that they had left it in better shape than they had found it.

"I want Mr. Lawrence to know," he told the twins one year when they rebelled on Sunday morning, "that we can be trusted, that we can be depended on. People that are depended on can amount to something."

★★★ **4** ★★★

**G**enie answered the door, on the third ring, just when Lucky and Tom Ed were beginning to think their parents had forgotten they were coming. Tom Ed seemed not to grasp the fact that pushing the bell harder wouldn't make it ring any louder inside. It seemed to irritate him that he was standing on the porch of a suburban trilevel, with the neighbors probably looking through the slits in their blinds, wondering if he and Lucky were Mormons or Jehovah's Witnesses.

"Lord, Momma, did the door bell break?" he asked and walked past her before she could answer. Lucky gave her a hug and kissed her on the forehead.

Tommy came rumbling out of the den, walking too fast up the steps. Lucky wondered if having three different levels was the best thing for two people their parents' age, but this was a lot better than the house they'd left on Mingo Road, and he knew he didn't have the money to give them anything more appropriate.

Genie had fixed some of the twins' favorite foods. There was chicken and pastry, along with butterbeans, corn, and stewed tomatoes that she'd canned herself. Westlake didn't allow gardens at the homes themselves, on the grounds that corn and watermelons in the back yard looked tacky, but there was a common gardening area a short drive away, and Genie grew her vegetables there. She'd fixed corn bread—not the kind out of the mix, but the round cakes of it that she fried in the skillet. And she'd made banana pudding for dessert.

When Tom Ed and Lucky were children, Genie would ask them what they wanted her to make for their birthdays. Lucky would ask for lemon pie; Tom Ed always wanted banana pudding. So she'd fix one of each, and the twins would savor their birthday desserts, hoarding them and trying to make them last as long as possible. Once, when they were in the fifth grade, Tom Ed came home from school and found out that Tommy had finished off his birthday banana pudding. He cursed Tommy and threw one of his books at him; Tommy was so clearly in the wrong that he didn't even punish Tom Ed.

"I'd have made you a lemon pie," Genie told Lucky, looking worried, "but I didn't know you were coming down until yesterday."

"Don't worry about it," Lucky said. "If you and Tommy'll hold Tom Ed's arms so he can't get me, I think I will have some of that banana pudding, though."

She and Tommy laughed and looked expectantly at Tom Ed, who looked up, not getting it, then said, "Oh, yeah" and went on eating. Lucky knew his brother had already had a couple of breakfasts forced on him, and he saw him take a swig of Pepto-Bismol in the car. But he couldn't turn down Genie's cooking.

They went into the living room after lunch. Tom Ed turned on CNN as if he expected one of their national political reporters to be talking about Tom Ed Sweatt. Like magic, one of them was.

The Sweatts were sitting there, visiting and using the TV to fill in the dead space, when Lucky suddenly heard a man with a strange name and bad hair say something familiar:

"And, in the North Carolina gubernatorial race, the Democrat, Greensboro mayor Knox Cameron, is the favorite. The latest Mason-Dixon poll has him with a lead of ten percentage points.

"However, the Republican, Tom Ed Sweatt, was trailing by twice that margin a month ago . . ."

The man spent a few more precious seconds on Tom Ed, then went on to an Oklahoma senatorial race.

"Ten percent my foot," Tommy said, sitting on the edge of his recliner that he'd popped out of when he heard his son's name. "How they gonna tell how people will vote when they don't talk to but a few hundred of 'em? Hadn't nobody asked me how I'm voting."

"At least they got my name right," Tom Ed said, almost to himself. One of the networks was calling him "Tom Sweatt," and he was constantly yelling at Sam Bender because some newspaper had spelled his last name with only one "t."

By the time they had to leave, Tom Ed had calmed down somewhat, had gotten out of the full-throttle mode he'd be in most of the time from then until the election, and the Sweatts had as pleasant a visit as they ever hoped for anymore.

"Are you staying at the house tonight?" Genie asked him just before they left to pick up the M&M twins at the motel. "Lucinda called last night. We had a nice talk."

"Nah," Tom Ed said. "We have to be in Durham for a thing tomorrow morning, so I thought we'd just stay up there tonight."

At 2:25 by the TV clock, Tom Ed and Lucky said good-bye to their parents. It seemed to Lucky that Genie was on the verge of telling them not to stay out too late, or that Tommy might be about to give them one of those toothless warnings he used to issue about not drag racing with the family car. In other words, it felt, for a few seconds, like high school and one big, happy family.

It was still hard for him to believe that, with a little luck and a favorable political wind, his brother could be the next governor of North Carolina.

Lucky never believed that twins, identical or fraternal, could read each other's minds. But, over the years, he'd had to sometimes wonder.

He was thinking about what an unlikely thing Governor Tom Ed Sweatt was to consider when Tom Ed turned to him, just as they were getting ready to walk out the door.

"It could happen," he said, and the way he looked gave Lucky a little chill.

"Son," Tommy said when they were leaving, "I'm so proud of you I could bust. You done it. You're almost there."

Lucky got out of the way so their father could reach Tom Ed and squeeze his arm. Tommy was not into hugging men, not even Tom Ed.

They were supposed to spend Wednesday night in Durham, where Tom Ed was going to have dinner with Horace Morgan, one of his biggest supporters.

Tom Ed had a press conference at four, in time to make the evening news, then they checked into a hotel in the Research Triangle, near where Interstate 40 had finally been finished all the way to the beach.

Sam Bender was trying to talk Lucky into going to dinner with him and the M&M twins and a couple of the other workers when Tom Ed stuck his head in the door.

"Hey, Bo. How'd you like to come over to Horace Morgan's with me tonight? You do have a coat and tie somewhere in there, don't you?"

Lucky hesitated for a second and Tom Ed said, "Great. Be ready in fifteen minutes."

Sam and Lucky stared at the closed door. They could hear Tom Ed whistling as he walked down the hall to his room.

"Horace Morgan," Sam said and shook his head.

Lucky asked him what was wrong with Horace Morgan, and Sam said to ask him later, that he didn't want to prejudice Lucky's opinion. There wasn't any time to grill him, and Sam didn't seem to Lucky as if he would grill very easily. He was a quiet man who seemed to make other people do most of the talking; Barry Maxwell told Lucky that Sam had been a hell of a reporter, the kind people would spill their guts to.

So Lucky got out his best and only blue sports jacket, white shirt, gray slacks, and red paisley tie. Don't want Horace Morgan to think Tom Ed's brother is white trash, he thought to himself. About twenty-five minutes after he'd said to be ready in fifteen, Tom Ed knocked and entered the room.

"Ready, Bo?"

Lucky said he was.

"Hell, I'll drive," Tom Ed said when they got to the parking lot. "You been driving all day. Besides, I've near 'bout forgotten how. All I know how to do is ride anymore. Ride and talk."

"You're pretty good at it. Talking, I mean."

Tom Ed gave Lucky a sharp look, then seemed to relax a little.

"So what do you think of the political world so far?" he asked after they'd gotten on the main highway. "This is a long way from Mingo Road, ain't it?"

Lucky allowed that it certainly was, then asked him whether he thought he was going to win.

Tom Ed started ticking off all the reasons why he couldn't lose, then seemed to realize that he wasn't talking to the TV people or the newspaper reporters or even Harry and Barry.

"I tell you, Bo," he said, "I don't know. I'll wake up at night and start thinking about it. Just lie there and stare at the walls until I can make out the patterns in the wallpaper in the dark. What if I fail? I can't fail, Lucky. Dammit, I can't fail!"

Lucky told Tom Ed that he was still young, just forty-six years old, which felt young to Lucky at least. You're old enough to run four more times for governor if you want to, he reminded Tom Ed, but he knew as he said it that patience wasn't ever going to be a strong plank in his brother's personal platform.

"I got places to be, Bo," he said, putting on the turn signal and heading down a well-tended street divided by a median strip full of Bradford pears. "I ain't got time to wait around four more god-damn years."

Lucky remembered how, when they were children, Tom Ed would occasionally irritate some of their neighbors because, for instance, if Old Man Draughon offered him $5 a day to help him sell watermelons off a truck, and then Frank Carter told him he'd give him $7 to crop tobacco, Old Man Draughon was out of luck.

Tommy upbraided him for it once, when a jilted employer complained to him. Tom Ed, who was thirteen at the time, looked his father in the eye and told him, "I ain't got time to wait for nobody to give me no pot of gold. I got to go out and get it."

Now, thirty-three years later, Tom Ed seemed to Lucky not to have changed much. He was still, to his brother, the same boy who looked for the best deal, regardless.

Lucky thought this was as appropriate a time as there would be to ask what he'd wanted to ask all day.

"I heard you're going to go after that doctor in Charlotte."

Tom Ed's jaw muscles tightened.

"So?"

"So," Lucky said, trying to talk through a minefield, "do you think he killed that preacher on purpose?"

Tom Ed let go with a big sigh.

"Hell, I don't know, Bo. Thing is, he shouldn't have been in a position for that to happen."

"But the story said he was just trying to get out of his own driveway."

Tom Ed looked at his brother. They were pulling into the driveway of a house that sat some fifty yards off the street, a two-story Georgian made out of old brick not very long ago. Lucky figured they'd knocked down a warehouse somewhere for the bricks.

"Do you know how many members there are in the Church of the Rock?" he asked Lucky, who had no idea and said so.

"Well, there's about twenty thousand. That's a modest estimate, because it's growing every day. The Reverend Gary Thorne supported me. I hope to hell that whoever is his successor supports me, because I ain't got twenty thousand votes to give away. If I don't lose any of the votes I got right now, and I can manage to steal about fifty thousand more, then I might be the next governor of North Carolina."

Lucky plunged on.

"Well, do you believe in what they stand for? That there isn't any such thing as a good abortion?"

Tom Ed gave him what the M&M boys called his spotlighting stare, because they said he could freeze a deer in his tracks just like a pair of headlights.

"What the hell are you, my conscience? If you are, then you better get on back to Virginia. I don't need a conscience. If Harry Mavredes hadn't convinced me that these were votes just waiting to be plucked, I'd be behind by more than I am right now. Shit, let Knox Cameron have a conscience. He can afford it."

Lucky told him that going back to Virginia suited him very well, that being a chauffeur wasn't his idea to start with. He offered to get out right there and find the Durham bus station, go back to Port Campbell for his car and head north.

"Whoa," Tom Ed said. "Whoa. Damn, Bo, that's just the way I talk. Can't let nothing I say get to you. You're family. I want you here. Hell, I need you."

They got out of the car and started walking up a winding brick walkway to the double front doors.

"Bear with me," Tom Ed told his brother. "I got to get after that Dr. Crowell, but it ain't personal. And don't judge me by everything you hear me say between now and election day, or you might think I'm one sorry son of a bitch."

Their conversation was cut short when the front door opened and they were invited in by a man who appeared to be about fifty-five years old. He had silver-gray hair, bushy eyebrows, twinkly blue eyes, a flushed face, and an almost-empty highball glass in his left hand. He was wearing a blue-striped shirt that looked as if you could cut yourself on the creases, and his pants were held up by red suspenders. He looked to be about thirty pounds overweight.

Horace Morgan was the only child of one of those eastern North Carolina families who own most of their particular county. He was a lawyer by trade, but he didn't ever have to work a day in his life if he didn't choose to. Sometimes he wondered why he was willing to soil his hands with the kind of trash his profession occasionally foisted on him, and he supposed it was habit, a feeling that a man ought to do something.

Lucky, who had spent all his life in two states, was often struck by the superficial similarity of and ingrained differences between Virginia and North Carolina. A person in another part of the country might look at a map and say to himself, "Virginia, North Carolina. Same difference." But Lucky knew it wasn't so.

The main divider was money. You could even hear it in the way people talked. There was an accent, called Tidewater or High-

Tider, that was the mark of the old gentry. In High-Tider, "about the house," came out as "aboat the hoase." In Virginia, if you were on the richest street in town, the money carried that accent all the way to Martinsville, thirty miles from the Blue Ridge Parkway. In North Carolina, this carryover from the plantation society never even made it to the Piedmont. Durham was really too far west for it, unless you lived on Horace Morgan's street.

In Richmond, Horace Morgan would have been just well-off. In Durham, he was rich.

Tom Ed introduced his brother. When Morgan learned that Lucky was living in Virginia, he started reminiscing about his relatives in Fredericksburg, which was some three hundred miles from Willow Cove.

Lucky realized that Tom Ed's attention was starting to wane, as if he were waiting for something. Following his brother's eyes, he turned to see a woman who he assumed was Horace Morgan's daughter coming down the stairs.

"Susannah," Horace said to her as she approached, "this is Mr. Lucky Sweatt, Tom Ed's brother."

Then she kissed Morgan on the lips.

Horace Morgan's young wife drew away from him quickly. To Lucky, she seemed a creature of quick, fluid moves.

"Lucky Sweatt?" she said. "Lucky Sweatt? That's a great name. Your folks must have had some sense of humor, Tom Ed. They name you after a great inventor, and they name your brother Lucky."

Lucky explained to her that his real name was Jack Dempsey Sweatt, and she thought that was even funnier, indelicately snorting into her bourbon and water.

"You never told me that, Tom Ed," she said and turned accusingly to the candidate.

Susannah Morgan was twenty-seven years old. She had thick lips that reminded Lucky of Carly Simon in her prime. She had a perky little nose that probably wasn't original equipment but, if not, Lucky felt, was money well spent. Her breasts poked out just enough beneath a coral-colored sweater to make her sexy and athletic at the same time. She had ash-blond hair and green eyes, and she was a chain-smoker.

She was, Lucky would learn, almost exactly half her husband's age, and the same age as his younger son. She was what, even in Durham, the professionals called a trophy wife. She and Horace had been married three years, since they met when he was teaching a class in criminal law at the Campbell University law school. She was in her third year, working her way through and getting a little alimony from her ex-husband, when Horace Morgan, who at that time had been married for thirty years to the same woman and had three children, asked her out to dinner after class one day. They were married within a year.

Dinner was served by a black maid who made Lucky somewhat uncomfortable. He was a man who didn't even like being waited on in restaurants. It was a constant source of irritation to Barbara that they seldom had a meal at which they didn't have to serve themselves, but Lucky always felt that you couldn't sit at a table and expect another adult human being to wait on you hand and foot without running the risk of being thought an asshole.

Afterward, coffee and then cognac were served in the den. Tom Ed and Horace were knee-deep into the campaign, which left Lucky to talk with Susannah. Lucky told her about how he and Barbara came to run a bed-and-breakfast in the Virginia mountains, and how they'd assembled their family. Susannah seemed fascinated. Before the campaign was over, Lucky would become convinced that her one great gift was being able to make a person feel as if he were the center of the universe.

She was uninhibited, by Lucky's standards.

Most of the women he knew didn't care much for jokes, either telling them or listening to them. Barbara had told him once that this was probably because so many jokes make fun of someone or something, and women understood how that felt.

But Susannah was different. They'd been sipping and talking for a while when she asked the three men if they'd heard the one about the barber and the Pope.

"There's this guy," she began, dangling her cigarette for emphasis, "and he goes to his favorite barbershop, sits down in his usual chair, and his usual barber comes up.

"The guy says, 'I want you to give me the best haircut you ever gave me, because I'm going on the vacation of a lifetime.'

"'Vacation!' the barber says. 'I don't know why anybody goes on vacation. You spend all your money. You're more tired when you get back than when you left. You're broke. You gotta be crazy to go on vacation.'

"'Nah,' the guy says. 'This one's different. We're going to Rome.'

"'Rome!' the barber says. 'My God! You're going to hate it. They hate Americans over there. They'll cheat you, spit on you. You might even get kidnapped.'

"'Well,' the guy says, 'I think you're wrong. What's really going to clinch it is that we're staying at a great hotel. We're staying at the Excelsior.'

"'The Excelsior!' says the barber. 'Not the Excelsior! I know somebody that went there. They were overcharged for their room, everybody had their hands out for tips all the time. It was hot, noisy. You oughta stay home.'

"'Well, thank you for your advice,' the guy says, 'but you're wrong.' The barber shrugs, finishes the haircut, and the guy leaves.

"Three weeks later, the same guy comes into the barbershop, goes over to his favorite chair and sits down. His barber comes up, and he's got kind of a smirk on his face.

"'Well,' he says, 'was I right about vacations or what?'

"'Actually,' the guy says, 'you couldn't have been more wrong. It was the trip of a lifetime. Unforgettable! Rome is the most beautiful city in the world, the Excelsior was by far the best hotel I've ever stayed in, the people were wonderful.

"'But the most wonderful part was that I got to see the Pope. The Pope actually came up to me and touched me. The Pope spoke to me.'

"The barber is stunned. 'The Pope spoke to you? I don't believe it.'

"'It's true,' the guy says. 'We're at Vatican City, admiring all the beauty there, when suddenly we see this entourage of people coming toward us. It's the Pope and all his bodyguards and secretaries and all.

"'And the Pope and his party are coming right toward us. They get right beside us when suddenly the Pope looks my way and he stops. And all the other people stop. And the Pope comes right up to me, puts his hand on my shoulder, and then, the Pope leans over and whispers right in my ear.'

"'What'd he say?' the barber says. 'What'd he say?'

"'He said, "My son, that's the worst goddamn haircut I've ever seen in my life."'"

Tom Ed spit about half his coffee in the general direction of the table, Lucky broke up, and Horace, having heard the joke before, laughed politely. Women, thought Lucky, can do a lot of things for you, but making you laugh once in a while ought to be at least second or third on the list.

When they were ready to leave, Horace went to get Tom Ed's coat while the other three waited in the foyer.

Suddenly, Susannah reached up—she was a short woman, Lucky saw, no more than five three—and kissed Tom hard on the lips. He kissed her right back with equal enthusiasm, even while Lucky heard Horace Morgan's footsteps coming down the hall. It was pretty plain to Lucky that they had been practicing.

She said, "The Hilton, eight o'clock?" and he nodded. She winked at Lucky and stepped back just as her husband came around the corner.

On the way back to the hotel, it was quiet. Finally, Tom Ed broke the silence:

"It don't even matter to him, Bo. He knows all about it. When she comes a'knockin' tomorrow night in Winston-Salem, where do you think he thinks she's gonna be? Visitin' her grandma? They have an understanding. Hell, you ought to get out more."

★★★ **5** ★★★

The next day was Thursday. By the time Sam Bender roused Lucky at six-fifteen, they could hear Tom Ed on the phone next door, haranguing somebody somewhere. You could hear a little "ding" when he slammed the phone down.

It was more of the same. Before the day was over, Tom Ed would shake hands at a mill in Burlington, speak to the Jaycees in Greensboro, partake of a photo opportunity at a school in High Point, and get to Winston-Salem in time for a 4 P.M. press conference.

There was a new poll out, and this one had Tom Ed trailing by eight percentage points instead of ten.

"Hell," he grumped while he was reading the Raleigh paper in the van, "I know I can make up a point a day on that SOB."

Harry Mavredes told Lucky that Tom Ed had his own pollsters, and they showed him trailing by just four points.

"Why don't you use that, then?"

"We're saving that one for when a poll comes out that says Knox Cameron's gained a point, or things are getting stagnant, so it looks like we got some momentum. If this thing goes like I think it's going to go, we might not have to use our poll at all."

Lucky asked him wasn't Knox Cameron going to do the same thing, didn't he have his own pollsters, too?

"He might," Harry said, "but he hasn't fired off any shots yet."

"Maybe," Barry Maxwell said, "he thinks it's beneath him to do such a thing. Maybe he's waiting for God to come down and just appoint him governor," and he and Harry and Sam Bender laughed, kind of short and mean. Tom Ed didn't look up, just took a sip of his coffee and kept wading through the five daily newspapers he took on the van with him.

"See," Barry said, "you have to be very careful how you conduct these phone polls. If, for instance, we just ask them if they're going to vote for Tom Ed Sweatt, and we don't mention Knox Cameron, a lot of the great unwashed is going to say 'yeah' just to get us off the line. We've got our own people calling. They know how to ask the questions."

Lucky soon came to understand, though, that no paper other than one that was in the hip pocket of one candidate or the other would use these in-house polls.

"Hell," Sam said, perhaps more careless than usual because he wasn't fully awake yet, "half of 'em couldn't tell you who was running if you held a gun to their heads."

Tom Ed quit rustling the paper and the van got quiet. Lucky could sense the sudden tension.

"Well," Tom Ed said, drawling a little more than usual for effect, it seemed to his brother, "I sure hope they know who ol' Tom Ed Sweatt is. If I was to find out they didn't know who Tom Ed Sweatt was, I might have to fire me some press aides and campaign managers and such." His voice rose slowly and evenly as he spoke, the way it would at a rally, where he started out quietly and humbly and wound up banging his hand on the rostrum like some Primitive Baptist preacher.

"What the hell are you all doing, if the people don't know me from Knox Cameron? Do you think"—he paused and took a deep breath—"do you think that me and the Republican Party are paying you to sit around and be smug and crack jokes like you all are too smart for the poor, dumb old people out there? The people are what is going to carry me, and if they don't carry me, your asses are all back looking for some new sucker to try to ride to a full-time job!"

Harry and Barry tried to calm him down, which he eventually did on his own. But when Lucky glanced over at him to see if he was going to bite somebody, he winked out of his right eye, the one nobody in the backseats could see.

Tom Ed had always been able to get people to do what he wanted them to. Lucky figured his brother got what he and Barbara called his bullshit genes from Tommy, except instead of conning some black stoop laborer into unloading a truck for him, Tom Ed was charming his way into money and politics.

By the time he was talked into running for the Port Campbell city council in 1978, he'd already made a small fortune in real estate, which he went into after some college stardom and minor-league mediocrity in baseball.

He ran for mayor in 1984, when mayor of Port Campbell wasn't something that a lot of people even wanted. If it had been stock, Tom Ed said later, you could have bought a bunch for not much money. Everybody liked Tom Ed, and nobody paid much attention to his politics. "Hell," he told Lucky on Christmas 1983, when he was thinking about running, long before he started occasionally referring to himself in the third person, "how much damage can a mayor do, anyhow?"

He won handily, beating a Democrat from the Hill who was an old friend of the Balcoms. Tommy wanted to call his mother-in-law to gloat, but Genie wouldn't let him.

During the eight years that Tom Ed was mayor of Port Campbell, an amazing thing happened. The DrugMart chain, in New Jersey, was looking for a cheap place to move to, a town and state where they wouldn't be encumbered by a lot of taxes and regulations and unions. So they moved to Port Campbell, North Carolina, not six months after Tom Ed assumed office.

And then an even more amazing thing happened. Partly because Amos Weinberg, who still owned most of DrugMart, was charmed by Tom Ed, he started giving something back to Port Campbell.

Everybody in Port Campbell with sense, including Tom Ed, knew the drill when a Northern company moved to some tired, played-out old Southern town. The company would create some low-paying jobs for people who previously didn't have any jobs. In return, it would expect free rein and would eventually move somewhere even more depressed, such as Mexico.

Maybe Amos Weinberg was just an old Jew trying to get into heaven, as Tommy so inelegantly told Genie. But he started giving money away. They'd been trying to build a new library for years, but books weren't very high on the list of priorities around Port Campbell. So Amos Weinberg built them one that put Raleigh's main branch to shame. He put down $10 million toward a new coliseum and shamed the city and county into matching it, and all of a sudden Port Campbell had an arena that was a threat to pull in just about any country music act or college basketball tournament.

Amos Weinberg donated to the arts. He funded a new business school building at McDonald College. He built a drug-rehab center. He offered scholarships for his employees' children. He got Belks and Penney's to reopen their downtown stores, basically subsidizing them by moving DrugMart's corporate headquarters and a DrugMart down there, too, right by the new library, not far from the new coliseum.

As a favor to Tom Ed, he renovated the old ballpark so the Carolina League would move a baseball franchise to town.

So people started to look at Port Campbell, which had enjoyed its previous heyday sometime between the American Revolution and the Civil War, and they started talking about a miracle. And who did they credit for the miracle? Not Amos Weinberg, who was called to heaven in 1989, leaving a big chunk of what he couldn't take with him for his adopted town.

No, they laid credit for the miracle right at the doorstep of Tom Ed Sweatt. He was friendly, he had a kind of Will Rogers air to him, and he never really downplayed his role, always saying things like, "The Lord has blessed us by sending us opportunities, and we have made the most of them. We were given five talents and have turned them into ten." It always struck Lucky as funny, hearing all this on his rare trips back home, that the Lord sent a Jew to deliver Tom Ed and Port Campbell.

*        *        *

Some of the Republicans in Scots County started talking up Tom Ed for governor in 1991, a good fifteen months before the election. One night that summer, Barbara and Lucky were working in the kitchen, trying to get everything set up for breakfast the next morning, when Genie called, breathless, to say that some men wanted Tom Ed to run for governor. It took Lucky by surprise, because he still had trouble with the concept of Tom Ed as mayor. He didn't think about it very much until that Christmas.

The Sweatts were together for the holidays, something of a rarity: Tom Ed, Lucinda, and their two sons; Barbara, Lucky, and their mixed bag of three; Tommy, Genie, and even Felton, the only one of Tommy's siblings still living. It occurred to Lucky that, if they'd had this gathering at the home place on Mingo Road, the kids would have had to sit in another room.

Right after dessert, while Genie, Lucinda, and Barbara were getting ready to clear the table, Tom Ed dinged his spoon on the side of his glass.

"Can I say something?" He stood slowly, almost bashfully. "It's about this governor thing. They want me to run. If we can scrape up enough money, we're going to do it."

Tommy let out a whoop and almost upset what was left of the banana pudding.

"Great day in the morning!" he shouted. "I knew it! I always said you'd be governor some day."

Everybody was excited, except Lucinda and the boys, Kyle and Kevin, who must have already known about it, and Felton, who was not known to make a fuss about anything.

Lucky congratulated him, and he said, "Congratulate me after I get it, Bo. I don't even have much of a shot in the primary yet."

But things happened.

Tom Ed announced in January, and in February there was a televised debate. Tom Ed Sweatt was pitted against an odd mix of characters seeking the Republican nomination for governor of North Carolina.

There was D. Warren Gates, Jr., a man from the East whose

main credential seemed to be that his late father had been a U.S. congressman for twenty years.

There was a strange character from Hickory named Farris Baumgartner, who had once been the Grand Dragon of the Ku Klux Klan.

And there was Skip Fullwood. Fullwood, Tom Ed knew, was the one to watch. He had been in the state legislature for ten years and was well liked.

D. Warren Gates, Jr., it developed, had the personality of a stump. He came across as slow and plodding.

Farris Baumgartner was perceived as being too zealous even for a notably conservative state. He smelled, the *Charlotte Observer* said in a devastating editorial the day after the debate, of the gasoline used to light a hundred crosses of hate.

Tom Ed Sweatt and Skip Fullwood both looked and sounded acceptable, which was as much as the Republican Party of North Carolina could hope for in most gubernatorial elections. They both praised free enterprise and family values; they both damned big government and "something for nothing." Skip Fullwood seemed smoother, but Tom Ed was generally conceded to have more warmth.

After the debate, no one expected the nominee to be anybody but Tom Ed Sweatt or Skip Fullwood. Baumgartner soon dropped out, and D. Warren Gates, Jr., might as well have.

Lucky first heard his brother mention Horace Morgan some time in March, when he told Lucky that he and his campaign staff had found a sugar daddy in Durham, someone who might make it possible for him to run for governor and still keep himself, Lucinda, and the kids "out of the poorhouse." There hadn't been a poorhouse in Scots County for half a century, but it was still the downside of any risky venture for the first-generation middle class.

It was around the same time that Harry Mavredes, Barry Maxwell, Sam Bender, and the rest of the machine whose sole goal was producing a governor started "coming aboard," replacing enthusiastic but guileless amateurs.

The primary was in May. Smart money said Tom Ed Sweatt's chances were slim. Skip Fullwood was the fair-haired boy, and about the only thing you heard about Tom Ed was some analyst wondering if he could close the gap fast enough.

But Tom Ed couldn't seem to lose. Six days before the primary, word surfaced, courtesy of Harry Mavredes leaking it to a friend at the *News & Observer* in Raleigh, that Skip Fullwood had been a draft dodger. Lucky told Barbara that, best he could tell, Fullwood was like about every other college white boy in 1970, trying to save his ass from getting sent to a war nobody believed in.

But Harry Mavredes was able to dig up a photograph from a UNC yearbook and got people to identify Skip Fullwood. He had a bandanna around his head, he was wearing a tank top, and it looked as if someone had drawn a peace symbol on his forehead. The picture was of good enough quality to reproduce in various state newspapers, on flyers, and even on TV ads.

It turned out that Fullwood had been declared 1-Y because of a knee injury. Lucky and Tom Ed both knew the drill: Doctors in almost any college community were against the war, and enterprising students knew to come to the right one with a bogus knee or leg or shoulder problem their sophomore year and start building a history, so that by the time they graduated, they were "chronic."

Unfortunately for Skip Fullwood, he also got his picture taken two years later winning his age group in a Raleigh club tennis tournament.

Tom Ed Sweatt spent Vietnam in a National Guard unit. He whiled away six years, rarely doing anything more productive or dangerous than peeling potatoes and playing cards one weekend a month, two weeks every summer. If people hadn't liked Tom Ed, they wouldn't have accepted his reasoning that he was there for his country, available if his unit had been called into active duty. Anyone who had been in the Guard or reserves during Vietnam knew that Tom Ed had a better chance of being struck dead by a meteor than he did of being sent to the jungle.

The most action Tom Ed and his unit saw was when they were sent to Burlington to keep the peace after Martin Luther King, Jr.'s, assassination. But people wanted to believe him. People were heard to say, "Hell, old Tom Ed just did what everybody else did."

Skip Fullwood didn't get the same kind of understanding. Maybe the difference was the pictures—the one protesting the war, and the one celebrating the tennis championship two years after he was declared 1-Y.

Maybe it was the way Fullwood dug himself a little deeper by denying what any sighted person knew was the truth. By the day of the primary, he was dead and buried.

So Tom Ed Sweatt was the Republican nominee for governor. At the top of a hill no one thought he'd crest, he was faced with a larger one dead in front of him. The Democrats had run the state almost uninterrupted since Reconstruction, and Knox Cameron had many friends and almost no enemies.

"Bo," Tom Ed told Lucky after the primary, "I don't know what I'd do with a lead. Probably screw it up."

He did more televised debates, this time a series of three with Cameron in August, at Sparrow College. It seemed to Lucky, still viewing and reading about the campaign from the Virginia hills, that Tom Ed and Knox Cameron were almost as alike as Tom Ed and Skip Fullwood. They both promised lower taxes and, somehow at the same time, the balanced budget mandated by state law. The Republicans claimed that Cameron was soft on abortion, but soft on abortion in North Carolina meant you were hardwood instead of granite.

One night, after Lucky was coerced into joining the campaign, Barry Maxwell told him, after a few bourbon and waters, that the key to the election was Julian.

"Who," Lucky asked, "is Julian?"

"That hairstylist." Maxwell said it with a swishing movement of his right hand. "The boy that does Tom Ed's hair every couple of days. That's all it comes down to, man: whose hair looks better on TV."

The next morning, Maxwell fell into step with Lucky as they walked down the motel hallway and asked him to forget he'd ever said anything about hair, but Lucky thought he was mostly if not completely right. It was interesting to see how the two candidates worked toward the same goal from two opposite directions: Tom

Ed was about ten years younger than Knox Cameron, so while Tom Ed was trying to look "gubernatorial," Cameron appeared to be trying to look younger. The best Lucky could figure it, they both wanted to appear about fifty-one years old.

Other than hair, Lucky figured Tom Ed's best bet was his mouth. He had a kind of Ross Perot way of seeming as if he were really speaking to you through the TV set. He could, as Harry Mavredes remarked, do earnest better than anybody.

All through the late summer and into the fall, Tom Ed Sweatt and Knox Cameron hammered at each other. Lucky got most of his information from the Winston-Salem paper and through clippings that Genie sent him.

The Democrats couldn't really get anything to stick on Tom Ed, and the Republicans couldn't find any appreciable dirt on Knox Cameron, a well-meaning, second-generation North Carolina politician who'd known he was going to run for governor some day since his father, forty years before, first told him he would.

Cameron's lead, which was 20 percent in early August, kept shrinking. By October 23, there was hardly any cushion left at all.

On Thursday night, Lucky and Sam were sitting in the room at the Hilton in Winston-Salem, waiting for Harry and Barry so they could all go to dinner, when they heard Barry kick the wall that separated their rooms, then scream something. There was a door between the rooms, and Sam rushed through it, Lucky right behind him.

Barry was watching the six o'clock news on the local station. A reporter in a raincoat was talking. He appeared to be standing outside a housing development somewhere. It looked vaguely familiar to Lucky.

". . . and so the question remains: Why did Westlake Development Corporation, of which Tom Ed Sweatt was president, continue to build houses on this beautiful stretch of land west of Port Campbell, even after state inspectors warned that much of the soil here was not appropriate for building? It's a question the Republican candidate for governor will no doubt often be asked during the next few days."

Lucky didn't know Tom Ed had come into the room until he spoke.

"Shrink-swell. Shrink-frigging-swell!"

He looked as if he wanted to hit someone, but Lucky was pretty sure that the one he wanted to hit was already dead.

★★★ **6** ★★★

They wound up ordering from room service. Lucky knew he wasn't any help in this sudden brushfire that the M&M twins, Sam Bender, Tom Ed, and the rest were trying to put out, but he didn't know anyone else in Winston-Salem, so he planned to hang around while they all tried to figure out what to do with something Tom Ed thought he'd buried along with Bobby Marsh.

"You were the president of Westlake, right?" Harry asked Tom Ed.

"You know goddamn well I was the president. Hell, they knew that on the evening news. But Bobby Marsh was chairman of the board. You think I'd've let all those houses get built if I'd known everything?"

"Tom Ed," Barry said, with about as much patience as he ever showed, "we have to come up with something that sounds plausible. We have to come up with something that will make people think you were just doing your job, but that somebody higher up was doing something you didn't know about. We need to get all the facts right. We can't screw this up and we can't let it sit, in my opinion."

"You want me to lay it off on Bobby."

"Well," Sam said, "he does seem convenient."

Barry gave a short little laugh and added, "You can't libel the dead."

So Tom Ed told them the sad story of the Westlake Development

Corporation and shrink-swell soil. They'd stop him every once in a while to double-check something or other. Tom Ed didn't like being cross-examined, but he could see their point. They were writing Tom Ed's speeches, and if they put anything in them that didn't wash, the press would be all over him, and he'd be all over them.

They were in Tom Ed's room. When the phone rang, he picked it up.

"I'm sorry . . . No, something's come up . . . You heard it, too, huh? . . . Hold on just a minute. Be right back."

Tom Ed started for the door and motioned to Lucky, who set down a cold, greasy french fry and followed him.

Tom Ed shut the door behind them.

"I got something I want you to do, Bo," he said, standing so close that Lucky could smell the bourbon on his breath. "I want you to go down and keep Susannah company for a while, 'til we get this wrapped up. I'll come get you."

He might as well have taken out an ad in the paper, it seemed to Lucky. Everyone in the campaign knew about Susannah, but Tom Ed seemed to be trying to fool himself into believing that it was a secret.

"Where is she?"

"Down in the lobby. Take her to dinner, something. Hell, I don't know. It's seven-thirty; I promise I'll be down by nine-thirty . . . No, wait. Just tell her to come on up at ten. If we ain't done by then, we ain't got a chance, anyhow."

The lounge of the Hilton had leather couches thrown here and there among the potted plants. There were little glass tables in front of groups of two or three of them to set your drinks on.

Susannah was sitting by herself, with a gin and tonic on the table in front of her. She was wearing a purple silk blouse and a short black skirt. She had her knees crossed so that, coming up from the side, Lucky could see several inches above her knees. Her legs, like the rest of her, looked good.

"Tom Ed sent me," he said.

She turned around.

"Well, as long as it's in the family." She laughed as if someone had told a dirty joke.

Lucky ordered a bourbon and water. They talked a little, steering clear of embarrassing subjects like Tom Ed's family and her husband.

"So," she said, uncrossing her legs, "tell me about shrink-swell soil while I can still say it."

Tom Ed went to the University of North Carolina for two years before the St. Louis Cardinals offered him a contract to play professional baseball.

He spent two years in the minor leagues, but he was a 'tweener: He wasn't quick enough for shortstop and couldn't hit well enough to play first base, so he never got past Class A. He got in trouble, the first time he ran for mayor, when he let his campaign manager claim he was "an ex–St. Louis Cardinal" when the closest he ever came to the big leagues was getting Bob Gibson's autograph at spring training one year. Tom Ed said it was a mistake and fired the campaign manager.

He graduated from McDonald College. Lucky figured it would have been Genie, so strong on education, who would have nagged him to finish. But it was Tommy.

Tommy had little use for book learning, but he knew Tom Ed would need that college degree some day. Lucky felt that it was miraculous that their father didn't remember a particular haranguing he'd given Tom Ed one Thanksgiving after they were all speaking again. Only Tommy's poor memory saved them all from having to hear it retold, with embellishments, at least five thousand times, he was sure.

"What's gonna happen if you're running for president one day," he said, waving a turkey drumstick, "and they say, 'That Tom Ed Sweatt, I don't know about him. He's a good old boy, but he can't stay the course. Couldn't even finish college.'?"

They all laughed at Tommy, but Lucky had to concede that he was probably right. Tom Ed's man-of-the-people aura had carried him far, but it might make the people of North Carolina feel inferior to elect a governor who was a college dropout.

By the time Tom Ed graduated, he was twenty-five years old, and he'd already been a Bible and encyclopedia salesman, an insurance salesman, and a real-estate agent. He would take whatever he made and find a way to spend it, either on some Amwayesque get-rich-quick scheme or a car, it seemed to Lucky. Once, when Lucky was making a rare visit to Tommy and Genie's, Tom Ed came home driving an enormous Buick Electra that he bought just before the first oil embargo.

"Bo," he told Lucky as he was showing off the tape deck, "I'm just a nigger when it comes to cars."

They had both known Bobby Marsh since high school. Bobby was a slightly chubby boy whose family was a little better off than the Sweatts. His father was a surveyor and his mother taught school.

Bobby was bright and charismatic. He and Lucky worked together to help keep Tom Ed in the Beta Club. Tom Ed was what they had in common.

Genie didn't approve of Bobby Marsh. He'd been arrested for siphoning gas out of school buses and was always in danger of losing his driver's license. But Tommy saw him as a boy who could help his son achieve great things, and he encouraged him to come around.

Bobby Marsh's gift was that he made people want to please him. He and Tom Ed had that in common. But while Tom Ed did it by making them like him, Bobby would do it, somehow, by being impatient, short-tempered. Some days, he'd seem like Lucky's best friend, then he wouldn't speak for days, and even though Lucky knew he'd done nothing wrong, he'd find himself trying to appease him.

Lucky eventually cut off Bobby Marsh along with everything else he'd known, and he'd look with teenage contempt as Bobby worked his magic on those around him. He only spared Tom Ed, who Lucky felt may have been the only true friend that Bobby

Marsh allowed. He had to admit, even as he despised his cunning, that Bobby was good. When he did deign to put someone in his good graces, it was as if the sun had suddenly come out. Even in high school, he had a fat man's infectious laugh, and he was an athlete with his words, quick and mobile.

Bobby went to college at Tennessee. When he came home in 1968, Tom Ed was just back from his second and last season in pro baseball, and he and Bobby again fell in together.

Bobby got into real estate first. When everybody else their age was turning away from making money and starting to let their hair grow long, Bobby Marsh didn't have much competition. And when Tom Ed saw how much money Bobby was making selling lots at a new development outside Charlotte, he quit his insurance job and went to work for Bobby, who was already assistant sales manager.

Somehow, Bobby Marsh and Tom Ed found enough people with extra money to buy almost two thousand acres of land west of Port Campbell, around Bethel Lake, where they had gone swimming and double-dating in high school.

Tom Ed and Bobby had been thinking about that lake for some time. They had been selling lots on one just like it outside Charlotte, and they realized that the most run-down, weed-choked millpond in the world could be made into a luxury development with a little imagination and a lot of somebody else's money.

So Tom Ed and Bobby Marsh came back to Scots County in 1975, when they were both twenty-nine years old. They had made a killing in Charlotte, and they both knew older, richer men in Port Campbell who would take a chance on them.

They called it Westlake. The plan was to have about 2,400 houses and condominiums, all sold as either "lakefront," "lake view," or "near the lake." They sold about three fourths of them before the trouble started.

They divided it into four communities: Mossy Creek, Mt. Nebo, Ransom's Branch, and Peach Orchard. They spent a couple of years putting everything together, clearing the land and damming up what was now called Westlake. The land they bought was five miles west of town, in an undesirable direction. The terrain was sand hills; the trees were mostly scrub pines and pin oaks, except around the lake.

The first time Lucky saw Tom Ed and Bobby's dream, it hadn't changed much from when they were kids. You still had to drive a mile down a dirt road to get there. But by then, Tom Ed and Bobby had already torn down the old bathhouses and concession stands, and there were little fires going all over the place from where they were clearing and burning.

Despite his unabated desire to see one of his sons amount to something, Tommy had little faith in the project. Every time Genie called, she'd tell Lucky how worried he was that Tom Ed would go broke. Tom Ed never shared his father's concern. "Hell," he told Lucky once, "we got a corporation. They can't take but so much. The old man thinks they still put you in the poorhouse if you go bankrupt. Bobby says everybody he knows that's amounted to shit has gone bankrupt at least once.

"The old man kills me," he went on. "He's always pushing, pushing, do this, do that, but when push comes to shove, he ain't got the stones."

As little sympathy as he had for Tommy Sweatt at the time, Lucky knew, but didn't say, that Tom Ed had "stones" because his father had spent the bulk of their childhood making sure at least one of his sons had them.

The lots sold slowly at first. Tommy's worrying even seemed to carry over to Tom Ed for a while.

But then came the eighties. Tom Ed and Bobby, who was now calling himself Robert Marsh, had both campaigned for Reagan, and it was Lucky's impression that Tom Ed credited the Republicans with saving him.

Something certainly saved them and the Westlake Corporation. The economy got better, at least for the kind of people who could build on Tom Ed and Bobby's upscale lake.

Soon, every builder in Scots County wanted a piece of Westlake, and Tom Ed and Bobby, as would be revealed later, didn't say no to anybody. You could see, in retrospect, that the first homes were constructed with care and pride. Those were the ones around the lake, where there were some sycamores and the kind of good-postured pines that people were used to seeing around the resorts at Pinehurst. The houses around the lake had a lot of brick in them, two-car garages, lots of "extras." Most important, they had good foundations.

The problems that came up later got progressively worse the farther away from the lake one built, although it was in patches. One house would be perfectly fine and the one next door would have to be abandoned.

By the mid-eighties, Tom Ed and Robert Marsh were rich, at least by Port Campbell standards. And Tom Ed had done the one thing that every poor boy dreams of doing: He had bought his parents a new house.

It wasn't right on the lake, but it was a fine house nonetheless, a large rancher, three bedrooms with a big screened porch at the back that looked into a small wooded area where Genie planted dozens of azaleas. Tom Ed had gotten a special deal from one of the builders, Camp Construction, which was one of the last to build at Westlake.

Genie was against leaving their old home on Mingo Road. She wondered how she was going to get to the Baptist church and if she'd see all her friends. Tommy, though, had been waiting for this all his life. He finally talked his wife into abandoning their old tin-roof house and moving to Westlake. Genie knew, too, that it would hurt Tom Ed if he couldn't do this for her.

Every time somebody from Arsenal Hill would move to his new neighborhood, Tommy would point it out to Genie and Tom Ed, as if this was even better than the Hill, as if his mother-in-law and her ilk wanted to move into his neighborhood now. He would go for long walks every day, and everybody for blocks around knew him. Tommy, who had never met a stranger, was in his element. He vehemently denied ever doubting the viability of Westlake.

The trouble started in 1985. The *Port Campbell Post* did a story on one house whose foundation was so cracked that the owners couldn't shut some of the doors. It was going to cost them more than $15,000 to fix it, and nobody was taking responsibility. The county inspector had okayed it, but they weren't allowed to sue the county, so they were stuck.

But then more people started coming forward. It seemed to Lucky that Genie and Tommy blamed the *Port Campbell Post* more than they blamed Tom Ed or Robert Marsh.

"Damn paper near 'bout won a Pulitzer Prize on poor old Bobby Marsh's corpse," Tommy said more than once.

By early 1986, it was in the paper almost daily. Tom Ed was already mayor, and he was feeling the heat.

The most damning evidence the paper produced came from a soil scientist from N.C. State who said he'd warned the Westlake Corporation back in 1977, when they were just getting started, that the land wasn't really meant for construction. The soil around the lake was mostly clay, so thick that it could pull people's shoes off their feet when it was muddy. It didn't perk very well; in some parts, water would stand for days after a rain. If you must and will build out there, he said he'd told them, you'd better make the foundations very deep and very wide.

An old farmer who was interviewed by the paper said that they used to call the land around Westlake "drunkard's clay" because of the way you had to weave about in the wet, unsteady muck, fighting to keep your balance, trying to gain solid footing.

But Tom Ed and Robert Marsh were in a bind. They'd lose everything if they didn't build, so they built. The land around the lake was developed mostly by high-quality builders who built their houses wide and deep, good solid foundations under all of them.

But it got a little dicier after that. The *Post* turned up stories about county commissioners who were given incredible deals on land around the lake. In exchange, it seemed that the inspectors' idea of examining a foundation was to drive by the house and blow the horn.

By this time, it was pretty obvious that Tommy and Genie's house was part of the problem. When Lucky saw it in April of '86, there were stair-step cracks running from the top to the bottom, all down the foundation, which was about half as thick as the foundations of the houses down by the lake.

The paper got a break when one of the reporters went to see Doc Tatum. Doc had been a county commissioner since World War II; everybody in the county knew him. They didn't think he was necessarily the most honest man in the world, but he did a lot of favors for a lot of people.

When the *Post* reporter went to visit Doc Tatum, the commissioner was dying of prostate cancer. Either he was trying to be honest on his deathbed, or he was so used to the way things were handled in Scots County that he didn't see anything wrong with what had been done. Whatever the case, he told the reporter about what Robert Marsh had given him and James Batts and Billy Sinclair, the three commissioners who had backed the Westlake project while the other two had expressed some concerns.

The one councilman who was still alive and healthy, Billy Sinclair, was indicted on a variety of charges relating to Westlake Corporation by the end of 1986, and so was Robert Marsh.

The top-rated drive-time radio station in Port Campbell had a field day, even composing a send-up song called "Foundation Blues" that was the talk of Scots County for a few weeks.

Lucky sang to Susannah, in a low, unsteady tenor, the verse he remembered:

> "Got a crack down in my basement
> That gets wider every day.
> What I thought was solid footing,
> Ain't a thing but drunkard's clay.

> Got the blues,
> Foundation blues,
> Got them Westlakin', belly-achin',
> Cracked-foundation blues."

The fact that Tom Ed Sweatt was able to run for governor six years later hinged on one fact: Robert Marsh liked to handle everything. What little correspondence there was with the three commissioners had Marsh's signature at the end of it. It was Marsh with whom the soil scientist corresponded.

There was little doubt in Lucky's mind that Tom Ed knew

about the shrink-swell soil, knew about the bought-off commissioners, knew that, with every generation of builders that came to Westlake, the warning about building stronger foundations was given in a little softer voice. And, with no county inspectors to watch over them, some of the builders, in the words of the prosecutor, did it cheap and wrong.

Everything had Robert Marsh's fingerprints on it. He was the man to whom Billy Sinclair and the soil scientist pointed. He was the chairman of the board. With every story, Tom Ed's role of president seemed to shrink just a little as Robert Marsh's culpability swelled. When the IRS got into it, there was Robert Marsh again.

The way Lucky saw it, when push came to shove, people just liked Tom Ed more than they did Robert Marsh, who had made some enemies along the way. People were afraid of him, and when they had a chance to put the boot to somebody who had made them crawl, most of them didn't hesitate.

It didn't hurt Tom Ed that he had friends at the newspaper. The man who was sports editor when Tom Ed was a three-sport star at Geddie High and North Carolina was now the editor of the whole paper. He and Tom Ed knew each other socially. The paper had backed Tom Ed the first time he ran for mayor and seemed to feel protective toward him.

There were stories that Tom Ed was prepared to testify against Robert Marsh if it came to that, to swear under oath that he had known almost nothing about shrink-swell soil.

But it never came to that. Robert Marsh surprised everybody. Maybe it was because his wife and kids left him. Maybe it was seeing Westlake crack and fall apart like one of its poorly constructed houses. Maybe it was the idea of hard time, which, between the state and the IRS, was a likelihood.

When Robert Marsh didn't show up for the preliminary hearing, they sent a sheriff's deputy around to get him at his home on the point at Westlake, a two-story Georgian containing four thousand square feet and commanding a view from a twenty-foot bluff. They found his body in the basement rec room. None of the neighbors had even heard the shot. It was a closed-casket funeral, and his wife and children didn't even come back for it.

What would Robert Marsh have said if he'd stood trial? He'd left no note. Tom Ed claimed he'd lost his best friend and said he wished that he'd kept a closer eye on him, that Bobby was just like him, a poor boy who wanted to amount to something, but that he'd just gone astray. He said a prayer at the funeral.

Genie and Tommy finally had to move out of their house when Tommy realized that a marble he dropped on one side of the living room would roll all the way across to the other side, pretty fast, on the slowly tilting hardwood floor, and that the chimney was separating from the side of the house. Tom Ed found them a new place, the place they were still living, and neither Tommy nor Genie would talk about the other house. Genie told Lucky once that Tommy didn't go for walks like he did before, though, and that the neighbors weren't as friendly.

Tom Ed did have to file for bankruptcy, or the Westlake Corporation did, but he'd socked enough away elsewhere that he barely seemed affected. He was reelected as mayor in '88 with a lot of help from the Weinbergs. It seemed to Lucky that, in no time at all, he'd gotten back to where he was before drunkard's clay. While there were still people who at least partially blamed him for Westlake, there weren't enough of them to hurt. In 1992, there were still almost four thousand people living at Westlake, many of them next to abandoned houses.

"Tom Ed just has to pick his friends better," Tommy was heard to say just after the 1988 election.

The one thing that was most interesting to Lucky about the whole affair, though, was that Tom Ed never lived at Westlake. When he and Bobby Marsh were trying to get started, Tom Ed and Lucinda and the boys rented a place on Arsenal Hill. When they hit it big, they bought a place on Arsenal Hill, among the old money and not far from Genie's mother.

By the time Lucky had told Susannah Morgan the sad story of Bobby Marsh and shrink-swell soil, it was close to ten o'clock and

they had charged four rather expensive drinks each to Tom Ed's
room.

"Man," she shook her head. "Some story. Well, I better see if the
next governor of our great state has got time for me, or if he's got
them old foundation blues."

When they both started to get up, Lucky's leg buckled and he
fell back into the soft leather chair.

"Are you okay?" she asked, and he made a joke about not having to drive very far.

Lucky barely limped at all anymore, unless he had to sit for a
couple of hours and the leg got stiff. He was glad most of their
campaign hops were short. He told Susannah to go on up, that he'd
just sit there for a minute. He felt sure that his brother and the
M&M twins had already figured out what to do about shrink-
swell.

He knew that if he started talking about the polio after four
strong drinks, he'd wind up telling her how he vanished from the
world of Tommy Sweatt at the ripe old age of eight.

## 7

On Friday, the campaign bounced from Hickory to Asheville to Boone, a whirlwind touching down at a school here, a furniture factory there, trying to suck voters into its growing mass. Lucky planned to meet Barbara after Tom Ed's afternoon speech at Appalachian State and then spend Friday night and Saturday with her in the mountains, catching up with the van Sunday morning in Salisbury.

Kim and Chris, who were eighteen and seventeen, would be taking care of Benny, who was six and had recently told Barbara that he wanted a dog "so I can be the boss of somebody."

This morning, there was a surprise. Susannah Morgan had officially joined the campaign. She was an attorney, Lucky reasoned, so maybe it didn't look as suspicious to outsiders as it did to the M&M twins, Sam, and the rest.

They were getting ready to board the van after breakfast when Sam took Lucky aside.

"Can you talk to him?"

Lucky asked about what, although he knew.

"You know damn well what. She can ruin everything we've built so far."

"Tom Ed's got a mind of his own. He's not likely to pay attention to anything I say."

Sam sighed. "Well, see what you can do. It's not just me. Harry and Barry and the rest are worried. It's okay to screw around—excuse me, I know he's your brother, but this is important—it's all right to screw around on the campaign. Hell, if he gets elected governor, he can marry her. But the Cameron people will bury us if this gets out."

Lucky said she seemed to him to be less of a risk with an official title than she was just showing up at the hotel.

Sam shook his head. "Do what you can."

Barry had set up a press conference for that morning at eight, at the Hilton, to answer the shrink-swell charges, so they would be leaving town later than usual.

Tom Ed handled it as well as anyone could have. He never damned Bobby Marsh, calling him a childhood friend who had been there when Tom Ed needed him. Lucky thought he left the impression that he went along with an old friend out of loyalty, that he wouldn't desert him when things got tough, and that he was never aware of the soil scientist's report or any of the illegal dealings with the county commissioners until it all came out in the newspapers. There was no paperwork to refute him, and nobody wanted to dislike Tom Ed. His eyes were wet when he talked about Bobby's suicide.

Tom Ed sealed it when he told the news media about his dream of buying his parents a nice home.

"And I bought 'em the nicest home I could," he said, "right in a good neighborhood in Westlake. And you know what? The foundation cracked on it, and my momma and daddy, who worked all their lives so I could be here today, had to move out.

"Do you think," he said, and he paused, as if to compose himself, "do you think that I would have bought my momma and daddy a house out there if I'd of known about any of this? If you think I'm that kind of man, then you ought not to vote for me or support me."

And he stepped back and walked out of the room.

By nightfall, most of the editorial writers would be praising Tom Ed for being so forthcoming, although Lucky felt sure he'd have paid a princely sum to never have had shrink-swell come up at all. He'd be tweaked some for not being more aware of what Bobby Marsh was doing, and the Democrats would try to make hay out of it, but it was pretty obvious that Tom Ed Sweatt was still very much politically alive.

At Hickory, Tom Ed was interviewed and then spoke at a rally. It was after one when they stopped for lunch at a diner outside Marion. It wasn't really lunch, just a photo opportunity. The diner claimed to make the best western North Carolina barbecue, and Tom Ed was supposed to compare it with the eastern kind that had contributed so much to his present full figure.

Tom Ed's mission was to avoid insulting anybody's barbecue. Lucky had long known that his brother had a knack for being able to kid people without offending them, and Tom Ed again rose to the occasion.

"Well," he said after he'd taken a bite of the sloppier, wetter pork barbecue they served west of Interstate 85, "this here reminds me a little bit of some stuff we have over in Scots County. We call it barbecue. You know, with a little work, this stuff could be as good as barbecue." And he reached over and put his arm around the man who owned the diner, at the same time that a couple of photographers started snapping.

There was good-natured moaning and groaning from the crowd.

"Now, you all know I can't deny my heritage," he said, holding his hands up in protest. "They'd sic the dogs on me back in Port Campbell if I said this was better than what they make back home. Tommy and Genie Sweatt would disown me."

Lucky saw Susannah standing off to one side. Their eyes met and they both laughed and shook their heads, and Lucky knew it had always been like this when Tom Ed turned on the brights.

The barbecue opportunity broke up, and they began heading back to the van for the trip to Asheville. Lucky saw Tom Ed duck into the kitchen, and he followed. There was a back room where the cook had prepared a plate of barbecue with some coleslaw and hush puppies and a big Styrofoam cup full of Pepsi—Tom Ed's lunch.

Lucky had few chances to talk with his brother in private, so he sat down across the picnic table from him.

Tom Ed looked up. With his mouth full, he asked Lucky if he wanted some.

"No, but can I have a minute instead?"

Tom Ed shrugged. "The barbecue'll be a better deal."

So Lucky told him how worried everyone was about Susannah, feeling guilty for spoiling his five-minute lunch. He told Tom Ed that everyone else was afraid to talk to him about it.

"Who? Who's afraid to talk to me?"

Lucky wouldn't tell him.

"They think they can butt into my business, tell me how to live my life?" His face was turning red; he was losing the battle to keep his voice down. People were peeking through the glass door to the kitchen, wanting to get a glimpse of Tom Ed.

He soon calmed down, as he always had. Tom Ed's like a summer storm, Genie had said more than once: He blows up in a hurry and then in ten minutes the sun's shining.

"These other people," Lucky told him, "they're trying to keep something from happening that'll ruin the campaign. I got bigger worries, though. I don't want anything to happen to you, yourself, no matter whether you get to be governor or not."

Tom Ed's face softened a little.

"It's okay, Bo," he said, patting Lucky's hand and lowering his voice some. "I know what you're saying. You think I ought to be worried about Horace Morgan. If Horace wanted to, he could squash me like a bug. Hell, I know that. But Horace likes me. That's the funny thing about it. He don't even care that much about Susannah, truth be known. He uses 'em and loses 'em, like he said. Told me that him and Susannah had an understanding.

"Know what he told me one time? He said that I'd save him a lot of alimony if I could get her to go quietly."

Lucky, feeling bold, wondered about Lucinda and the boys.

"Lucinda and me haven't been getting along so good, Bo. Between you and me, I've been waiting for the boys to get away from home. Felt like I owed them that much. But this might be it.

Might be time to cut the ties. And it ain't a one-way street, let me tell you something. She's give me some lumps."

Tom Ed got up, accidentally knocking over his half-full Pepsi in the process. He was on his way out even before a waitress came rushing in and told him to never mind, she'd get it. He stopped long enough to take the owner aside and tell him that that was the best barbecue he'd ever eaten, then stepped back and said, "But if you tell that to anybody in Scots County, I'll swear I never said it," and they both burst out laughing.

They were almost to the van, where everyone else was waiting, when Tom Ed turned to Lucky.

"Don't worry, Bo. She's official now. If we have a late-night strategy meeting, who's going to know?"

Tom Ed had been telling him not to worry as long as Lucky could remember.

He couldn't help it, Lucky knew.

What, after all, had Tom Ed Sweatt ever had to worry about? He hadn't ever become invisible.

Lucky and Tom Ed had the same teacher in the third grade, just as they had in the first two. They were Mrs. Culbreth's pets. It was the first year they were given real grades, and they both got straight A's the first two report periods, the only ones in their class to do so. They were always on each other's teams in softball and then, when the weather got colder, football. Even though they were the two best athletes, it was understood that the Sweatts were always to be on the same team.

By then, it was taken for granted that they could walk home from school. Genie and Tommy knew they were trustworthy.

They would race, if there wasn't any traffic. Either Tom Ed would win by half a step or it would be a tie. Lucky could only remember beating his brother once.

But one day, in early November, Tom Ed won by two steps. When they raced the next day, it was four steps. Lucky wouldn't race him again after that. But by the middle of the month, it was hard for Lucky to keep up with Tom Ed walking, and he couldn't seem to do anything right when they played football. It wasn't such a disadvantage anymore to play against the Sweatts.

They were fearless, heedless boys. Tom Ed kept trying to get Lucky to race him again; Lucky kept refusing, but he was still under his father's spell, still convinced nothing bad could happen to Tommy Sweatt's sons.

Finally, Genie took Lucky to the doctor. Tommy kept trying to talk her out of going, as if bad news couldn't be actualized if it wasn't confirmed.

Dr. Squires knew right away that it was polio.

Lucky was one of the last children in Scots County to fall before the Salk vaccine made iron lungs and leg braces almost obsolete. Years later, reading the story of the last GI to die in Vietnam, he knew how the man's family must have felt.

There was the usual horror: weeks and weeks in bed, nurses and Genie massaging a leg that had gone dead, then the hated, heavy braces, the lost year of school, the knowledge that he would never again be one of the golden twins.

When Lucky was in the hospital, he saw children who had been in iron lungs for a very long time and weren't ever going to be any better. The wasted, pain-wracked red-haired boy sharing his room died the first week after Lucky was admitted. He came to understand that loss was relative.

What really changed was different from what he might have expected, as much as eight-year-olds expect anything.

Lucky came home in early January. His parents had set up the guest room as his bedroom, mainly because Tommy felt it would be difficult for Tom Ed to have to be there during all the extensive "doctoring" that still had to be done on his brother. Except for the hospital, it was the first time in their lives that Tom Ed and Lucky had slept in separate rooms. It seemed to Lucky that this bothered Tom Ed more than it did him; there was plenty for Lucky to think and fret about other than his twin's absence.

There was a split second, coming home, with Tommy sitting next to him in the back of the ambulance, when Lucky saw his future. He looked up and over at his father, and what he saw in

Tommy's eyes was what a corpse might expect to see if he could look up out of the casket at one of the mourners. And then Tommy looked away, without saying a word.

When they got home, it became clear rather quickly that Tommy wasn't going anywhere near "the sickroom" if he could help it. Lucky would see him about once a week.

Tom Ed visited often at first, and they'd talk just like they always had. But one day they were in Lucky's room, talking about baseball, when Lucky heard his father call Tom Ed in a sharp voice.

"I gotta go," he said, and then he blurted out, "Daddy doesn't want me to catch it."

It was some time before Lucky came to understand that polio wasn't really contagious. He wondered, later, if it wasn't something else that Tommy was afraid Tom Ed would catch, like bad luck.

Everything changed. By March, Lucky could get up and begin his therapy. By late spring, he could walk around and was already making plans to repeat the third grade in the fall.

But Tommy had taken Tom Ed and gone on. Competing in sports and much of the roughhouse play that was so much of their lives before polio came was out of the question, of course, but there was more. They didn't play Parcheesi anymore, or checkers. Tommy had enjoyed playing games with the boys, before polio. Tom Ed or Lucky would play checkers, with the winner taking on Tommy, and then the winner of that playing the other one. And Tommy would cheat. He would roll a seven when he needed eight to send his opponent home in Parcheesi, then try to take eight, roaring in mock outrage when he was caught.

It was the same in baseball. He had shown the twins the hidden-ball trick, where the first baseman goes up to talk to the pitcher and the pitcher slips him the ball so he can tag the man at first as soon as he takes his lead.

"You got to watch the other feller," he'd say, winking. "Everybody's trying to win, any way they can."

Now, though, it was mostly Lucky and Tom Ed or Lucky and Genie. One of Lucky's sharpest memories of that spring was of playing some card game with his mother and being able to hear the crack out in the yard as Tom Ed connected with a baseball. He could hear Tommy yell something, and he knew his father was out there with Tom Ed, pushing him from one level to the next, underhand to overhand pitching to fast overhand. Learn one step and move up to the next. And now they were moving on without him.

In a strange way, it was a relief to Lucky. It took all his strength just to get through the therapy. It was, for quite a while, almost pleasant not to have Tommy directly in his face all the time, pushing for more, better, faster.

It wasn't until warm weather, when the worst of it was over, that it really hit him. There wouldn't be any more pep talks. There wouldn't be any more of Tommy telling both twins how they were going to amount to something. Now he was in the next room telling Tom Ed that. All he told Lucky, when he looked in at all, was good night.

Tommy had an extra room built on the house so that each twin could have his own room, something neither of them wanted very much.

That fall, wearing a brace, Lucky had to either catch the bus or get Tommy to drive him to school, something that didn't please his father at all. Tom Ed offered to ride the bus, too, but he tired of that pretty quickly. They'd always told the others kids, who had no choice, that riding the bus was for babies.

Before polio, Lucky had usually been a half-step ahead of his brother in the classroom. Now, with time on his hands, he turned more to reading, and the gap widened a little. By Christmas, the third-grade teacher let him move into a combined third-and-fourth grade room, where Mrs. Spivey let him do fourth-grade homework.

At the end of Lucky's second third-grade year, he was allowed to skip to the fifth.

It wasn't the same, though. Lucky somehow knew he would always be, after that, "the one who had polio." He discovered the meanness of children, and he had more than one fight that ended when someone pushed him down and ran away, calling him a gimp or a cripple. Gradually, and then not so gradually, all the self-confidence that he had acquired by being king of the hill the first eight years of his life melted, until there was nothing left but a dirty pile of slush to remind him of all that bright promise.

Tom Ed did a lot of fighting on Lucky's behalf, and Lucky did a fair amount of Tom Ed's homework.

Tommy didn't seem to mind Tom Ed getting into fights defending Lucky, as if Lucky were now part of what Tom Ed was supposed to overcome, like being poor or learning to hit a curve. It was, Lucky knew, a long fall from his prior grace.

By seventh grade, he'd already had three operations, and the doctor said he was about the best he was going to be, the implication in his sigh after the last surgery being that this "best" was none too good. There was no more need for a brace, but he still limped a little, even walking.

Now seeing himself as one instead of half of two, Tom Ed seemed to begin compensating, the way a man who has lost his legs might build up powerful arms or a blind person might hone his other senses. He became more and more driven, determined to be the best in whatever he tried, making up for Lucky's not being there. And Tommy pushed all the harder, now that he could concentrate on one instead of two. He seemed to lose some of the bubbly, mercurial good humor that made people want to be around him.

Tom Ed was always captain of the football, basketball, and baseball teams. Two years before he got to high school, the coaches at Geddie High knew who he was. They would stop by to see a game his elementary school was playing, and they'd go sit with Tommy, and Genie, if she was there.

Lucky was the manager, washing towels for kids he wouldn't even have chosen for his team when they were in second grade.

The twins were both in the safety patrol, joining the other students of sufficient grades and character. They wore white belts that crisscrossed their chests and helped direct traffic before and after school.

It was a given that the twins would be in the safety patrol. Tom Ed had A's and B's all the way through, and Lucky hadn't had a B since the fifth grade.

Lucky, in fact, had the best grades of anyone at Mingo Elementary School. And they always made the seventh-grader with the best grades the captain of the safety patrol.

That year, they had an assembly the second day of school and announced the new safety patrol members. All the chosen students had to walk up to the stage. Then the principal, Mr. Green, said that they'd had a hard time picking the captain, and he looked over in Lucky and Tom Ed's direction. The twins were standing side by side because it was all done alphabetically.

Something told Lucky to watch out. Maybe it was because Mr. Green, who'd just come there the year before, was what people called a "man's man." He attended all the sports events, sometimes sitting on the bench like an assistant coach. The principal before him, Miss Downing, was seventy when she retired and didn't seem to know that Mingo Elementary had a baseball team. Mr. Green was the kind of principal who liked to give all the spankings himself.

"This year's safety patrol captain," he said, "is a boy who best exemplifies everything that a leader should be. He excels on the athletic field as well as in the classroom."

Lucky knew then that Tom Ed was it. They hadn't talked about it beforehand, but they had both assumed all along that the captaincy was Lucky's. Because the safety patrol captain had to sometimes represent the school, like in the Christmas parade in Port Campbell, Lucky worried about how his leg would hold up. But until Mr. Green started talking about excelling on the athletic field and "a strong mind in a strong body," he had taken the honor for granted. He promised himself afterward that he'd never, ever, take anything for granted again, that hope was too much of a long shot.

From the corner of his eye, Lucky could see his brother swallow hard as he stepped forward to receive the silver bar that would set him apart from the other patrol members.

Afterward, at lunch, the twins sat together, something they didn't always do anymore.

"That damn Mr. Green," Tom Ed said. "He cheated you. You ought to have been the captain. I'm going to tell him, too."

But pretty soon Mr. Green was calling Tom Ed out of class to help him with this or that, and nothing ever came of it except that Tom Ed was safety patrol captain.

Genie knew what had happened, and Lucky assumed that Tommy did, too, although, despite his insistence on good grades, his heart really wasn't into books.

But nobody talked about it. Lucky would have felt better if Mr. Green had called him in and told him, straight up, that he wasn't sure he could handle all the physical demands of this seventh-grade perk. He knew that Genie and Tommy, assuming he was aware, were in a bind because they would be pitting one of their sons against the other, but he wouldn't have minded if someone had been a little upset.

Finally, though, Lucky chewed it down to where it was just a tiny lump that he could swallow. He was getting good at swallowing things.

By the time they'd gone from Hickory to Asheville to Boone, everyone was a little cranky. Tom Ed snapped at a TV reporter who asked him about shrink-swell soil again, asking him if he hadn't "read the damn press release." Harry and Barry tried to smooth things over.

The last straw for Tom Ed, though, was when someone told him that Tommy had been quoted in the *Port Campbell Post* as saying that shrink-swell wasn't that bad, anyhow, and that the people who sued the Westlake Corporation were "just a bunch of soreheads," that he and Genie were "real happy" in their new place. Lucky figured the newspaper people probably swooped down on them right after Tom Ed's press conference.

"That damned old man," Tom Ed swore when they returned to the van. Sam Bender was in the back. The rest hadn't returned yet. Susannah, on Tom Ed's instructions, was riding in the other van with three of the campaign workers.

"Why doesn't he just keep his mouth shut, like I told him to do five hundred times? Goddamn, goddamn, goddamn. I don't believe the Democrats can hold us off, Bo, but Tommy might save 'em yet, if he keeps running his mouth."

Even with the tinted glass, some of the crowd could see in, and Lucky guessed that they could tell that the candidate wasn't exactly in a gleeful mood.

He told Tom Ed that it probably wouldn't amount to much, that nobody was going to pay much attention to Tommy one way or the other.

Tom Ed looked as if he were about to ask his brother what the hell he knew about politics anyhow, but then he seemed to catch himself. He patted Lucky on the knee.

"I know, Bo," he said. "But it's always going to be something. If we win this thing, if I get to be governor of the great state of North Carolina, he'll be after me to be a senator or something. If I was president, he'd want me to run for king of the world, I swear to God."

It was Lucky's considered opinion that, if Tom Ed won the election, Tommy Sweatt would die a happy man. But he conceded that Tom Ed probably knew their father better than he did, since he was the one still being pushed.

"He's been trying to help me all my life," Tom Ed said, sighing, his face going slack as he stared straight ahead. "If he helps me much more, they're going to have to fit me for a straitjacket."

Lucky almost felt like apologizing for leaving Tom Ed out there to deal with Tommy all by himself.

## 8

Friday night, Barbara's waiting at the hotel in Boone, in the lobby full of campaign workers and reporters and camera crews and young Republicans, and Lucky can't find her at first.

He spots her, finally, sitting at a table in the coffee shop that is set in the middle of the lobby itself. She's reading a P.G. Wodehouse paperback. She devours them the way some people do murder mysteries or spy thrillers; Lucky can't understand the attraction.

He envies his wife's lack of anxiety. He knows that, if he were waiting for someone in a hotel coffee shop, he'd be looking up every thirty seconds, walking around, checking out the magazine stand, sure the person he was supposed to meet had forgotten, or he had the wrong hotel. But Barbara could sit in a place like that for two hours, knowing that whoever she was supposed to meet would eventually find her.

Barbara has dark, straight hair, parted down the middle, the same way she's been wearing it since the late sixties. It's going a little gray now, just as Lucky's is, but while he's gained thirty pounds since high school, she still resembles her yearbook pictures. She complains, when she and Lucky are in bed, that she's sagging and slipping, and she says she's afraid he'll leave her for some twenty-year-old coed, but Lucky knows she's too smart to think a thing like that could actually ever happen.

Lucky tells her sometimes that he wishes he'd known her in

high school, or even grammar school, but she tells him that he doesn't want that, because she was a mess back then. Lucky tells her he doesn't trust anyone who wasn't a mess in high school.

Barbara looks up when her husband is about five feet away. She reaches up and brushes a strand of hair away from her face, and Lucky realizes how much he's missed seeing her do that for the better part of a week.

"What?" she asks when she sees him staring. She reaches up with her hand again. "Do I have something on my mouth? Tell me."

He gives her a substantial enough kiss to draw a small round of applause from those around them.

The next day, Saturday, they're having funeral services for the Reverend Gary Thorne in Charlotte, and Tom Ed is one of the featured speakers. According to Sam Bender, he'll be flanked by a well-known right-to-life advocate and James Barnwell, the TV evangelist who has his own college.

Lucky and Barbara go up to White Top in the morning and take a four-mile hike to the summit. It's a gradual enough slope that Lucky can make it fairly easily; they do most of the climbing with the car, just getting to the trailhead.

It's misting when they start out, and Barbara has to coax Lucky out of the car. They disappear into a laurel thicket and eventually walk into a hardwood forest that doesn't give them much of a view. But then, when they come out near the top, it opens into a bald. They're walking on part of the Appalachian Trail, but they don't see another soul all the way up. Too late in the season, Lucky figures. Late enough to get snow this high up. If it was his choice, they'd never go up this late, but Barbara, the mountain girl and the adventurer, had her heart set on climbing White Top today.

At the top, they've outclimbed the mist, and the sun breaks through. Barbara figures they can see Kentucky off in the distance, about six peaks away. Lucky has to admit that, as with so many of Barbara's ideas, this one had more merit than he'd originally thought.

They share a picnic lunch on one of the rocks on the other side of the summit. Then they slip behind the rock, she lays out the blanket on the ground, and they make love right there, Barbara on top. They're still wearing all their clothes except she's got her jeans pulled down and had the foresight not to wear any panties. They can see just about forever, and Lucky figures forever can see them if it has a mind to.

Later, back at the hotel, they're in bed eating room-service food when the six o'clock news comes on. The first item is the Reverend Thorne's funeral, and Tom Ed gets most of a minute of airtime. The funeral was held at a college gymnasium, and the TV reporter says that about five thousand people showed up. Probably every TV station and newspaper in the state, too, Lucky guesses.

Tom Ed's wearing a navy-blue robe; it looks to Lucky as if the Church of the Rock has made him an honorary minister. And he sounds as if he's working a revival. One of Tom Ed's strong points has always been blending in. Lucky tells Barbara that Tom Ed can talk Ph.D. or he can talk ditch-digging. Barbara calls him the lizard, because she says he can change colors, but Lucky tells her a politician that was the same color all the time wouldn't ever get elected.

"The Reverend Gary Thorne," Tom Ed booms out, "shall not die in vain. You weep for the crucifixion today, but I tell you, brothers and sisters, that the resurrection is coming soon. The Reverend Thorne is with us."

They can hear amens and moaning from the crowd. They only get the abridged version, but Lucky can see Tom Ed starting out slow and low and measured, the way he does, then gradually raising the heat until he's boiling and the audience is in the palm of his hand. Tom Ed, his brother knows, can make you want to do something.

Barbara sets down a drumstick and wipes her mouth with the back of her hand.

"Does he believe that crap?" she asks, and Lucky knows she means the antiabortion stance.

He tells her what Harry and Barry and Sam Bender are telling him, that Tom Ed is doing just about anything right now to get elected.

"But isn't he going to have to answer to those people, if they're all supporting him?"

Lucky tells her he guesses he will, but that if Tom Ed will lie about supporting their point of view in the first place, he might lie again.

Barbara sighs. "I guess that's the best we can hope for from Tom Ed, that two wrongs will make a right."

Lucky doesn't say much, one way or the other, because he knows he's caught in the middle. There probably isn't much that Tom Ed and he agree on politically anymore. But Tom Ed is still Tom Ed, the mirror image he slept and played and dreamed with, and he knows that if they don't somehow connect now, if he doesn't help Tom Ed get this thing he thinks he has to have, then they're history.

There were years and years when history was all Lucky ever wanted him and Tom Ed to be. Some of it was justified, but Lucky has come to feel that some of it was just pride and hurt feelings.

He and Barbara go around and around about that one. If your family is just dead wrong, do you write them off for dead and reinvent yourself, or do you stay with them like you do a marriage, for better or for worse?

She'll ask Lucky sometimes what he'd have done if he was Hitler's brother, or Stalin's son. Lucky tells her that neither his brother nor his father has exactly been Hitler, and Tom Ed is who he's been brought up to be.

Lucky gets angrier about wrongs done to Barbara than he ever does anything that he's experienced personally. He resents her parents for kicking her out of their home when she got pregnant in high school, even though they've made their peace now. Similarly, he knows she will never forgive Tommy for things that happened long before she knew Lucky Sweatt existed.

He tells her that this is a one-shot deal, that whether Tom Ed wins or loses, he'll be counting the days until he can go back to Willow Cove.

"That's all I'm living for, too," she says, and he wonders if all the words and deeds he's employed in all the years they've been together are enough to let her know the magnitude of his debt to her.

From 1963, when Lucky was bailed out and left Scots County, until 1974 seems to him to be more than a lifetime.

The army wouldn't take him, and most colleges preferred high school graduates.

But college towns somehow appealed to Lucky, and he knew a boy who was working construction in Chapel Hill, so he fell into the life of sweat and Schlitz. He and Buddy Gardner lived in a house trailer off the Pittsboro Road for three years.

Some of it was pure spite. Lucky knew that Tom Ed was going to college at UNC, and he knew his brother would be a little uneasy just having Lucky living in the same town.

On Sundays sometimes, the newly minted construction worker would go into the main campus library just to browse through the books.

Tom Ed knew where Lucky was, more or less, and Lucky knew where Tom Ed was, saw him coming out of his fraternity house one morning with two other boys, all three of them looking to Lucky as if they knew the sun was shining just for them. Lucky would slip over to the baseball field occasionally and see Tom Ed play. He saw him hit two of the longest home runs he'd ever witnessed in a game one day against Duke. When everybody else stood up and cheered, Lucky just sat there and smiled.

They didn't try to patch things up until just before Tom Ed left college for minor-league baseball, in the spring of 1966. Lucky heard a knock on the trailer door one Saturday morning about ten. He was scrambling some eggs and yelled for whomever it was to wait a minute. After he spooned the eggs into a bowl, he ran and opened the door.

"Hey, Lucky," Tom Ed said, "it looks like you ain't going to come see me, so I thought I'd come see you."

Tom Ed was a little hesitant, which Lucky understood, considering how they'd been the last time they'd seen each other. He told his brother to come in.

"I got this offer to play for the Cardinals," he blurted out. "They think I can get to the big leagues in three years."

Lucky told him that sounded great and asked him if he was going to stay with college.

"Hell, this isn't for me," he said. "The old man is going to raise hell, but he'll raise more hell if I flunk out."

Which is what he was close to doing. It was the first time that Tom Ed had been solely on his own, and he'd gone a little wild. Between partying with the jocks and partying with his fraternity brothers, there wasn't much time to study. He told Lucky he was afraid he'd be kicked out, drafted, and sent to Vietnam if he stayed at Carolina much longer. The Cardinals could pull some strings and get him in some soft National Guard unit that wouldn't interfere with his baseball career.

So a month after Tom Ed visited Lucky, he was gone again, to a rookie-league team down in Florida. They met two more times in that month, had a few beers together. Tom Ed said he was going to marry Lucinda Stallsmith, whose mother came from one of the Arsenal Hill families. Lucky thought to himself how happy this would make Tommy.

They didn't ever talk about what had happened in 1963, and it seemed to Lucky that they could build on what was left, but that it wouldn't ever be the same.

Just before Tom Ed left, he told Lucky he wished that he would go visit Tommy. Lucky had gotten several letters from their mother, who wrote as soon as she found out where he was, but he hadn't been back at all. He told Tom Ed that, as far as he was concerned, Tommy was dead. And he meant it.

Tom Ed tried to plead their father's case in absentia, but Lucky was having none of it, not then.

"Look," he told Lucky, "it ain't exactly heaven being me, either. I don't think that old son of a bitch has ever been satisfied with anything I've done. And it's worse now . . ." and he stopped, letting it hang there like a poison cloud in the air.

The Budweiser clock Lucky and Buddy had conned from the beer distributor hummed loudly in the background. There was a dog barking next door, the same dog that barked all day while its owners were at work. The owners never believed Lucky and Buddy when they complained.

Neither brother said anything for the better part of five minutes. Either of them could have said he was sorry and each had enough to be sorry for, but they were twenty and not good at apologizing.

Finally, Tom Ed rose to leave. He offered his hand and his brother took it, but it seemed to Lucky that something was lost forever.

Lucky left Chapel Hill the winter after Tom Ed did, because he'd met a girl, Lorrie Chambers, and she was leaving home to go to Wilson College, an all-women's school in Wilson's Draft, Virginia. She was a townie; her father ran a grocery store and had his heart set on her going to UNC, but she didn't want any more of Chapel Hill, so she got her parents to send her to Wilson.

They didn't know Lucky was part of the deal. He had gotten his GED by then, but he understood how a man who works all his life to make a go of a grocery store, putting up with all the arrogance of college kids looking down their noses at him for being a storekeeper, wouldn't want to see his only child marry a construction worker.

Lucky got work with a contractor who was building houses in Wilson's Draft and rented a room not far from the campus. He and Lorrie lasted less than two months, until she fell for an upperclassman from Virginia Tech.

But the town and the mountains around it somehow suited Lucky. Wilson's Draft wasn't a college town like Chapel Hill. Most of the people there were blue-collar, working hard or drawing unemployment. There was a furniture factory that employed about half the adults in town, and Lucky wound up working there himself for two aimless years.

He had been an honors student all through high school, right up to the day he quit, but for the first four years after he left home, it didn't cross his mind to do anything more academically ambitious than get his graduate-equivalency degree.

Some of it, he came to understand later, was that he linked studying with all the bad times, especially toward the end. In high school, he couldn't play sports and he made good grades, so he was considered, by Geddie High standards, to be a "brain," what Kim and Chris and Benny would call a nerd.

So he was out to prove that he wasn't a brain at all, no matter how Pyrrhic his victory. The years in Chapel Hill and the first one in Wilson's Draft, he devoted his life mainly to partying. He and Lorrie were smoking marijuana before it was fashionable, in the days when that seemed the most dangerous thing the young and the restless could do, when the game of sex and drugs was strictly a low-stakes affair, no AIDS, no crack, no sweat.

Lucky had one rather pathetic date the entire time he was in high school, with a girl who was a Jehovah's Witness and didn't believe in kissing. He knew he was the gimp, the brain, and his lack of confidence radiated off him like a neon sign.

But leaving home threw Lucky into another mind-set, the James Dean mode, and it gave him the confidence of the hopeless, the confidence of nothing to lose. He would go into dormitories at the women's college at Greensboro and ask the girl at the front desk if anybody wanted to go out with a boy from Chapel Hill, not mentioning that he was a common laborer there, not a student. And it worked, as often as not.

Buddy Gardner and he would go to Durham and Raleigh, prowling the drive-ins and bars for nursing students, business-college girls, secretaries, whatever. Women were prey.

It took Lucky about six months in Chapel Hill to lose his virginity, to a hooker. He and Buddy were out one night at the Burger Palace in Durham when two women in a red Mustang pulled up beside them. They had shellacked hair that reminded Lucky of cotton candy, and they looked to him to be a little rough. But Buddy started talking to them, went around their car to the driver's side, and leaned his head in.

In a couple of minutes, he returned. He cranked up his Chevy Impala and followed the Mustang out of the parking lot.

Lucky asked him where they were going.

"To get some pussy," Buddy said.

Lucky said that sounded good, although the cut-and-dried aspect of it didn't appeal to him.

"You got any money?" he asked, and Lucky finally caught on, but it was too late to turn back. With Buddy, Lucky knew, you didn't back down on a fuck or a fight.

The women led them to an old cinder-block house where a fat black man lay sprawled out on a couch in the front room watching "Gunsmoke." There was a bedroom off to either side. Buddy took the dark-haired one and Lucky got the blonde, who, he couldn't help but notice, was actually wearing a wig.

Lucky was self-conscious; it scared him to think of the shame of not being able to perform, of the blonde laughing and of Buddy finding out, but the woman—a girl, really; she seemed to Lucky to be younger than he was—was good at her job, and Lucky and Buddy were both out the front door in less than ten minutes. The man on the couch said, "Come again."

It cost $15, and it gave Lucky more confidence than all the A's he'd gotten in high school. It wasn't romantic, but it was a small measure of warmth in an otherwise cold stretch of life.

He dated a lot of girls in Chapel Hill and then up in Virginia, and treated most of them badly. Even Lorrie, he finally conceded to himself, probably wouldn't have dumped him if he had treated her as anything but a piece of meat. But that was Lucky, post–Scots County, pre-Barbara, determined to make up for what he thought he'd missed, sure that he was getting his just due for past grievances.

He had been in Wilson's Draft for about a year and a half when something happened. He was coming home from the graveyard shift at the furniture factory on a freshly minted April morning. The campus was between the factory and his apartment, and sometimes, if the weather was good, he would walk to work.

Half-asleep, he took a shortcut across one of the quads on campus. It was about eight-thirty, and the students were just beginning to stumble out of their dorms, headed for class. Lucky's path took him past the campus bookstore.

Maybe it was spring, or maybe it was just time to do something. He went inside, surprised that the store would be open so early, and began browsing. Lucky didn't turn his back on the printed word when he left Scots County. In some ways, not having to read anything made it easier to enjoy books. But he had had an eclectic education up to that point. Whatever caught his eye was what he read next, whether it was a cereal box or *War and Peace*.

He was working his way through the fiction shelves, looking for a paperback to take home, when he heard a voice.

"Can I help you with anything?"

Lucky mumbled a no. He was fairly certain that he wasn't even supposed to be there. After living in two university towns, he was beginning to feel decidedly inferior to all the college kids whom he and his coworkers cursed during long nights at the factory.

Something in her voice made Lucky turn around, though. The girl he saw had straight black hair, a dark complexion, and brown, kind eyes. She seemed to invite conversation, even from a boy in a dirty work uniform with his name in red cursive script over his heart, a boy who looked as out of place as a lug nut in a jewelry box.

She asked him if he had read *Sometimes a Great Notion*. Lucky had never even heard of Ken Kesey, but he wound up buying a copy.

Barbara Bates introduced herself, holding out a perfect, tanned wrist that Lucky grabbed awkwardly, feeling the warmth that he knew he'd give his right arm to lie next to.

"And I guess you're Lucky," she said. Seeing his surprise, she nodded toward the name on his pocket. He nodded dumbly, then said, "Sometimes."

Lucky couldn't get Barbara Bates out of his mind. Almost every day, coming home from the graveyard shift, he would stop and talk with her about what he had read so far of the book she'd recommended.

He learned that she was divorced, even though she was just twenty-one, two years younger than Lucky, and that she was going back to college. She was a freshman, taking twelve hours and working at the bookstore forty hours a week. Her parents, she told him, were pretty much fed up with her, and she with them.

She was going steady with a boy from Emory & Henry, and near the end of the semester, unable to risk asking her for a date and being turned down, Lucky stopped coming around. When he returned in June, she wasn't working there anymore.

Barbara had, however, shown Lucky how inexpensive it was to take classes at Wilson, which had gone coed just the year before.

The last thing any shift worker at United Furniture wanted to do was let anybody know he was taking courses at Wilson. Lucky's peers thought any boy who would go to a "girls' school" was severely suspect.

But Lucky knew he had to do something, even (and he realized as he thought it that it was Tommy's phrase) if it was wrong. He had always assumed, without telling anyone, that he would go to college someday, even if he didn't know how or when.

When the rest of the graveyard shift found out Lucky was enrolled at Wilson, he brazened it out and told them he was meeting a higher caliber of woman than he was used to rubbing up against at the Mountain Dew Inn, which the workers had unofficially dubbed the Mad Dog.

The fall of 1969 and spring of 1970, Lucky took two courses each semester, then another one in the summer. He had qualified for in-state tuition, and he made up the rest by taking out a student loan.

By the fall of 1970, Lucky was twenty-four years old and halfway through his freshman requirements at what was now Wilson University.

The sixties didn't really get to Wilson and its part of the world until the early seventies, but Lucky figured he was ahead of the curve, since he'd been acting as if there weren't any rules since he'd left home seven years before. He was finally fired from the furniture factory because he wouldn't cut his hair and talked too loudly against the war in Vietnam. By September 1970, he was working with an independent contractor, trying to squeeze classes around work. He'd grown a beard to go with the long hair and fancied himself to be good-looking.

That fall, he was taking two courses again, Modern Civilization II and a course in English Restoration comedy. When he walked into the classroom for the English course the first day, he saw Barbara Bates right away. Her hair was almost to her waist by then, and she was wearing an Indian headband.

She had her back to Lucky. The desk behind hers was vacant, and he slipped into it.

"Are you still going steady?" he whispered before he even had time to think.

She didn't even turn around.

"I was wondering when you were going to catch up with me," she said.

Then she did turn.

"No," she said, "I'm not going steady." And she smiled. "You know, I had a dream about you the other night." And Lucky silently prayed that he would, at least once, live up to his name.

Barbara and he had lunch at the school snack bar after class, and it was if they had known each other their whole lives, could read each other's minds.

It was not some campus fairy-tale romance, at least not like anything Lucky had ever heard or read about. Barbara taught him about commitment. Up until that time, he realized later, he had been using the late-breaking sixties for his own selfish purposes, as an excuse to get laid as often as possible and experiment with the relatively innocent drugs that were available.

But Barbara, Lucky soon learned, was serious. She was one of the first students at Wilson to really try to do something to help end the war, while Lucky was just talking about it, and by 1970, she was vice-president of the campus National Organization of Women chapter and was spending much of her spare time protesting everything from South Africa to tobacco.

She'd get Lucky to come to various meetings with her, and sometimes he would tell her that he thought something or other that she was championing was full of shit. She would turn thoughtful and tell Lucky, chapter and verse, why it wasn't full of shit.

"You know, Lucky," she told him one time the first winter they

were in love, "if you can't work up some sympathy for the underdog, after all you've been through, what hope is there for us?"

Until he really got to know Barbara Bates, Lucky thought
everything bad that had happened to him was just an excuse to
raise hell. But she told him about her own life, about getting an
illegal abortion at eighteen. She told him how it affected her to see
an abused child or abused wife or some black guy who was buried
so deep that he would never get out from under. Finally, over a
period of months, it started to sink in.

Lucky realized, at last, that he was a follower. He wanted to do
right, beneath all the bitterness, but he needed someone like
Barbara to show him what right was.

Lucky often wondered what made Barbara Bates want him. She
was beautiful. She was smart. She was ambitious without being
greedy. Sometimes, he suspected that he was a project, that if she
could get some furniture worker like him to see the light, then
there was hope for humanity. But he knew that reciprocal, requited
love, if it wasn't there at the outset, did grow, and for that he would
always be thankful.

Barbara got her degree in sociology, with honors, at the end of
the fall semester of 1973. That spring, with Lucky still a year and a
half short of his degree in English, they got married. They'd been
living together for three and a half years already, and they'd never
talked seriously about making it legal. Barbara's family was in no
position to harangue her about morality, and Lucky was as far out
of Tommy and Genie's orbit as he ever would be.

When Lucky went home for Christmas that year, all Tommy
asked him was to not do anything that might embarrass Tom Ed.
By then, Lucky had the look and mind-set peculiar to those who
come to activist politics late and are trying to play catch-up. He
had the impression that his father feared he might try to blow up
the Capitol, thus severely limiting Tom Ed's political aspirations.
Lucky's brother was already an officer in the Scots County
Republican Party; only memory and regret kept them from fighting over Nixon.

Barbara refused to come with him. She knew that the anger she harbored for people she hadn't even met would ruin any chance of reconciliation.

Lucky wanted to get married but doubted that Barbara did. She was the best thing that had ever happened to him, he was sure, and he was afraid he would awaken one morning and find just a note on her pillow. He knew he was the happiest he'd ever been, and he was loath to do anything that might alter that happiness.

Barbara had strong feelings about traditional marriage, which she felt was about nine tenths of the reason why women didn't get any showing. Proposing to her, Lucky believed, would be almost an insult.

In April 1974, though, he came home one Sunday afternoon from doing some overtime work, helping a man build a custom house up in Glade Springs. Barbara was sitting on one of the two beanbag chairs that were the greater part of their living-room furniture. She had the Sunday *Roanoke Times* spread all around her, and she appeared to be on the verge of tears.

Lucky approached cautiously and saw that she was holding the brides' section, row after row of young women looking better than they'd ever look again in their lives.

She heard Lucky and turned toward him.

"I am such a fake," she said. "All I want to do is put on one of these goddamn white dresses and walk down the aisle in a church somewhere."

Lucky told her that that was all he wanted her to do, too, and that he didn't think marrying him would be quite as hard on her as indentured servitude.

She laughed and told him she couldn't screw up as badly as she had the first time.

She hadn't even gotten to wear a bride's dress for that one. She'd already told Lucky the story about eloping to South Carolina, about how she and her husband-to-be had shown up at his older sister's, Barbara in jeans, a T-shirt, and no underwear. The sister had taken her to Belk's and paid for something that wouldn't offend the sensibilities of the Heavenly Bliss Wedding Parlor in Freedom Hill, South Carolina.

So Lucky did what he had wanted and feared to do for so long. He got down painfully on one knee and asked Barbara Bates to marry him, and she said she would. They even found a Baptist church, in the village where she was doing social work, that would let her wear white.

## 9

Sunday morning, Barbara returns to Willow Cove. Lucky catches a
ride to Salisbury with a campaign volunteer who calls him "sir" all
the way there. Tom Ed is in Salisbury long enough to address what
Harry calls the Big White Folks Baptist Church. From what little
Lucky has seen of the campaign, it seems obvious that his brother is
getting the lion's share of church-related opportunities. Knox
Cameron is an Episcopalian, and there aren't many of those in North
Carolina. The Baptists and Methodists and country Presbyterians,
Lucky can see, feel more comfortable with Tom Ed Sweatt's muscu-
lar Christianity.

From there, they'll head for Durham and Raleigh, then go
down east the next day.

Susannah is still there. While Tom Ed is being interviewed by a
Durham TV station that afternoon, Sam confides to Lucky that she
stayed over the night before, and that Tom Ed threw one of his fits
when Barry Maxwell tried to advise caution.

"Jesus," Sam says, talking low and not looking at Lucky. "Those
fundamentalists find out what's going on here, they might even
convert to the Democrats."

It seems that Tom Ed has heeded Barry Maxwell's warning
when Susannah gets off the campaign van in Durham to "catch up
on things at the office."

Lucky is struck, not for the first time since joining his brother's campaign, by the casual way his new acquaintances treat what is almost holy to him. He, who once lived with his future bride with no solid prospects of marriage, is now among matrimony's more fervent disciples. When Tom Ed tells him that Horace Morgan will be throwing a fund-raiser that night at his club in Durham, he feels sad for Susannah, of whom so little is expected, and for Tom Ed, for whom so little is being offered.

Tom Ed borrows a car, and he and Lucky ride to the fund-raiser together.

"Did you catch the speech in Charlotte?" Tom Ed asks. Lucky says just the short version.

"We knocked their dicks off," Tom Ed says, looking satisfied. "The Democrats don't know this state like I do. I can get these people so fired up over this mess with Nate Crowell that we'll pass old Knox Cameron like he's standing still. When I'm through, they'll be lucky if they don't lynch Crowell and run Cameron out of the state."

Lucky is silent.

"Aw," Tom Ed says, "you don't think I believe all this shit, do you? This is just politics. Look, they aren't going to wind up doing anything to Nate Crowell but maybe giving him three years, and he'll be out in nine months. Hell, they give Uncle Felton more than that for self-defense. But by the time they do it, I'll already be governor.

"Don't worry about the rich folks, Lucky. They can take care of theirselves."

He says he's supposed to speak at a pro-life rally in Charlotte on Saturday, "and that'll be the crowning blow for Mr. Knox Cameron. There's going to be twenty thousand people there, and it's going to be televised live."

Lucky tells him to be careful. Careful of what, his brother says, and gives him a suspicious look. Just in general be careful, Lucky answers.

All the black people at Horace Morgan's club appear to be waiters, but Lucky's fairly certain that the places where they're having fund-raisers for Knox Cameron aren't strong on ethnic diversity, either.

Tom Ed immediately strikes up a conversation with one of the waiters, and in about thirty seconds, they appear to be fast friends. Lucky can tell when black people are just playing polite because they have to, when some rich white guy is trying to cozy up. The white guy walks off like he's just solved the race problem, and the black guy goes around the corner shaking his head.

But it isn't that way with Tom Ed. On one level, Lucky can see that what his brother is planning to do if he becomes governor is nothing but bad news for anybody who's down and out, the likely status of an African-American living in North Carolina. But on that personal, small-group level, Lucky knows that Tom Ed can talk with black people better than any liberal he's ever come across. He likes their food, he's lived where they live, he has the same sense of humor, he has the same feel for what it's like to have rich people dumping on you.

Lucky saw a picture in the Sunday paper of Knox Cameron shaking hands with a state-level NAACP leader. They both looked as if they were handling snakes. But Tom Ed can go up to a black person, rich or poor, and just seem to click immediately, which is going to get him some black votes, Lucky feels. It is his opinion that most people vote for whoever seems to like them the most. And Tom Ed could always make people think that he liked them.

Horace Morgan has a man with him who seems to be trying as hard to be seen as anyone Lucky's encountered lately. The man is wearing a suit about one notch too loud for the low-key political crowd around him, and the only one who ever seems to speak to him is Horace himself, from whom the man doesn't ever stray more than a few feet. He's short, no more than five foot eight. His hair is black and slicked straight back, and his complexion, in late October, speaks more of tanning salons than the beach. He is wearing sunglasses, and there is a bulge in his pocket that is almost comically obvious. He reminds Lucky of a very loyal, somewhat dangerous pet. He can't shake the notion that Horace Morgan is going to reach over, pat the man on the head, and assure them all that he doesn't bite.

Morgan rushes up and pumps Tom Ed's hand when he comes in. He talks to him for a minute or so, then Tom Ed turns to address the man hanging on at Morgan's elbow.

"Lord, Bo," he says, his eyebrows rising, "didn't I see you on 'Miami Vice' the other night?" This draws a muted chuckle from those around them but not the least twitch of a smile from the man himself.

"Oh," Morgan says, "I'd like you to meet Sonny Lineberger."

It's obvious to Lucky that Tom Ed's heard the name before. "Oh, yeah," he murmurs. "Little Sonny Lineberger. Well, I'll be damned. Heard a lot about you."

Little Sonny Lineberger, Lucky learns later, became acquainted with Horace Morgan when Morgan extricated him from a world of trouble. Tom Ed tells his brother, on the way back to the hotel, that Little Sonny shot a man five times—twice in the knees, twice in his private parts, finally in the head. One of the dead man's friends said at the trial that the deceased and Little Sonny had gotten into an argument over a woman in whom they each exhibited an extreme proprietary interest. The friend felt fairly certain that it was Little Sonny who followed the victim home and used him for target practice. Big Sonny, Little Sonny's father, owned a trucking company, and he paid Horace well, Tom Ed said, to get enough people to swear that his son was nowhere near the scene of the crime.

Now, according to what Susannah has told Tom Ed, Little Sonny and Horace are as thick as thieves. Horace has told her that Little Sonny can do some errands he wouldn't entrust to a man who didn't owe him his freedom. It's hard for Lucky to imagine two people having less in common than Horace Morgan and Little Sonny Lineberger, but it isn't the strangest arrangement he's seen on his brother's campaign, and he doesn't say anything.

The fund-raiser lasts about two hours. Tom Ed works the room, leaving everyone smiling. The brothers are barely out of the driveway when Tom Ed drops his big news on Lucky.

"She's leaving him as soon as the campaign is over," he says. "I'm leaving Lucinda. Soon as this damn election is over, we're home free. I might wait six months to actually make it legal, but it's a done deal, Bo, come Tuesday week."

That was why Susannah was going home: to tell her husband. Lucky can't believe it. Horace Morgan could not have been more pleasant and courteous, bringing rich friends over and introducing them to "the next governor of North Carolina," taking Tom Ed aside for a heart-to-heart chat at one point.

Lucky comments on this.

"I told you already, Bo," Tom Ed says, turning his head toward his brother and leaning forward, looking as if he's talking to a backward child, "those kind of people, they don't care about stuff like this. They got different rules. He'll thank me for taking her off his hands. Don't worry."

Horace Morgan reminds Lucky of his and Tom Ed's two uncles.

Dorothy Canfield Balcom, the twins' grandmother, had two sons, both older than Genie. James helped his mother run the family business, and Franklin, Jr., became a lawyer. Together, they knew anyone worth knowing in Port Campbell.

They had immaculate manners, courteous to Tommy even while his mother-in-law treated him, Genie, and the twins as if they were dead. Lucky can remember their father coming home one day when he and Tom Ed were twelve. Tommy smelled of liquor, and he'd run into the Balcom brothers somewhere, probably at the bootlegger's.

"I wish that old lady had as good a manners as your brothers do," he told Genie. "Me and them is just like that." And he held his index and middle fingers together.

No more than three months afterward, Tommy had one of his occasional ideas to make him and his family rich. Genie was sometimes charmed, sometimes exhausted by the childlike exuberance with which her husband approached life. That Sunday, the Sweatts rode all the way to the beach because Tommy had an urge for fried shrimp. On the way back, he said that if somebody who knew what they were doing was to open a place like those Calabash joints right there in Port Campbell, why, they could make a million dollars.

He'd talk himself into something like that, even after he'd settled on the best job he'd ever hold, at the lumberyard. It seemed to Lucky that his mother didn't have the heart to throw cold water on Tommy's schemes.

He talked to James and Franklin Balcom, and he said they told him they'd back him on his plan to build a seafood restaurant in Port Campbell, right on High Street.

So Tommy rented a place that had already gone broke four times as a restaurant, one of those buildings that seem to have "born to lose" written on the walls with the kind of paint Tommy Sweatt could never seem to see. He even did some repair work on it, with Felton helping him out.

Then he went back to James and Franklin, and they hemmed and hawed and then said they couldn't do anything for him right then, maybe later.

So Tommy went to all the banks, and nobody would loan him a drink of water.

He lost about $1,000 on the deal, which was a lot of money at that time, especially to the Sweatts, and word got back to him that the Balcoms had told all the banks not to loan him a cent.

But Tommy and Genie and their sons met the Balcom brothers on High Street less than a month afterward, and James and Franklin couldn't have been nicer.

When the Sweatts had walked half a block farther, Tommy stopped, turned and faced the twins. He said, "That's the way you do it, boys. Don't never get mad. Just get even."

Even then, Lucky could see that their father admired something in the way the Balcoms had stuck him. He never forgot it, and he was damned sure Tom Ed hadn't, either.

Wherever James and Franklin Balcom got their talent for duplicity, it didn't come from Dorothy Canfield Balcom, who pulled no punches.

Lucky and Tom Ed would see her, almost always from a distance. She would cross the street to avoid coming face-to-face with any of her daughter's family. However much all this might have hurt Genie, she never let on, standing faithfully by Tommy Sweatt through some alliance of love and stubbornness.

However, the area of his mother-in-law was one of the few in which even Tommy Sweatt, the most callous of souls, knew to tread lightly. Not even he knew to what extent time had healed or worsened Genie's wound of separation.

Dorothy Canfield Balcom wore black all the time, summer and winter. Lucky and Tom Ed were embarrassed for their friends to know that the apparition Port Campbell children called the Black Widow from a safe distance was their grandmother.

Once, when they were fourteen, the twins had gone downtown to see a movie, catching a ride with Genie, and Tom Ed had talked his brother into climbing up Arsenal Hill and then turning down a couple of side streets so they could see where Grandmother Balcom lived. Tom Ed knew the address from looking up her number in the telephone book.

Her house sat on the very edge of Arsenal Hill. The boys could see the space above downtown through the maples in her backyard. Genie told them once that in the summer it was the coolest place in Port Campbell. Lucky reckoned that she must have missed it often in her hot, sandy exile by Mingo Road.

"Watch this," Tom Ed said after they had stood silently for a couple of minutes. Before Lucky could stop him, he ran up to the front door and rang the doorbell.

While Tom Ed's hand was still on the buzzer, with Lucky standing thirty feet behind him on the walkway, the door opened with a jerk and there stood Dorothy Canfield Balcom, dressed in black even in the privacy of her home.

She glared down at Tom Ed, who was already stepping backward.

"I don't receive Sweatts here," she said in a voice as cold and final as a killing frost. Then she shut the door, firmly.

The twins never told anyone about their brief encounter with their grandmother, and they never went near her house again until Lucky was invited.

It was two years later, in May. Lucky was in Port Campbell one day. Already, he had begun to drift from Tom Ed, whose new high school friends seem to tolerate Lucky more than like him.

So Lucky drove into town one Saturday afternoon and went to a movie by himself. It was *Cleopatra,* and he went in the afternoon so that he wouldn't have to face all his classmates and all their dates when they went to see it that night.

When he came out, half-blinded by the sun, he felt a bony hand, cold even in the heat, grab his elbow.

He turned with a jerk, and there was Grandmother Balcom, a mass of blackness and chill amid the glare and heat. Lucky never understood how she knew he would be there, coming out of that theater at that time.

"Jack Dempsey Sweatt," she said, not a question at all.

"Ma'am?" he said, though he seldom even said "Yes, ma'am" to his mother anymore, and never answered to his given name.

"I want you to do something for me. Be at my house at five o'clock on Wednesday. You know where I live." That wasn't a question, either.

She walked away, hobbling slightly, and it occurred to Lucky that here was someone who was in even worse shape than he was. Dorothy Balcom was sixty then, but to Lucky she looked much older.

Ten feet away, she turned around.

"And don't tell anybody," she said.

On the appointed day, Lucky was evasive, which made his parents suspect that he had a date. By this time, they were pleased to see the boy whom they referred to more and more as their other son do anything of a social nature.

To Lucky, his grandmother's house was just as frightening as it had been two years earlier. She was alone; her sons lived a few blocks away.

She answered the door, dressed in black as always. She didn't invite Lucky to enter, instead brushing him to one side and locking the door behind her.

"I want you to drive me somewhere," she said, and that was all.

Lucky wondered, then and later, why he came running when the most unfriendly person in Port Campbell beckoned. But there was something about his grandmother; she assumed that others would do what she said to do, and they usually did.

She stood by the side of the used red Buick, which Tommy had bought for the whole family but had let Tom Ed pick out, still as a stone until Lucky realized that he was supposed to open the door for her.

"Where we going?" he asked as he turned on the ignition.

"We're going to see your great-aunt Ida," she said. Lucky didn't know he had a great-aunt Ida.

Dorothy Balcom directed her grandson to the nursing home. It was the good one, which didn't smell so much like wet beds and decay. It wasn't far from where Tom Ed and Bobby would build Westlake.

Lucky started to ask a question, then realized that he didn't know what to call his grandmother, having never called her anything to her face.

"You're my grandmother, right?" he said, looking for a hint.

"Call me Grandmother Balcom," she said. "I'm not Granny or Grandma or any of that nonsense. Grandmother Balcom."

And so she was, from then on.

Great Aunt Ida, Grandmother Balcom's sister, was a frail old woman. She was fifteen years older, but she was dressed to the nines, sitting up in the more comfortable of the two chairs in her room, prepared to entertain guests.

She embarrassed Lucky by the fuss she made over him. She asked many questions about his mother.

They stayed for an hour. Neither grandmother nor grandson said anything on the way back to the car. Lucky opened the door without her having to wait this time and then got in himself.

"She wanted to see you," Grandmother Balcom said. "She's about to die, and she doesn't have much family." It was true. All of

Ida's and Dorothy's siblings were dead, James had never married, and Franklin, Jr., and his wife had no children.

"You can come and visit me sometime if you've a mind to," she said when Lucky was helping her out of the car back on Arsenal Hill. "But don't you tell any of them about this." She fixed Lucky with a gimlet eye.

Lucky promised, and he kept his word. And he did return to her house several times afterward, spending long afternoons on the back porch that overlooked the town or in the sitting room, to which Dorothy Balcom still carried wood for the fireplace.

The last time he'd seen her, just months before she died, was in 1968. Lucky had moved to Virginia and was living as close to the edge as he ever would. He had a temporary construction job that took him, of all places, back to Port Campbell, where they were building Scots County's new hospital. He had cursed his hometown as he left it, and now he saw it like a spy looking through a telescope. Lucky had few friends when he left. Now, with a full beard and long hair, he felt sure he wouldn't be recognized. He was living in a trailer south of town, near the construction site.

One afternoon, though, it began to rain, the soft, steady rain that meant no more framing for that day. Lucky's crew knocked off at two. Instead of getting drunk or stoned, Lucky, on a whim, took the old van he was using and went up Arsenal Hill.

It took him half an hour to find the right street. It was raining hard now, and Lucky had to run as well as he could to the front porch with his head half-tucked inside his shirt. He didn't see her until he hit the top step.

His grandmother was sitting there, rocking, looking as peaceful as she ever looked, watching the rain.

"Thought it was you," she said, and she sounded a little weaker, a little less scary, than before. When he got a good look at her, he saw that she looked twenty years older, and her hand trembled noticeably.

"Sit," she said.

Neither of them spoke for several minutes.

"Heard you were in Virginia," she said at last. She seemed to Lucky to be doling out words, as if she had a finite number left.

He told her that there wasn't anybody in Scots County who likely cared much one way or the other where he was.

"Your momma does," she said, and Lucky wondered how she would know that.

"I see her," Dorothy Balcom said, seeming to read his mind. "She looks beaten down now, like she's carrying the weight of the world."

It occurred to Lucky that the bond he and his grandmother shared was Genie, separated from them both by stubbornness and old wounds.

Dorothy Canfield was born to cotton farmers living west of town. She finished high school when she was fourteen because she'd started when she was five and had skipped two of the eleven grades available to North Carolina students at that time. She was the valedictorian for the entire county.

"And do you know what it got me?" she asked Lucky. "A job at the mill. My daddy said he wasn't going to waste money sending girls to college." She sighed and shook her head, as if even now trying to dislodge the injustice of it.

She worked in the mill until she'd saved enough to move to a boardinghouse off High Street. She borrowed from Ida to start business school. Before she finished, she took a job as the book-keeper for Balcom's, the biggest hardware store in town.

"I didn't have any intentions of ever getting married," she said. "I was not a beauty at all. I had never dated before I met Franklin Balcom."

She thought he was teasing when he asked her to the Christmas party at the Balcom house, but he assured her that he was serious. Dorothy had to buy the material and make her own dress, with just two weeks to do it in.

"That night was wonderful to me," she said. "I had never been in a house that nice. They were not unkind to me; I guess they were happy that Frank was seeing girls. I found out later that he hadn't dated more than two girls in his whole life, and he was almost twenty-four then."

They dated for two years before they were married, she said, and then they moved into her in-laws' house.

"I thought living in a room with two other girls back on the farm was hard," she said. "But many's the time I wished I were back there."

They lived with the Balcoms for almost twenty years, in the house where Dorothy Canfield Balcom still lived. She had to stop working because her in-laws didn't think that it was proper for their son's wife to do "menial labor."

She said that she had no privacy at all, that her mother-in-law would walk into a room without knocking, whether it was bedroom, bathroom, or whatever. She said that she never heard a compliment from her husband's mother the entire time she lived there.

Frank, she said, would not stand up to his mother, and it soon became apparent that he would always owe first allegiance to his birth family. When their sons were born, Frank's mother was allowed to name them, laughing off Dorothy's wish to name the second one Thomas, after her father.

Genie was the baby, two years younger than Franklin, Jr., and four years younger than James. She was allowed to give her the middle name of Canfield.

"She was the prettiest thing anybody had ever seen," Dorothy said, seeming to be talking less to Lucky than to the air in front of her. "Don't know where she got it from. Surely not from me."

Her husband died of congestive heart failure while their sons were away during World War II, not long before Genie and Tommy eloped. Her mother-in-law died not long afterward, and Dorothy Canfield Balcom threw her considerable energy and intellect into running a store in which she had been only tolerated up to that point.

"I found my calling then, what I'd been waiting to do," she said.

By the time James and Franklin, Jr., came home from the war, she had already seen the future and borrowed the money to invest in it. By 1968, there were twelve Balcom's, located all over North

Carolina, that sold everything from mulch to light fixtures. Her sons, it was said, could not make a move without her approval, even then, and were constantly afraid of being excised from her will.

Lucky asked her, at last, because he saw that he was the only one who could, how she could turn her back on Genie.

She gave him a sharp look.

"I might ask you the same thing," she said, then paused a moment before she continued:

"Tommy Sweatt was trashy. We weren't rich like people thought, at least not until I made us rich, but I couldn't bear the thought of my Genie living her whole life in squalor. She might as well have spit in my face as run off with that Tommy Sweatt."

She asked him about Genie, whom Lucky had seen once in five years himself, driving home on a last-minute whim, half-drunk, the visit serving no purpose other than to assure the four family members that they were still linked, however feebly. He told her what he thought she wanted to hear, about a picture Genie had somehow saved of her mother, about how he was sure Genie would want to see her again.

Dorothy Balcom said nothing to this, just continued to rock. After a while, the rain stopped and Lucky helped her out of her chair and into the big old house. She offered him iced tea, but he told her he had to get back to work.

He never saw her again. He learned of her death the next spring from Genie, who would discern his whereabouts when he moved and write him four letters for every one he wrote her.

"Momma passed away Tuesday," she mentioned two thirds of the way into a four-page summation of the Sweatt family's life in the five days since she'd written last, stuck between a critique of the new minister's pulpit skills and a glowing report of Tom Ed's latest business venture. "I thought you might like to send some flowers."

Lucky made a rare phone call home. He and his mother talked for twenty minutes, and he finally asked her if she and his grandmother had made their peace.

He could hear a sigh on the other end of the line.

"Peace? I don't know about that. We did talk, though. That was something. We decided we didn't hate each other.

"Momma wanted so much," Genie went on after a pause. "She couldn't understand why everybody wasn't as smart as her. She didn't see how some people just wanted to be happy."

Lucky thought about what his grandmother had said on the porch, that last day he'd seen her. She was walking him out, as best she could, when she suddenly grabbed his wrist, digging her nails in so hard she drew blood.

"I wanted your mother to be somebody," she said.

At that moment, to Lucky, she might as well have been Tommy Sweatt.

★★★ **10** ★★★

Monday, they head off into the rising sun.

This is Tom Ed Sweatt's home field. He knows he has the eastern third of the state locked up, so he pays it little attention.

Eastern North Carolina begins within eyesight of what passes for Raleigh's skyline. Harry Mavredes says it's the land of collards, cotton, and conservatives, and Tom Ed asks him what the hell's wrong with that.

"Bo," Tom Ed says to his brother, "I love these people. These are my people. But there just ain't enough of them."

They attend a Jaycees breakfast in Clayton and a mid-morning rally outside a tobacco warehouse in Dunn, then plunge into the heart of it, past dark green ponds and old farmhouses surrounded by sycamores and live oaks, with sons' and daughters' mobile homes in side yards bearing hard witness to farming's diminishing returns in the 1990s.

There are four vans now, carrying experts on everything from the news media to makeup.

"I sure hope Tommy and Momma don't hear about this," Tom Ed says while a young woman tries to darken his almost-invisible eyebrows. "It'd kill 'em."

Then, suddenly, as fast as a thunderstorm, his face changes.

"Shit!"

He throws down a towel he's holding and bolts from the van.

They are outside a television station in Greenville, and there's a phone booth across the parking lot. Tom Ed walks quickly toward it.

Five minutes later, he returns.

"Momma's birthday," he says. "How come you didn't remind me?"

"How come you didn't remind *me?*" Lucky asks him, then has to borrow quarters so he can call her, too.

"You know," Tom Ed says when his brother returns, "if she killed the old man in his sleep tonight, you couldn't find twelve people in Scots County that would convict her."

Genie, in the photos Lucky used to look at, in which she would be holding him or Tom Ed or both, was a beautiful woman with her green eyes and brown hair. She had a Lauren Bacall look to her. The night she was introduced to Tommy Sweatt was one of the few times he had ever been even momentarily tongue-tied. Finally, to keep her from thinking he was an idiot, he blurted out, "Lord, girl, I'm about five miles inside them eyes of yours, and I can't get out." He wasn't even trying to flatter her, which flattered her all the more.

She and Tommy were as attractive as any couple in Scots County in their day, but while Tommy's hairline and waistline had betrayed him, Genie still had the eyes, lights to remind former beaus that she had once broken their hearts by marrying a Sweatt instead of them.

They eloped to Dillon, South Carolina, two days after the war ended. They told everybody they did it on a whim, because Genie's best friend, Ruby Dowd, and her boyfriend were also eloping. They drove down together, Tommy telling jokes all the way down and half the way back, when they all began to consider the parental wrath that awaited them.

Genie was an excellent student. Her mother would have sent her to any college that money allowed. But she married Tommy instead.

Tom Ed and Lucky were in high school before they did the math and figured out that their mother had to have been pregnant at her wedding. Lucky never told anyone until he and Barbara were already married themselves.

Tommy Sweatt has squandered most of Lucky's love and respect, but Lucky feels that his mother and father were as meant to be, in their own way, as he and Barbara, that they would have married no matter what. He didn't always think that, didn't want to believe that a woman as bright as Genie would put up with Tommy slipping around with waitresses and throwing money away on ideas that made lottery tickets seem like sound investments. But, at forty-six, Lucky is getting a clearer and clearer picture of how absolutely stone-blind love can be.

One of his secret childhood memories is of the time Genie was taking him back from a doctor's appointment when he was ten. With no warning, she jerked the old car into the parking lot of a cinder-block building on Route 47 that Lucky had not noticed before. He was already aware that it was not his mother's way to do things in such an unexpected, violent manner. She had a grace about her that Lucky thought he could see in the way his brother fielded ground balls. When they picked peas in the garden in back of their house, Tommy would start out like a house afire, then stop to wipe his brow or complain about the heat, then tear off again. Genie would go along, smooth and seamless, economy in motion, and her foot tub would be full before Tommy's, every time.

The place into which Genie turned so abruptly was a diner, and Lucky still remembers seeing all these people sitting on stools inside, then noticing Tommy in a booth beside the window. Just as he realized he was watching his father, Tommy turned and kissed the woman beside him. She had blond hair and wore a blue dress.

All the silence, all the changes that had come since the polio, didn't feel as bad to him as that.

Genie got out of the car. She walked calmly over and tapped on the glass, which was the first either her husband or his friend had seen of her. And then she walked back to the car, got in, and drove off. Lucky looked out the back window and saw Tommy burst out the door and then stop, just watching, his hands held awkwardly together in front of his belt.

Lucky didn't say anything, and he never heard his parents fight about it. Tommy was home for supper, and Genie had it ready for him.

They spend the night in Kinston. There's good news: The latest poll, one commissioned by the Sweatt campaign, says that the race is almost dead even.

Everyone's in a good mood except Tom Ed.

"It's too easy," he says. "We hadn't ought to be catching him this quick. We got to keep our momentum."

Susannah's back with the campaign now, but she's staying in another hotel tonight. In spite of what he says, Lucky is sure Tom Ed knows he has to be careful now.

Tom Ed calls about ten, asking Lucky to come down to his suite. He and the M&M twins, Sam Bender, and the rest have done about all the damage they can do for this one day, Tom Ed says. He tells his brother to bring a bucket of ice with him.

When Lucky gets to his suite, Tom Ed puts some ice in two bathroom glasses, fills them halfway with Early Times, and then adds tap water.

He hands his brother one glass, then lifts his to it and offers a toast, as solemn as he might look on inauguration day.

"You'll never amount to anything, Bo."

Lucky laughs. "You neither, Bo."

It had been a running joke since grammar school. Tommy always told them how they had to amount to something, meaning get rich or famous or both. He used the phrase a thousand times, pumping them up for the next ball game or better grades or a class election. Except that, after the polio, Tommy seemed to realize that there were some things a pep talk wouldn't fix, so he reserved all of them for Tom Ed.

One of the twins would come up behind the other at his locker or in the school lunchroom, lean down and whisper in his ear, "Son, you'll never amount to anything." They even signed each other's junior yearbooks that way, not knowing how far they'd be from each other in six months.

Lucky could see, now, that the idea of "amounting" was still nipping at Tom Ed's heels like a fox terrier. He could see it working on him the way it worked on their father, except that Tom Ed had the tools to do more amounting than Tommy Sweatt ever dreamed of.

They talked about high school and summers and things they'd never discussed. Lucky and Tom Ed hadn't had a lot of long talks in the past twenty-nine years, Lucky realized.

"Bo," Tom Ed said at some point before 2 A.M., when Lucky left and staggered down the hall, drunker than he had been in years, "remember the beach, how we used to come sneaking back in from the boardwalk, way past curfew, and how Momma would always be waiting up for us?"

One time, the summer after Tom Ed talked their father into getting the red Buick, the twins came back two hours past their midnight curfew. The cottage that Mr. Lawrence loaned the Sweatts each summer gave them one more week at the beach than most of their neighbors on Mingo Road. It was six blocks from the boardwalk at White Oak Beach, and Tom Ed cut the ignition more than two blocks before they got home. They coasted in, crawled out the windows so they didn't have to close the car doors, tiptoed through the sand to the front porch, then put the key soundlessly into the front door just as Genie opened it and asked them why they cut off the ignition.

They laugh, too loudly for 2 A.M. in a quiet hotel room where a World War II movie blinks away soundlessly.

Lucky, though, remembers things Tom Ed either doesn't remember or just doesn't talk about. Lucky knows he should forget it or talk about it, but he doesn't know how to do either.

The summer they were fourteen, they were downtown at the beach with their parents, Felton and his new wife, and her two daughters. Tommy liked to invite all the family and friends he could to stay all or part of the week, a largesse he seemed to relish as much as the beach itself. The daughters were within two years of the twins' age, close enough that Tom Ed and Lucky wanted to impress them.

It was the year they installed a basketball free-throw shooting game on the boardwalk, and it was very popular. Hit three baskets in a row and win a teddy bear.

Tommy saw it first. He walked over to the booth and told the man running it, whose job it was to tease teenagers into trying to win prizes for their dates, that he had a son "who can put a serious dent in your bear population there."

Tom Ed had no choice, with his family, plus Felton, his dyed-blond wife, and her two daughters standing there. So he looked at Lucky, shrugged his shoulders, and took the ball from the man.

Tom Ed Sweatt would set a county record his senior year by hitting forty-two free throws in a row, and the tighter the game, the better he got. Before he was through, he had won a teddy bear for each of the girls, Felton's wife, and Genie, plus a big one to take back home to Susan Culbreth. For not the first time, Lucky secretly and shamefully willed his brother to fail.

Finally, exasperated, the man running the booth looked over at Lucky, who was trying very hard to be invisible.

"Hey, buddy," he said, "your brother's gonna win all my merchandise before you get a chance. Come on up here and give him a break."

There wasn't much choice. Lucky had long since quit shooting baskets with Tom Ed, feigning lack of interest, but he was stranded now between the smirking carny and a crowd that had been augmented by a few gawkers.

He hit one of the first three, none of the second three, and he could see Tommy drifting down toward the cotton-candy stand.

"I get it," the carny said, "he takes all my profits away from me, and you give 'em back."

Tom Ed told him to watch his mouth or he'd be eating one of those teddy bears, and the man threatened to call the police if they didn't leave.

But how, Lucky wonders, can a grown man talk about shooting free throws for teddy bears over thirty years ago? And, failing that, why can't a grown man just forget it?

In high school, they were thrown in with kids from all of eastern Scots County, most of whom never knew Lucky before he had polio, when he was still golden.

Tom Ed was an instant favorite of the coaches, the combination of natural leader and natural athlete they seldom found. He was captain of the junior varsity football, basketball, and baseball teams in the ninth grade. Lucky was the manager. He had slightly better grades than his brother, and he still helped him with his homework, because here Tom Ed wasn't a natural, struggling for his A's and B's. And Tom Ed still fought Lucky's fights for him. Lucky resented, he came to realize too late, the help he received more than the help he gave.

The twins began drifting apart in the tenth and eleventh grades. Tom Ed played every sport, was in every club. Lucky was in the Beta Club and the Future Farmers of America, not because he was a future farmer, but because that was where all the other male students with a grudge seemed to gravitate. He continued to be manager of the football team, because no one else wanted the job and because the coach, a man named Black who seemed to actually like Lucky, asked him to.

So Tom Ed and Lucky would ride to school together, then go home together after practice during football season. The rest of the year, Lucky had to take the bus home. They still had some laughs, but like a fan belt put to too much hard use, their brotherhood was less and less capable of standing the strain.

Tom Ed and Lucky were both gone by the time Geddie High was integrated. But, between their tenth- and eleventh-grade years, McDonald College in Port Campbell offered a speed-reading course, and one of Lucky's teachers nominated him for it. Tom Ed was already gone to a summer basketball camp, paid for by Tommy, so when Lucky said he wanted to learn to read two thousand words a minute, there was little resistance.

Lucky never really embraced speed reading. It made reading, a previously pleasurable activity, into a task or a contest. He also could see that the fix was in, that the point was to prove that everyone should learn speed reading. The night before they were to show off for the TV and newspaper reporters, they were allowed to take the next day's texts home with them, to ensure that everyone would be properly impressed. One fifth-grader read 32,000 words a minute.

McDonald College's speed-reading program was where Lucky met Eugene Solomon. Eugene wasn't the first black person he had ever known. Tom Ed and he had both worked in tobacco, and they both spent time helping Felton sell watermelons off the back of a truck in Frenchtown, Port Campbell's black quarter. But Eugene Solomon was the first black person Lucky had ever known who didn't seem likely to bite a tobacco worm in half.

Eugene Solomon was five feet, five inches tall. He wore thick-framed, thick-lensed black glasses. He was in the speed-reading program because McDonald College had insisted on having Carver High represented along with the white schools, some of which chose not to send anyone to an integrated class.

The first day, Lucky was next to Eugene, the only black student in a class of fifteen rising juniors and one of the few in the whole program, for no loftier reason than alphabetical seating. On the second morning, though, he arrived late. As he walked in the classroom door, he saw thirteen white students on one side and Eugene Solomon on the other, just as far apart as they could get.

Lucky felt a bond with this strange-looking, smallish scholar. He knew, without having to think, that Eugene Solomon's burden was heavier than polio.

"I hope I ain't taking anybody's seat," he said as he took the seat beside Eugene's. The black boy giggled, Lucky guessed out of nervousness, and then the mask that warded off cold, mean times came back down.

"Well," he said, "you got to be pretty special to sit over here, as you can see. We don't hold much with integration over here on Rastus Row." Lucky figured it was Eugene's way of saying it before somebody else did, a preemptive strike against their cruelest jabs. It was sad, but it was funny, too. Lucky soon came to appreciate one of the truly funny people he had thus far known in a world where humor was mainly used to inflict pain. He saw that it could be the weapon of the otherwise defenseless as well.

Eugene and Lucky became as close as black and white people ever got in Scots County in 1962. Lucky would go to the Solomons' house, and sometimes Eugene would visit the Sweatts. Neither of them felt especially welcome. Mrs. Solomon treated Lucky better than Tommy, Genie, and Tom Ed treated Eugene, but Lucky wondered sometimes if it wasn't out of some gene-deep fear of doing otherwise.

Tom Ed acted strangely toward Eugene. He would laugh and joke with him when he visited, whereas Tommy would simply leave the room. But then he would ask Lucky, after Eugene left, why he was wasting his time hanging around with niggers. Lucky told him, more than once, that it wasn't a nigger, it was Eugene.

It was Eugene Solomon who made Lucky and Tom Ed both see that they wouldn't be bonded for life, that there was something down there under the surface, a wall that grows up between the well-liked and the tolerated.

Eugene's sense of humor was as dry as dust. Out of necessity, he had become a master at putting people on so well that they didn't realize they'd been had until he'd already left the room. The problem, he told Lucky in about as candid a moment as they ever had, was that "half these crackers never get it. They just go home laughin' about the crazy spade."

The few blacks in the various classes that summer were all treated as pariahs. The students were fed at the McDonald College cafeteria, where the only previous black people worked behind the food lines. Eugene Solomon, older than the other black students and a loner to boot, usually had only Lucky for company.

One Friday, the week before the class ended, Eugene came in carrying a watermelon that seemed to Lucky to be about half as large as Eugene himself. He set it beside his desk like some green-and-white striped pet at show-and-tell. Nobody said a word to him about it, and he was deadpan enough to be holding aces and kings.

Then, at lunch, he went to the table where Lucky already sat.

Eugene reached into his secondhand briefcase and pulled out a butcher knife a foot long. He put paper towels all over the table, and then he sliced the melon lengthwise and split it apart. It made a wet, ripping sound that got the attention of the few students who weren't already staring. Then he dug into it, using his fingers and the knife, like a field hand who hadn't eaten for two days.

He motioned for Lucky to join him, and they both attacked the melon. By the time they were finished, they had the red juice smeared all over their faces, watermelon seeds all over the table, and a melon corpse stripped of all nourishment.

Eugene had tucked one of the brown lunchroom paper towels into his shirt like a napkin. He took it off and wiped his hands, and he and Lucky left the table and walked out the door as if nothing had happened, watermelon carnage in their wake. He never said a word about it, and neither did Lucky. That would have spoiled the coolness, and Eugene and Lucky knew that they had nothing if they didn't have cool. Not the approval-seeking cool of the jocks and rich kids, either, but the genuine stuff that gave no quarter, the cool of the nothing to lose.

Lucky knew Eugene all through his last year and a half of high school, up until Lucky left. Eugene would leave, too, through a scholarship to the University of Maryland. Once, during Lucky's time at Wilson's Draft, he went with a friend to College Park, Maryland, to visit a boy the friend had gone to high school with. Lucky hadn't thought of Eugene in more than a year, but he suddenly remembered his partner in cool when they drove by the Maryland campus. He figured that, if Eugene Solomon were still around, he would have been a junior then.

When they reached the boy's apartment, Lucky called student information and got Eugene's number. Another black voice answered and seemed not to know any Eugene Solomon, an evasiveness that reminded Lucky of his youth in Scots County, where black people knew that if someone white wanted to see them, it probably wasn't to deliver good news.

"If he's anywhere around," Lucky said, "please tell him it's Lucky Sweatt."

The voice said to wait, then Lucky heard the receiver drop. A couple of minutes later, as Lucky was beginning to believe that the voice had just walked off and left the receiver dangling, Eugene came on the phone.

"Lucky," he said, without commitment or even warmth. Lucky explained his unexpected proximity, said he wanted to see if Eugene was still alive.

"Yeah," he said, sounded tired. "Still alive. Still alive."

It was quickly evident to Lucky that Eugene Solomon didn't have much of a sense of humor anymore and that chewing the fat with white folks from back home wasn't high on his wish list. But he pressed, got Eugene to agree to meet him for a beer. Eugene gave him the name of a place on Route 1. Lucky went there and waited.

It was the spring of 1967. When Eugene Solomon walked in, Lucky suddenly realized how long ago they'd known each other. He barely recognized his old friend, who was now wearing a bas-ketball-sized Afro and the thinnest, flimsiest gold-rimmed glasses Lucky had ever seen. Lucky, whose hair hung halfway down his back, had to wave to get Eugene's attention, although there weren't a dozen people in the little bar, and only four of those were white.

Eugene sighed, gave a half-hearted wave, and walked back.

"What it is?" he said, and sat down.

They bought a round of beers each and talked about their fami-lies and about Port Campbell, a couple of expatriates. Eugene had spent time in Mississippi and Alabama, trying to sign up voters. He had a scar across his right cheek. He looked, to Lucky, as if he had been boiled down to the very essense, to where there wasn't an ounce of fat on his body or in his spirit.

At some point, struggling upstream to make some kind of con-tact, Lucky ventured that things were probably a lot better "all around" than they had been when they were growing up in Scots County.

Eugene Solomon stared at him for a long ten seconds.

"They'd better be getting a lot better yet," he finally said, "or somebody better get a lot more fire trucks."

Lucky wanted to ask Eugene if he didn't get any points for being better than the average, better than the people who kept blacks in second-rate schools and forced them to go two states away to get into a half-decent college. But he knew it wouldn't wash. Even as a kid, Lucky knew that nobody was standing up and saying, "This ain't right." To him, there had been Eugene, and there had been niggers, and he guessed that Eugene knew that now.

There wasn't much else to say. Lucky never heard of Eugene Solomon again until he read about his death. By then, Eugene had moved to California, and had apparently joined the Black Panthers. Genie sent a clipping about "Port Campbell native Eugene Solomon" being killed in a police shoot-out.

"He seemed like such a sweet boy," Genie said. "I don't know what gets into colored people sometimes."

Since Horace Morgan first heard the phrase "jumped-up" on "Masterpiece Theater," he had used it often.

It sounded a lot better, he felt, than "white trash" or "nigger." No doubt about it; the English had class.

Horace had been dealing with jumped-up people all his life, long before he even knew what to call them. People who didn't have any respect for their betters, didn't appreciate it when a man with an Ivy League education tried to do something nice for them.

His father had known what to do with them. How many times had Horace Senior told him, "Son, you give a dog dog food every time, his whole life, he won't ever want anything else, won't ever know the difference. But you give him a little bit of biscuit with some red-eye gravy one time, he'll resent it from then on every time you don't give him the whole ham. Might as well shoot him right then. Don't raise people's expectations."

But Horace had tried to be fair, more than fair, even.

He had done pro bono work with the law school at North Carolina Central, and all he got for it was a bunch of surly black activists asking him all kinds of rude, impudent questions in class, plus getting his tires slashed.

He did work with the prisons, until he got tired of being insulted by these dregs of society questioning his manhood every time he walked in the place.

He'd tried to take a girl like Susannah Horne, first one in her family to get out of the swamp and go to college, and teach her how to be a lady.

He'd tried to take a rube like Tom Ed Sweatt—God sakes, he needed a stage name, or something—and turn him into a responsible leader of the state, introduced him to all the right people, the ones who wrote the checks.

Sometimes Horace had to admit that his father had been right. The hell with them all. Use 'em, just like he'd been using that Lineberger cretin, then throw 'em away. Don't even get your hands dirty with them. Let 'em eat each other.

Let 'em rut like pigs.

Horace wouldn't give anybody the satisfaction of knowing they'd gotten the best of him. That was how you showed you had class. You didn't get all rednecked about it. You just got even.

## ★★★ **12** ★★★

Tuesday morning, Tom Ed has a briefing and throws what Lucky has come to think of as his daily fit.

Lucky counts twelve other people in the small meeting room Harry and Barry have been able to commandeer. He sits at the back, amazed that Tom Ed can look as if he's had eight good hours of sleep instead of half a fifth of Early Times. Lucky sips a cup of bad coffee and munches on a doughnut that's as glazed and stale as he is. Being just the driver and a poorly paid one at that, Lucky feels a freedom, an entitlement not to catch any of the abuse that Tom Ed is slinging at everyone within earshot and eyesight. He isn't sure if twins can really read each other's minds, but he's pretty sure that Tom Ed senses how little it would take this morning to make his critically hung-over brother return to Virginia.

Tom Ed hammers home the fact that it's just one week before the election. Lucky can see, though, that what's really gotten his brother's goat is the latest poll the Democrats have come out with that has Knox Cameron leading by three points.

"By God, we're blowing it!" he yells at the dozen staffers who sit pretending to scribble in their reporters' notebooks. "If we don't get off our butts and get going, we're going to be the laughingstock of the state! They're going to say we had it in our hands and then just sat back and let that son of a bitch Cameron steal it from us!"

Sam Bender has told Lucky that the only thing to do when Tom Ed gets like this is to just ride it out. Before the campaign, Lucky had never seen his brother so overbearing and irascible, but the advice sounds to him like what the twins used to tell each other when Tommy Sweatt would throw one of his patented tantrums. After a few minutes, Tom Ed runs dry, and he's more considerate than usual the rest of the morning, as if to silently apologize.

Lucky remembers his brother from their shared childhood as having a sweet disposition. He almost never lost his temper for long, and Lucky can't help but feel that these tirades are just part of what Harry once called "the package," the whole Tom Ed Sweatt package. The voters would see this good-natured, likable man who spoke their language and was never too busy to stop and talk, but they'd hear about the tantrums, too.

Lucky can see the sense in it. The kind of people the Sweatts grew up around respect a man who will throw the occasional fit. They don't seem to trust people who don't wear their hearts on their sleeves. If Lucky were inclined to give Knox Cameron advice, from what he's seen of the Democratic challenger so far, it would be to let people see him get mad once in a while.

After Tom Ed stops yelling, Barry Maxwell does the daily briefing.

They're supposed to go to Burgaw and then to Wilmington, where Tom Ed will do a photo opportunity with some veterans at the USS *North Carolina*.

After that, the plan is for him to go hunting with some Republican ward heelers in Bladen County. Lucky knows Tom Ed never liked hunting when they were kids, and that he'd as soon miss this part of the day. He knows that Sam Bender has taken his brother out and given him some pointers on how to use a rifle, because it wouldn't look good for the candidate for governor of North Carolina to not know how to hunt. The night before, when Tom Ed was too drunk to care, he'd told Lucky that he didn't want to look "like Dukakis did in that tank, all goofy and silly."

Susannah's at the briefing, too. She comes up to Tom Ed on his way out, and they talk for a couple of minutes, finally stepping back into the meeting room. The rest wait about five minutes before Tom Ed comes sauntering out, waving at some of the guests who recognize him. He's almost smiling when he gets into the van, and nobody has the guts to chastise him for holding things up.

They're ten miles out of Kinston, on Route 258, when Lucky sees three black children playing alongside the highway. They're waiting for the school bus, running around to stay warm; it's turned unseasonably cold.

They have what looks to Lucky to be a cheap dime-store rubber ball. When the van is almost too close, one of them throws it up in the air, tries to catch it, and misses. The ball apparently hits a rock, because it takes a crazy bounce right into the highway.

The boy goes running after it, doesn't even seem to think about looking for traffic. Lucky jams the brakes, but not enough to make the van slide, just enough to keep from hitting him.

Lucky looks back, paying little attention to Tom Ed, who's complaining loudly about the splash of coffee he spilled on his shirt. The boy who crossed the road is standing on the other shoulder, still happy, still ready to play. He doesn't seem to have any idea how close he came to being killed. Kids never do, Lucky thinks to himself.

"Gawd damn, Bo," Tom Ed's yelling while an aide hands him a wet handkerchief. "You gonna try to throw me through the windshield every time we see some little spearchucker playing beside the road?"

Lucky jams the brakes again. This time they do slide a little, just enough to be worrisome, and come to a dead stop in the middle of the road. Everyone's in an uproar now. They soon become quiet when they see that Lucky has no intention of budging just yet.

"I thought he looked like Benny," he says. Tom Ed's mouth is already open, but he doesn't say a word.

Lucky puts the van into first gear, and they're off again. It's quiet for a while.

It was Barbara's idea to adopt.

They both liked children, but they'd never talked about having any. After they were married, she told Lucky that she had a plan, if he'd go along with it.

If everyone who could afford it took responsibility for two children that no one else wanted, she told him, it might make a difference. Lucky, whose great debt to Barbara was the mellowness with which she seemed to have imbued his chaotic life, told her that he would as soon spend what little money they made on children as on anything else. They both felt, without saying, that they could improve on parenting as they had known it.

So they began trying to adopt. The Presbyterian church Barbara was cajoling Lucky to attend had a foreign missions program. The hardest part for him was the probable irreversibility of the vasectomy that would give them some control over their plan. Lucky was making ends meet as a carpenter, which paid better than any honest work he felt he could get with his newly acquired history degree, and most of the crew he worked with seemed to have a yard full of their own progeny. They looked somewhat askance at anyone who chose to raise other people's children. But the woman running the program said the surest way to get pregnant yourself was to adopt.

Over the following years, Lucky and Barbara got at least as much from their assembled children as the children received from them. A woman stopped them in church once, after the first adoption, and told Barbara how "brave" she thought they were. The brave ones, Barbara said to Lucky later, were the couples who were adopting the disabled children, the ones born addicted, the ones with Down's syndrome.

What Barbara and Lucky got was Kim.

She was four, the product of some anonymous coupling between an American GI and a Vietnamese woman. This was in 1978, after they had been on the list for two years.

When they first met her, she seemed to be all eyes, all terror, scared to death either that the Sweatts would take her home or that they wouldn't. They couldn't speak more than a few words of her language and she couldn't speak theirs, and they made up a rather intricate sign language that Kim would remember even as a teenager.

They thought she was the prettiest little girl they'd ever seen. Despite coming from the kind of life that leads to an orphanage door, she was well-behaved. Kids, Barbara warned Lucky before the adoption, were naturally selfish. But Kim wasn't. They would invite other children over to play with her, helping her get used to life in Willow Cove, and Kim would give them her toys. When she could understand enough English, they explained to her that she ought to try to keep at least some of what was hers.

She had learned English better than most of her classmates in their Virginia hill town by the time she started school. Barbara worked with her constantly, and sometimes Lucky felt that she had become too Americanized. She learned to get by with the best of her native-born classmates. She made nearly 1,300 on the SAT but wouldn't be able to get into the University of Virginia because of her grades. She told her parents, with perfect American insouciance, that she found homework a bore.

Once, Lucky started to read Kim the little-used riot act for not taking advantage of her great opportunity. Barbara pulled him into the kitchen and told him, in no uncertain terms, that just because Kim was an orphan and had had it rough didn't mean she was supposed to work harder than anybody else's children.

"Lucky, you quit berating that girl," she told him. "If anything, she ought to take it easier. She deserves a break, don't you think? We're going to raise these children the way we wish we had been raised."

He guessed she was right. He knew Barbara wouldn't accept anything below a certain level, anyhow. If Kim had just quit going to class altogether, that would've been different. Besides, it had worked out. She'd be going to James Madison University on a basketball scholarship.

Kim had been with them for four years when they adopted Chris, but because he was seven at the time, it meant that he was just a year younger than Kim. He was Vietnamese, too. The adoption agency was hesitant about their adopting two children of opposite sexes so close to the same age, but they had done so well with Kim that they let Chris come to Willow Cove, too.

Chris struggled more than Kim had. He came with a cleft palate, which was finally corrected after a long, painful ordeal that included many operations. Lucky knew that his adopted son must feel a double outcast, a Vietnamese and, in the graceless cruelty of other children, a "harelip."

By the time he reached high school, though, he had turned out to be a reasonably normal kid, even good-looking, Barbara and Lucky agreed. The thing Lucky learned was that, living somewhere like Willow Cove, where people tended to look like each other's first cousins, someone from another race and another world was more a novelty than a threat.

When Chris was small, and he'd come home crying his heart out because someone had teased or bullied him, Lucky would tell him about the polio.

"They call me Lucky," he told him once when Chris was ten years old, "but you're the lucky one. By the time you get to high school, you'll be as normal as they come. I started out normal and then went backward."

Even though Lucky was pretty sure his son wasn't buying this rationale, it did appear that the cleft palate, and then its absence, made Chris appreciate life more. Never an A student, he appeared, as a high school junior, to be reaching some kind of turning point. His first report card, Barbara told Lucky over the weekend, contained four A's and a B. Lucky just hoped it wasn't too late for him to get a nice, fat college scholarship somewhere. And Lucky was also aware that it was Chris's ability to take anything in the house apart and make it run better, his sheer handiness, that enabled Lucky to chase a piece of his own lost and mismanaged childhood back and forth over North Carolina.

For four years after they adopted Chris, it was just the four of them. The kids were getting big enough to help out at the inn; everything was running as smoothly as clockwork.

And then, Benny.

A black teenager named LaChaundra Hairston was helping out at the inn. They let her go in January 1986 over a matter of some missing cash that they didn't believe anyone else could have taken.

That October, she was murdered by her boyfriend.

They apparently got into an argument over drugs, the boyfriend's occupation. They found her body in the cabin that the two of them were living in. It had no indoor plumbing; there was a pump in the front yard for water and a privy by the woods.

She was sixteen years old, and she had a baby boy who appeared to be about a month old. When the mailman saw the front door open and went up to investigate the next day, he found LaChaundra where she had bled to death, stabbed twenty-nine times, on the cabin floor. And there was the baby, too weak even to cry, on a blanket beside her.

Lucky had heard that babies can remember everything, right from the first light. He hoped that was wrong.

Barbara, who always seized the blame for everything that went wrong, anywhere, took it worse than Lucky, who had been greatly relieved when they had let LaChaundra go. He could see that she was going to be somebody's problem. He could not have guessed that LaChaundra Hairston's troubles would come back to them in a baby blanket.

If they had been living in a larger city, what came next might never have happened. The baby probably would have been put in an orphanage or a foster home awaiting passage to an appropriate African-American family.

But LaChaundra had no family in or around Willow Cove. It turned out that she ran away from her aunt's home in Martinsville with her boyfriend when she was thirteen, and that no one back there had much interest in taking on another baby, especially one who none of them had ever seen or even known about. This somehow made Lucky sadder for LaChaundra than even the murder had.

LaChaundra's body was shipped back to Martinsville. The baby stayed with the Sweatts in Willow Cove.

The county welfare department was delighted for them to take care of him "for a while," and the while, in the absence of bureaucracy, soon turned into forever, which suited the Sweatts very well and seemed to suit the baby, too.

There were six black children in Willow Cove Elementary

School, and there weren't more than twenty in Kim's grade at South Valley High. Lucky knew all the arguments: how they were taking Benny away from his heritage, robbing him of his identity, and he knew the same could be said for what they'd done by adopting Kim and Chris, that white America had done its share in making them orphans.

But he didn't care, and Barbara cared less than he did.

"Lucky," she told him one time, after they found out how much surgery Chris was going to need and were wondering where the money was going to come from, "if we can leave it just a little better than we found it, I'll feel like we have led good lives. Hell, some days I'd settle for breaking even."

They let Kim and Chris name the baby, although Barbara did veto three of the earlier offerings: Moonbeam, Volvo, and Chris, Jr. That they even had to name him saddened Barbara to tears. His birth father, serving a life sentence in the state penitentiary in Brunswick County, said that they had never bothered to name "it."

There was a lot of sentiment for Moses, because he'd been more or less found in the bulrushes, and the two older children had seized on Christianity harder than Barbara or Lucky, who were both deacons in the Mount Carmel Presbyterian Church, ever had. Barbara said she was a humanist, and Lucky guessed he was, too.

Finally, though, they settled on Benjamin Moses Sweatt, because they liked the story of Joseph and his brothers in the Old Testament. Kim and Chris agreed to call him Benny and see if he grew into Ben. In the fall of 1992, he was still Benny, but Lucky felt he might be a Ben soon. He still believed in Santa Claus and he still thought his mother named him before she died of some mysterious ailment. For both of those things, Lucky often thanked Kim and Chris, who responded, almost always, "No trouble, Pop," and gave embarrassed teenage shrugs.

Guests at the inn would sometimes do a double take when the Sweatts all sat down at the long communal breakfast table. Lucky felt that it was good for the kids to see themselves as others, all the way from Florida to Canada, saw them, the inn being right off an interstate highway.

Kim and Chris were old enough now to sometimes get irritated over the surreptitious looks. They'd been known to tell a paying guest that they were kidnapped from their true parents and forced into slave labor. And now Benny was old enough to join in.

"Me, too," he'd yelp when they began pulling some stranger's leg. "I'm a kidnap, too."

Once in a while, someone in town or at church would say how nice it was that Barbara and Lucky had adopted Kim, Chris, and Benny "since you all couldn't have kids of your own," as if the three were consolation prizes. Lucky held his tongue, usually, and the Sweatts and the town of Willow Cove coexisted peacefully.

Sometimes, Lucky would come in late from some hopeless, thankless project like trying to make the roof last another year, mad at the world and wondering when he was ever going to catch a break, and he would see them all through the picture window, there at the table, Chris reaching across Kim for more peas, Kim carrying on a depressingly adult conversation with Barbara, Benny inspecting a spoonful of something he was not likely to eat voluntarily, and Lucky would have to step back into the darkness for a couple of seconds, not wanting to alarm them at how much the sight of their togetherness unhinged him.

It's almost two o'clock by the time the appearance at the USS *North Carolina* is over. They reach Elizabethtown too late for dove hunting, so Tom Ed makes a token appearance. Lucky's thinking his brother is somewhat relieved, although Tom Ed complains bitterly to the businessmen and farmers and lawyers about how "them damn boy geniuses of mine" made him miss out on the high point of his year's social calendar. Tom Ed has a couple of drinks, tells a couple of mildly off-color jokes, making sure no one is taking notes, and then they're off to Port Campbell. The campaign is supposed to be in Charlotte by the next afternoon, but Tom Ed tells Lucky that he wants them, "just us two," to do something the next morning. When Lucky mentions that Tommy and Genie would be hurt if they knew they were in town and didn't at least drop by, his brother seems peeved and says he sees more than enough of Tommy Sweatt as it is.

"Just you and me, Bo," he says, and Lucky guesses that something like this is why he agreed to do this fool's errand to begin with.

The Holiday Inn north of town says WELCOME/TOM ED SWEATT/DOGBODIES. Dogbodies, they find out, is the house band.

Tom Ed shakes his head. "At least they're spelling my name right."

When they were in Wilmington, a reporter from the Raleigh paper asked him about the antiabortion rally in Charlotte scheduled for Saturday, and whether he was still planning on speaking at it. Tom Ed was quiet for a second or two. A couple of TV crews were taping.

"Let me ask you something," he said to the reporter. "If I was to come out here and say I supported killing baby seals, that it was okay because women need something to keep 'em warm, you all'd be on me like a duck on a june bug, wouldn't you?"

The reporter said he didn't know, but Tom Ed was already off and running.

"But you all think it's okay for some doctor to kill some innocent, unborn baby? Hell, you show more sympathy for some ax murderer up on death row. You're damn right I'll be there on Saturday. I'll be in the front row, and proud of it."

Some of the veterans behind him were eavesdropping, and they let out with a big roar that carried across the Cape Fear River. For a minute, it looked to Lucky as if they were going to pick him up and carry him off like the kids in Geddie had done a couple of times in high school after he'd hit the winning basket or driven in the winning run. Looking at his brother wave to the men, Lucky saw that Tom Ed had the same kind of glow in his eyes he'd had in those magic days when it seemed he couldn't screw up if he tried.

After dinner, Lucky and Tom Ed are alone in Tom Ed's room. Lucky watches his brother puff on an enormous cigar, looking as pleased as he's seen him in a long time.

"Tom Ed," he asks, seizing the rare mellow moment, "I have to ask you something. Do you really believe that a three-month-old fetus is just the same as a baby?"

Tom Ed looks for a second as if he's going to erupt. But either the residue of a good day or brotherly love stills him.

"Hell, Bo," he sighs, "I don't have a clue. The Church of the Rock people have showed me some awful pictures of babies in trash cans, look like they're as human as you or me. But I don't know how old they were.

"Tell you what," he says, "I wish there was some panel of experts somewhere that could tell me what's a baby and what's a fetus. Just tell me and I'll go along with it."

Lucky tells him that he might, but that he doubts the Church of the Rock would.

Tom Ed gives him a look that has something foreign in it—indecision. Then he gets up, dragging his chair with him, and sits down directly in front of Lucky, leaning forward so far that his brother can smell the cigar stench on his breath.

"I'm going to tell you something, Bo," he says. "It's something the goddamn M&M twins don't know, and you probably hadn't ought to know either, but you're going to."

Susannah had only missed two periods when Tom Ed sent her to the only doctor he could trust, an old fraternity brother from Chapel Hill who could keep a secret. That was in August.

Two things, though, made the difference: Susannah didn't care much for secrets, and Tom Ed kept things.

When Susannah slipped a scented note in his hand two weeks later, full of erotic promises and mentioning, almost in passing, "the procedure," Tom Ed read it twice and put it in among the morass of papers in his briefcase, as if the note itself would entitle him to the favors of which she wrote.

The next week, Tom Ed made a rare overnight stay at home. How could he have foreseen that Lucinda would take the trouble to ransack his briefcase, looking for what Tom Ed figured she knew already?

When he came downstairs after showering, she confronted him

with the note. Tom Ed had no choice but to concede what was obvious, and he spent the rest of the night at the Holiday Inn. He was barely able to get his shirt and pants from Lucinda on the way out, and it took him a week to retrieve the briefcase.

Tom Ed regretted the way things had turned out, but he didn't worry. He felt sure that Lucinda wanted to be the governor's wife more than she wanted revenge. She had always been patient, and she would have plenty of time to settle scores.

It wasn't revenge that caused her to tell Tommy. She wouldn't have told another soul, not for a while, if Tommy hadn't upbraided her, or tried to, eight days afterward.

The old man had come over one night, by himself. She didn't like Tommy Sweatt, wouldn't have even if he'd liked her, and she realized the two of them had probably never been alone before in that house or any other.

He hemmed and hawed, then finally got to the point. He thought she wasn't doing enough "electioneering."

"Tom Ed needs you, Lucinda," he'd said, trying to make it sound like pleading instead of demanding. "Can't no man get to that governor's mansion by himself. He needs a helpmate to stand by him."

Lucinda had a short fuse, and the word "helpmate" alone might have been enough to set her off.

"If he wants a damn 'helpmate,'" she told Tommy, "tell him to recruit that slut he bought an abortion for. He's getting most of his 'help' elsewheres these days."

She'd halfway assumed the old man knew anyhow. The minute she mentioned "abortion," she knew he didn't. He lost his temper, called her a liar, said she was just a rock dragging Tom Ed down.

But he knew it was probably true.

"You can't tell nobody," he said, really pleading now. "It'll ruin him. It'll ruin the whole family."

She told him to get out. He tried to extract a promise, and she had to threaten to call the police before he finally gave up.

That same night, Tommy reached Tom Ed by phone and confronted him.

"Goddammit, Tommy, shut up!" Tom Ed exclaimed. "We'll talk about this some other time. This is a public phone. You watch what you say, now."

The next day, he made a special trip down to Port Campbell just to take his father aside and stress to him, as if to a child, how important it was that he not tell a soul, even Genie, about this. He told him not to worry about Lucinda.

"I wouldn't tell Genie, nohow," Tommy muttered.

"So," Tom Ed is looking straight into Lucky's eyes in the hotel room, "that's where it is. I figure, what the hell, if Lucinda and Tommy both know it, you might as well, too. You're less likely than either one of them to call a press conference. If this gets out, though, won't all the king's horses nor all the king's men be able to put Humpty Dumpty back together again."

The phone rings. Lucky can tell from his brother's voice that it's Susannah.

Tom Ed hangs up and rises to leave.

He pauses at the door.

"I don't like it, Bo. I feel like the biggest damn hypocrite in the world, but what else am I goin' to do? Roll over like a puppy and just give up?

"Seven more days," he says as he opens the door, holding up his right hand and the index and middle fingers of the left. "Six, if you consider that I ain't likely to lose too many votes on election day itself."

Lucky starts to say something, then decides not to push his luck.

## ★★★ 13 ★★★

Wednesday morning, Tom Ed borrows a car from Cody Barrett and Johnny Ray Roberts, who are taking a semester off from Wake Forest to work for Tom Ed Sweatt. Just a couple of young, idealistic Republicans trying to keep America safe for millionaires, Harry Mavredes once described them within earshot of Lucky, who's now driving the Ford Taurus Johnny Ray's father bought for him out of the hotel parking lot. Tom Ed teases them, calls Cody "Muffy" and Johnny Ray "Sunbeam," but he also depends on them and several other college-age volunteers to help woo what he publicly calls "North Carolina's future" and privately refers to as "the young and the witless."

Lucky can remember how much he hated Republicans when he was Cody and Johnny Ray's age, how a cynical professor at Wilson had passed on to him the old saw: If you're not a liberal at twenty, you don't have a heart; if you're not a conservative at forty, you don't have a mind. He wonders what Cody and Johnny Ray are going to be like in twenty years. He knows why he's here—family, for better or worse. But he has an itch to shake Johnny Ray Roberts occasionally when he starts acting smug about homeless people or homosexuals or women's rights. He wants to tell him that he's got a whole lifetime to get fat and ugly. Why start early? Part of him yearns to ask Cody Barrett what in God's world an educated woman would stand to gain from the Tom Ed Sweatt platform. Kids, he sighs to himself. They probably think we want them to rebel, so they'll be conservatives just to piss us off.

He's tried to rear Kim and Chris to fight for the underdogs, but before he left Willow Cove, Kim let him know that she considered her uncle Tom Ed to be "somewhere to the right of Pat Buchanan."

Other than family, Lucky didn't have an answer for her. He still doesn't, but he knows Tom Ed isn't the same Tom Ed he sees doing the TV commercials. And, he tells himself, Knox Cameron isn't exactly going to bring socialism to North Carolina.

The more he thinks about it, the more he's convinced that Tom Ed's taking the only route he can take and hope to be the next governor of North Carolina. If he had come out as some wild-eyed, idealistic liberal, champion of the underdog and the oppressed, Lucky can see that he would have been just one more lunatic fringe candidate with no money to back him.

If you're a Kennedy, Lucky plans to tell Kim when he gets back home, you can afford compassion. If a poor boy does it, though, he doesn't have any fat-cat money to back him and he looks like a sorehead, because that little guy he's fighting for looks an awful lot like him.

There's something else, too, that Lucky's starting to understand. If you grow up, in Tom Ed's words, "poor as shit," you get a little uneasy sidling up to the welfare cases and the dirt farmers. It's too close to the quick; if you admit that all these folks haven't had a fair shake, you're just a baby step from conceding that you're where you are because you did get all the breaks, and not because you personally pulled yourself up by your bootstraps. The only difference between you and me, says the thought balloon above all those boys' heads at the country store where Tom Ed stops to shake hands for the cameras, is that you got good teeth, you used to play ball, and you kissed a lot of ass.

Tom Ed can talk the down-home talk, but it's no secret to Lucky that he'd rather spend the rest of his days living next to some country club golf course.

★     ★     ★

So Cody and Johnny Ray are headed for Charlotte in the van, where the Sweatt brothers will catch up with them by mid-afternoon. Tom Ed and Lucky are tending to business, although exactly what business Lucky doesn't know.

Also part of the caravan headed for Charlotte is Lucinda. Tom Ed hasn't seen her since Lucky joined the campaign, and he's fairly certain that his brother isn't looking forward to the reunion in Charlotte.

Tom Ed and Lucky have left in the Taurus before the rest of the entourage hits the trail. Lucky is driving, and Tom Ed's giving directions. Soon they're up on Arsenal Hill, and Lucky can tell that they're headed for Tom Ed's house, where Lucinda is waiting for the van to pick her up.

Lucky parks in Tom Ed's driveway. His brother gets out and tells him to wait.

Tom Ed returns to the car twenty minutes later, and he doesn't say anything at first, just slams the door, red-faced, as if he's been yelling.

Finally, sounding as defeated as Lucky's ever heard him, he mumbles, "She ain't going, Bo. She says she ain't going anywhere where I might be at."

They sit there for a minute, the engine idling. Finally, Lucky asks him, "Where to, Governor?"

Tom Ed shoots Lucky one of his slit-eyed looks, designed to melt junior campaign workers. Then he seems to remember who he's looking at.

"Mingo Road," he says, and Lucky thinks maybe they might be getting somewhere.

Tom Ed Sweatt and Lucinda Stallsmith dated in high school, but then they broke up for the third time when everything else was more or less falling apart the twins' senior year. They got back together just about the time Tom Ed dropped out of Carolina to play pro ball. The Stallsmiths seemed to think they were a cut above the Sweatts, but Tom Ed charmed their pants off, the same as he did everyone else.

They got married before her senior year at UNC-Greensboro, just after Tom Ed had finished his year in the Appalachian League, when he was already starting to suspect that he wasn't going to be able to hit a major-time curveball. Lucky was invited to the wedding. He made a point of staying in Virginia and getting especially drunk that weekend.

Lucinda taught school for two years around Port Campbell, waiting for Tom Ed to come home for good. His second year in the minors, Tom Ed played in the Western Carolinas League and only hit .208. Lucky would buy the *Sporting News* to see how he was doing, half pulling for him, half hoping he'd fall flat on his butt.

At any rate, Lucky figured somebody must've pulled Tom Ed aside at the end of that second year and told him that it was time for a career change, because when Lucky came home for Christmas in 1968, Tommy was telling everyone that "the prodigal has returned," and Tom Ed wasn't saying anything.

Kyle, their first, was two months old, and Lucky gave Tom Ed credit for not going back or trying to catch on with another organization. It would take Tom Ed twenty years to be candid enough to tell him, "If you hit .208 in Granite Falls, Bo, the only way you're ever going to make the major leagues is with a ticket."

By early the next year, he was in sales and on his way to getting somewhat rich in real estate and becoming Your Future Governor, Tom Ed Sweatt.

To Lucky, there had always been something strange about Tom Ed and Lucinda. To his eyes, they never seemed to even like each other that much. His main memory of them, back in high school, was of the two of them sitting together at a table in the lunchroom, apart from everyone else, not speaking and acting as if they were mad at the world in general and each other specifically. Lucinda was fully capable of going a day at a time without speaking; Lucky had seen her do it at family gatherings. Genie said it was just the Stallsmith in her, as if, Lucky thought to himself, there weren't any crazy Sweatts and Balcoms running around loose.

Lucky asked Tom Ed about her one time, their junior year,

when he and Lucinda had broken up again, this time because she wanted to date a college boy from N.C. State. How, Lucky just blurted out one night when they were by themselves, can you go steady with a girl who acts like she can't stand you half the time?

He gave Lucky a look more of hurt than anger, and Lucky was already sorry and wishing he hadn't asked.

"Aw, Bo," he said finally, "she's not like that. We get along fine. She just ain't got much to say sometimes.

"And besides," he grinned and lowered his voice a little, "you haven't seen them tits of hers out in the open."

Thinking back, Lucky concedes that that might have been enough, at seventeen. When they finally got together for good, though, he was somewhat surprised, but he figured that maybe both of them had been with worse and appreciated each other a little more.

There had always been hints of an impending breakup. Tom Ed did move out of the house for a month once, when Westlake was blowing up in everyone's face, but nobody in the family ever talks about that anymore. Lucky wonders if Tommy and Genie know how bad things have gotten. He realizes that his unspoken advice to Tom Ed is the same that Tommy's would be: Keep your pants on 'til after the election.

They turn left at Geddie and head down Mingo Road. Lucky tells Tom Ed that it appears the Bullocks have added about six more house trailers since the last time he was there. The Bullocks, who live about half a mile from the Sweatts' old place, remind Lucky of the Amish whose farms he saw once up in Pennsylvania. No Bullock ever seems to leave home, but instead of building on extra rooms like the Amish, until the house resembles a small hotel, the Bullocks just haul another mobile home into the field out in back of the big house and extend the dirt road a little farther toward the swamp.

Tom Ed shakes his head.

"You know, Bo," he says, "I spent my whole life trying not to have to live next to Bullocks."

They pull into the driveway at the old house. You can tell, without even going in, that Genie has been coming out there about once a week and cleaning it, even though they haven't lived there for years. The first time Lucky realized she was doing that, he asked her why anyone would clean a house they didn't have to clean. Housekeeping at the inn seemed to take up about half of his and Barbara's waking hours.

"You don't ever know," she said, "when you might have to go back where you came from."

Tommy didn't want to have anything to do with the old place. Felton once told Lucky that he only came back to Mingo Road to go to the store and brag on Tom Ed.

They get out of the car, then both stretch and yawn. To Lucky, there's something about the old place, about this neighborhood, that makes him want to lie down and sleep, even first thing in the morning. He figures it's the quiet or the humidity or some combination. When he first left home and went to work in Chapel Hill, it seemed to him that he needed less sleep, had more energy. Tom Ed tells him it's magic dust the rich people sprinkle in eastern Scots County to keep the natives from ever amounting to anything.

They both reach for front-door keys and laugh when they realize they both still have the keys to a house in which they haven't lived full-time for almost thirty years.

"Maybe Momma's not the only one," Tom Ed says. "Maybe we're all afraid we're going to have to come back here and live someday."

They go inside and walk around for a while, as if trying to memorize the rooms or find something. They talk some, about the games they played, the raging tantrums their father used to throw, the way nobody makes chicken and pastry as well as their mother used to. Lucky opens a drawer in the bedside table of his old room and a 1958 Topps baseball card falls out, some nondescript utility infielder for the Kansas City Athletics with a candy-apple-red background.

"How much you reckon that's worth now?" Tom Ed asks. Lucky

says probably about fifty cents, then promises himself he'll come back sometime with Chris and scour the place to see if there are any more that Genie didn't throw away. But the rush he gets from the old baseball card is like walking down the street and getting a whiff of a fragrance once worn by a girl you hadn't thought of in twenty years.

They go outside and take turns retelling the story of how Tommy almost killed Lucky when he tried to make them walk across an old plank from the carport roof to the chicken-house roof. Lucky realizes that this is the first time they've ever really talked about it.

Finally, they just lean back against the borrowed Taurus and are quiet. They can hear the single engine of the Campbell and Cool Spring Railroad train shifting cars in Geddie.

Tom Ed clears his throat and says, "I hate losing people, Bo."

Lucky looks at his brother. Tom Ed is staring straight ahead, across Mingo Road.

"I mean," he goes on, "it didn't have to be like that with me and Lucinda, you know? She didn't always hate my guts, and I didn't always want to leave her. But she'd do stuff, and I'd do stuff, and neither one of us ever forgot a goddamn thing, I don't believe.

"You know, she'll throw up Greta Long to me sometimes now, if she's had enough to drink?"

Tom Ed had dated Greta Long out of spite his junior year when Lucinda told him she thought they should see other people. She was killed in a car crash fifteen years ago, Tom Ed adds.

"The old man was right," he says, and Lucky asks, "About what?"

"About how women are always trying to keep you from doing what you know you got to do. You know, Lucinda didn't want me to run for the legislature, said she didn't want me to be away that long, said she had everything she wanted already and didn't want to risk losing any of it. Didn't trust me to be away that long is more like it. But the old man told me that I wasn't ever going to amount to shit if I let Lucinda Stallsmith tie me down like that."

He looks at his brother.

"Bo," he says, "the old man ain't always wrong."

Tom Ed seems to catch himself, then bursts into laughter.

"What the hell am I saying? Of course the old man is always wrong. I must be losing it, Bo. It's been a long haul. I just ain't myself."

They both laugh, then it becomes quiet again. Lucky knows Tom Ed is about as relaxed as he's going to be, because he hasn't looked at his watch even once since they turned on to Mingo Road. A chilling wind is picking up across the garden, where they can still see the ridges from the long-abandoned collard rows, looking like frozen waves.

"Bo," Tom Ed says, finally, "you know, it like to have killed the old man and Momma when you left like that."

He stops for a couple of seconds, as if he's struggling for what comes next.

"Like to have killed me, too," he says, and Lucky puts his arm around his brother, much the way he might have coming home from school in the third grade.

Then, he does look at his watch.

"Damn," he says, "we got to be in Charlotte in three hours."

He's already shut the passenger door by the time Lucky opens the one on the driver's side.

They speak no more than a few sentences on the way to Charlotte, Tom Ed napping much of the time. Lucky listens to the radio and wonders if, contrary to everything he's made himself believe for most of his life, loss can be reversible.

## ★★★ 14 ★★★

It comes to Horace Morgan almost like a dream.

He is thinking about Susannah and Tom Ed Sweatt, about Dr. Nate Crowell and the whole mess in Charlotte. About secrets.

Horace's first wife bore him two children. He knew morning sickness when he saw it. When Susannah went away in the middle of the week, then came back with no explanations, just looking a little tired, he knew. But he bided his time. He sprung it on her one night in late September.

They were having a late supper together; they still shared some moments of intimacy, although fewer and fewer in bed.

Horace cleared his throat, then wiped his mouth delicately with his napkin. Susannah was worrying a piece of cold fried chicken for a last morsel of meat. Just like you used to do in that tar-paper shack you grew up in, Horace thought to himself.

"You know," he said, "I have a hundred dollars that says you had an abortion Tuesday."

She stopped chewing.

"I have another hundred that says Tom Ed Sweatt paid for it."

He had no proof, but he thought he could probably get it, and he was even more sure Susannah believed he already had it.

She put down the drumstick and reached for her own napkin. Horace saw that there was grease around her mouth.

"It's all right," he continued. "Better that than the alternative. I just wanted you to know my faculties are still relatively unimpaired."

"Some are more impaired than others," she said, not smiling, a little nervous. She was still, beneath it all, a country girl who sometimes, on the high wire of what she supposed to be sophistication, looked down.

He grunted.

"You really ought to be more careful, though, if you don't mind my saying so."

"Well," she said, "I guess I won't be your problem much longer."

"You could be if you want," he said.

"Stop. We said it was all settled. No more talk."

He nodded. It was as far as he could lower himself.

"Does anyone else know?"

She hesitated, then nodded.

"His wife. And his father."

"His father! That old gasbag. My lord, what in the world would make Tom Ed Sweatt tell him that. Has he lost his mind?"

"Aren't you worried about the wife?"

Horace said he wasn't, that he'd bet another hundred she'd swallow a gallon of pride to be the governor's wife.

"For a while," Susannah said, smirking.

"His father?!" Horace repeated, amazed all over again.

She told Horace what Tom Ed had told her, the whole sad history of a secret gone bad.

At the end, he shook his head.

"Well, you had better be sure nobody else knows. Forget you even told me. If we're going to win this election, somebody better zip up . . . in more ways than one."

Susannah laughed.

"You know," she said, "if we can ever get over being married, we might even get to be friends."

In hell, he thought to himself, smiling back.

Now, lying on his back alone, waiting for sleep to come, afraid to even look at the digital clock beside his bed, drifting in and out of consciousness, Horace Morgan has a vision, either a real dream or a product of the scattergun tangents insomnia sometimes visits on his brain.

Sometimes, it appalls Horace to think of the kind of people he must occasionally deal with, just to keep from being what his father used to call the idle rich.

Take Little Sonny Lineberger. He's like a bad imitation of a TV gangster, but he's proved helpful since Big Sonny paid Horace well to defend him. It's almost as if he thinks Horace did it out of the goodness of his heart.

Little Sonny has proved as faithful as a Labrador, glad to help when there are people to pay, people to collect from, sometimes even people to scare. Horace knows that, weird as Little Sonny might be, he can keep him from having to deal with people ten times weirder.

Sometimes, Horace just wants to move, to Virginia or England or somewhere. Some place where class is appreciated, where fast-talking trash doesn't carry the day.

Take Tom Ed Sweatt. Take him and his whole jumped-up type, he thinks, turning again and kicking the covers off one leg. And that father of his. Horace has met him just once. All bullshit and pretension, like he is somebody. He just about talked one of Horace's ears off before Tom Ed led him away to bother somebody else. Horace grits his teeth and thinks of the likes of Tommy Sweatt knowing about Susannah's abortion, wonders if Tommy knows her name.

And then something clicks. Horace's eyes fly open like a pair of venetian blinds.

He turns on the bedside lamp and sits up, walking it through his mind, a right-hand finger coming down heavily on his left palm as he ticks off each step. No stone, he thinks, unturned.

"Yes," he mutters to himself. "Yes."

He thinks about a commercial for the New York lottery he saw the last time he took Susannah up there to see a real play. The punch line made them both laugh.

"Hey," he mumbles to himself, repeating the line, "you never know," and he laughs almost silently in the empty house.

He resets the alarm for half an hour earlier, so he can reach Little Sonny Lineberger before Little Sonny leaves for the job Horace got for him.

Then he drifts into the most peaceful sleep he's had in months.

$\star\star\star$ **15** $\star\star\star$

Tom Ed makes an appearance at the memorial service for the Reverend Gary Thorne on Wednesday at two o'clock, then they head into the heart of the Piedmont.

The center of North Carolina seems to Lucky to be one factory town after another, each with just enough people to make it worth Tom Ed Sweatt's time to give a speech or visit the newspaper or indulge in whatever pork-product festival is going on at the moment.

Wednesday is an endless succession of such places. Concord. Kannapolis. Albemarle. Salisbury. Statesville. Lexington. Thomasville. High Point. By the time Lucky clears one town's stoplights, they're already in another that is a carbon copy of the last. Tom Ed never seems to tire of jumping out of the van with his million-dollar smile, ready and eager to shake a few hundred hands.

Getting back in the car after a rally at a church in Statesville, Tom Ed turns and winks at Lucky.

"If Knox Cameron is working this hard," he says, "I'll kiss his sorry liberal ass."

By now, the experts are saying the race is dead even, and they're trying to figure out how Tom Ed Sweatt, whom they've all buried several times, is doing it. Tom Ed is worried, though, because the momentum seems to have come to a dead stop, which is what Barry Maxwell says usually happens when neither one of the candidates gets caught having sex with a farm animal. The Democrats don't seem to be able to make shrink-swell soil or anything else stick to Tom Ed, and Knox Cameron doesn't seem guilty of anything worse than a generally unsubstantiated "softness."

The M&M twins want to push harder on abortion. They constantly tell Tom Ed that he can soft-pedal it after he wins the election, but that they've got to get him elected first.

Sam Bender seems to Lucky to be a little less sure that Tom Ed's doing the right thing. He tells them at lunch that the last poll he saw on the subject said most North Carolinians favored letting a woman make her own choice.

"That's the mind talking," Harry tells him. "We're going after their Baptist hearts."

Tom Ed seems to push himself and everyone else harder every day, and on Wednesday, it finally starts to show. At the end of the day, he goes to his room, shuts the door and tells Barry not to let anybody in, not even Susannah, who's staying on another floor.

Thursday, it's pouring when they awake, the kind of driving rain that will strip the hardwoods of most of what the tourism bureau calls fall foliage. They drive through Winston-Salem on streets slick with leaves, and the trees suddenly look old and tired.

Tom Ed is speaking at Wake Forest, a rare appearance before a university crowd. The students aren't completely friendly, despite what Cody and Johnny Ray and the others have done to pack the house.

Wake is a Baptist school, but not a hard-shell one. There are some pro-life demonstrators, but not as many as were in Charlotte at the Reverend Gary Thorne's funeral.

Lucky thinks about the Tom Ed he's seen eating chitlings and talking about cropping tobacco for the benefit of the country voters, and he cringes inwardly for him.

Once more, Tom Ed amazes him. He comes across not as an ignorant man, or even a naive one, but as someone who's been playing dumb but is letting you, college sophisticate that you are, in on his act because you're too smart to fleece. It's as if he's winking at them and saying, "Hey, you all know what you've got to do to get elected in North Carolina. Put me in there and then you'll see the real me."

At the end, he's got some of them laughing and some of them shaking their heads, the way adults will react to a rambunctious but likable child. The pro-choice people can't even work up much venom, and Tom Ed deftly low-keys the abortion issue.

He's also careful not to take any questions from the audience. He tells them a cornball joke built around the fact that it's worse for Baptists to be caught having premarital sex than dancing. Then, while they're still laughing, he says, "God bless you all. Let's make this a great state," and he's gone.

He, Lucky, and the rest are back in the van within a minute, headed for another college speech in Greensboro.

Lucky can see that Tom Ed enjoys leaving the college kids' mouths open. He has his degree, but he reminds Lucky of other people he's known who work their way slowly through school or drop out and go back later, too old or hampered by responsibility to savor the fraternities and keg parties and Student Prince aspect of the experience. They always seem to look at the "college kids" as some privileged lot laughing behind their backs. The only thing that kept Tom Ed from graduating in four years was Tom Ed, Lucky knows, but he understands how his brother feels, having conquered Wilson University with calluses on his hands.

Thursday night, Tom Ed appears to have gotten his second wind. It's stopped raining, and he wants to go for a drive. He and Lucky borrow Johnny Ray's Taurus again; Tom Ed hands his brother the keys and tells him, "Just drive, Bo."

They get on one of the four-lane streets leading into Greensboro from the hotel. Without conscious thought, Lucky has turned right because he thinks he sees something familiar, then takes a left and another right, and there in front of them is a small park that sits beside the UNC-Greensboro campus. Only then does Lucky realize what dim, distant signal has led him here.

Lucinda.

Tom Ed and Lucinda were split; she had given him back his

ring for the third time. He was at Carolina and Lucky was working construction in Chapel Hill. Sometimes, Lucky and a friend would drive the sixty miles to Greensboro, which had a ten to one female to male ratio at the time, and try to convince coeds that they were college boys from UNC.

This night, Lucky's friend was driving. He already had a date, but his girlfriend was unable to get one for Lucky, so Lucky told his friend to drop him off on campus, that he'd fend for himself and catch a ride back with him when the dorms closed at midnight. Lucky phoned two girls he'd dated before, but one had fallen in love and the other had a test the next day.

He thought of Lucinda. It was April of her freshman year, and there was no reason to think she might want to see Lucky Sweatt, of all people, other than maybe spite toward Tom Ed. Lucky thought they might have that in common. Standing in a phone booth with nothing to do for four hours, it seemed worth the risk.

He knew her dorm because he had run into another girl from Geddie two months before. So he walked across campus and up the steps and asked the girl at the front desk if he might speak with Lucinda Stallsmith. She paged her and told her who her visitor was. Lucky could hear Lucinda say, "Who?" and then, "Just a minute."

She looked as puzzled as Lucky had ever seen her, almost unimposing for once. Lucinda was a beautiful girl. She was five feet seven, with long, straight blond hair. The breasts about which Tom Ed had once boasted formed perfect points beneath her alpaca sweater. She was slender and graceful, a cheerleader at a college without a football team. She and Lucky had both been on the yearbook staff and in the Beta Club in high school, but she was always either Tom Ed's girl or was soon going to be Tom Ed's girl again. Lucky, who was never really in her social world anyhow, had treated her like someone with whom he might be sharing family holidays for the rest of his life.

But now, away from Geddie, away from Tom Ed, the old rules were invalid.

"Well," she said, sighing, "I guess one Sweatt's as good as

another." Lucky knew she said it in that bad-girl pose that she used most of the time to excite the boys, usually much more promise than delivery, but it still electrified his nineteen-year-old mind and body.

It was a Thursday night, but Lucinda said she didn't have any classes worth going to the next day. When she found out Lucky didn't have a car, she told him to wait a minute.

She came back down with a blanket, and she took him to the park, the same one where Tom Ed and he are sitting on this late-October night in 1992. She spread it out carefully on the ground, as if she were making a bed, and sat down, cross-legged, her miniskirt concealing little.

Lucky sat down beside her. She asked him what he was doing with himself, and he lied, telling her that he was taking two courses and working part-time, hoping to enroll at Carolina full time the next fall. She told him that he looked "different," which he figured had to mean better.

"I don't guess you see much of Tom Ed," she said, and he told her, no, that he didn't guess either of them saw much of him any-more.

"Don't want to," she mumbled, and suddenly she was all over him, and he was all over her. He'd fantasized about doing this while she and Tom Ed were dating, forbidden images convincing him, as if he needed more proof, that he was a twisted, broken vessel.

Lucinda had learned a lot, either with Tom Ed or someone else, and some part of Lucky told him even while they were locked together that there was more revenge than desire in her thrusts, and that the best thing that could come from this was nothing.

Still, he phoned her twice afterward, dazzled by his night of perfect satisfaction and retribution, but she never would go out with him again, and they never mentioned it. Before tonight, it had been at least three years since Lucky had thought of this park or that evening.

Tom Ed is sitting on the hood of the Taurus, looking out across the now-bare trees. The cold front that swept out all the rain makes it uncomfortable to sit outside for long, but Tom Ed seems so relaxed that Lucky hesitates to break the spell.

"You know," he says, "I believe to my soul that this is the very park Lucinda took me to a couple of times, after we got back together my sophomore year. It looks just like it, anyway."

Lucky tells him he's probably right.

## ★★★ 16 ★★★

The fall of Lucky and Tom Ed's senior year, Geddie had the best football team it would ever have.

Tom Ed was the quarterback. There were two running backs, one big and strong and the other small and quick, who would score twenty touchdowns apiece. There were three linemen, including another set of twins, who each weighed more than two hundred and twenty pounds and were said to be as mean as snakes. It was the perfect blend that a small school like Geddie gets once every twenty years if it's fortunate, the result of a dozen or so perfect little future athletes popping out of their mothers' wombs at approximately the same time.

Everyone knew Tom Ed was what made it all go, though. He had been quarterback in every game of football he'd ever played, from sandlot on. He was a magnet drawing the other kids around him. August before their freshman year, when most of the boys were trying on their first real football gear, the JV coach came in the locker room, walked up to Tom Ed, slapped him on the shoulder pads he was about to put on backward, and said, "You're my quarterback, son." It seemed right to everyone.

Lucky was the manager.

Tom Ed started three years for the varsity. His sophomore year, some of the seniors resented the fact that Sammy White, one of their classmates who'd been second-string the season before, was being passed over, but nobody could stay angry at Tom Ed for long.

And he won, right from the start. Tom Ed could throw a football seventy yards, and he could run when he had to. He had good instincts; by his senior year, Coach Black was letting him call most of the plays. Most important, he was the one who could look the other players, boys who had grown up with him, right in the eye and tell them to shut the hell up, that he was running this huddle, by God, without anyone sulking or holding a grudge.

The twins' junior year, the Geddie Rebels made the play-offs for the first time in living memory. They beat Sandhills 7–6 in the first round and then lost 14–13 to Mount Hebron on a disputed call. Just wait, everyone said, because Geddie was only losing two starters.

Tom Ed's favorite sport was baseball, and that's the one that he and Tommy had already decided was his best bet beyond high school. The summer of 1963, though, Tom Ed gave up a chance to play American Legion baseball so he could work out with the rest of the football team. They held unofficial practices all over their half of the county. Other coaches complained, but they could never catch Coach Black at any of those illegal off-season sessions. He'd just tell Tom Ed and a couple of the other seniors, who would then get the word out, and before long, there would be twenty-five kids, all from Geddie, running plays by themselves at Campbell River Park or one of the junior high schools.

As manager, Lucky would accompany Tom Ed to make sure they had extra equipment, to wrap ankles, and to take care of the occasional cut or sprain. Even he, their own age, was impressed that a group of seventeen-year-olds could work so hard for something.

The 1963 team never even came close to losing in the regular season. Geddie had only 350 students and was playing above its size in Group AA, but the Rebels played and defeated two larger Group AAA schools that year. Tom Ed already knew that he'd have a college baseball scholarship if he wanted one, but now North Carolina and N.C. State were sending football scouts to look at him.

Geddie got to play Mt. Hebron again, this time in the first round of the play-offs, and this time it wasn't close. Tom Ed threw three touchdown passes and ran an interception back for another one, and Geddie won, 48–6.

The next week, in the semifinals, the Rebels beat Barbersville, 21–12, and that put them in the state championship game.

The *Port Campbell Post,* which seldom paid much attention to the ragtag county schools, came to Geddie and did a big feature story on the "The Little Team That Could." Even the *Raleigh News & Observer* ran a small feature on the Rebels. Everybody, even a slightly gimpy manager, got special attention just by wearing the letter jacket. No one paid for anything at the Soda Shop all week when they went there after practice.

The only thing between Geddie and the state championship was a school from far up in the hills, Santeelah. Nobody knew anything much about these mountain boys except that they were supposed to be really small, although Coach Black tried to convince his team that they were as big as houses. They had lost two games in the regular season and had won their semifinal with a touchdown on the last play of the game.

Geddie was to be the home school. The state athletic association decided on Tuesday, though, to play the championship game at Port Campbell High, on Arsenal Hill, because it could seat five thousand people, and Geddie's rickety bleachers could barely hold five hundred. It was an unpopular move with a lot of the Geddie fans, who felt that their moment of glory was somehow being stolen by the city people who consistently snubbed them.

If they'd known how everything was going to turn out, Lucky thought to himself later, sitting in his cell, they might have wanted it played in China.

Being manager of the football team was one of the few links Lucky still had with his brother. He had kept the job as a favor to Coach Black, because he'd always treated him well, but Lucky already had one foot out Geddie's door. He had been accepted on early admission at Carolina; Tom Ed had, too, assuming he didn't get a better scholarship offer elsewhere, Tommy would gloat. Geddie had never, in Lucky's bitter eyes, done much for him except treat him as a cripple, and he could hardly wait to see it in his rearview mirror. He let everyone know that they wouldn't be seeing Lucky Sweatt much after graduation.

Tommy was already complaining that he couldn't afford to send two boys to college. Lucky would wonder aloud and sarcastically which one would get to go, and Tom Ed wouldn't say anything. But Lucky was fairly certain that, between student loans and part-time jobs and Genie, he would get his chance soon.

In the fall of his senior year, Lucky had succeeded in building a wall around himself. He had started wearing sunglasses to class, and his hair was two inches longer than any other boy's at Geddie High. Only Tom Ed's intervention saved him from an impromptu haircut by several players after practice one day. He and the school dress code were locked in mortal combat, and the principal, a rather prim man in his fifties, mourned the former Lucky Sweatt. He had already dropped out of the Beta Club and quit the yearbook staff and was hanging out with two boys who hated Geddie High almost as much as he did.

What drove the final wedge between Tom Ed and Lucky, though, was John F. Kennedy.

They were in the ninth grade when Kennedy was elected president. Just about every white voter around Geddie went with Nixon because Kennedy was Catholic and everyone knew that, if he was elected, they would soon be taking orders from the Pope. They little suspected how much they would come to hate him for more secular reasons.

The black vote hardly mattered, since few black people had been been allowed to vote yet.

Lucky, by now savoring his role as the outsider, was determined that if his family, his classmates, and the deacons at the church he seldom attended thought one way, he would think another. Anything that the majority of white Geddie approved of was anathema to him, so he quite naturally became JFK's best friend at Geddie High School.

Tom Ed reluctantly backed his brother up at school, although Lucky was beaten by three older students for handing out Kennedy campaign literature before a mock election. After the beating, Kennedy could have signed a pact with the devil on live network TV and still had Lucky on his side.

In the tenth and eleventh grades, with JFK and Robert Kennedy working to reverse 350 years of Southern custom and prejudice overnight, Lucky found even Tom Ed abandoning him. There were loud, ugly arguments at the Sweatt household, and Lucky seldom had an ally. He backed Kennedy at the outset because no one else did, but more and more, especially after he became acquainted with Eugene Solomon, it wore on him how Tom Ed would talk about "the niggers." Being an outsider of a different sort made him more sympathetic than most of those around him seemed to be.

But they could still stop at some point and say, "Hell, it's just politics." In spite of their differences, neither Lucky nor Tom Ed wanted to go to war with each other over someone in Washington, D.C., they'd never met.

If not for Lee Harvey Oswald, they might have made it through high school, graduating together and going off to college, best friends for life, although the older Lucky got, the more he felt that, if it hadn't been November 22, it probably would have been something else. Bile filled him like magma. And Tom Ed didn't seem to know enough to tiptoe at the appropriate times. He was used to being adored, and it never seemed to occur to him that he was living in close quarters with somebody who occasionally desired to hit him hard and repeatedly.

Lucky was in study hall when he first heard, his head down on the desk trying to sleep through one more hour of Geddie High.

He heard Mr. Sturdivant's voice and figured he was about to tell him to sit up, but the tone of his voice was all wrong.

"Ladies and gentlemen," he said, then he paused, as if trying to pull himself together. Finally, he just blurted it out. "The president has been shot. They think he's dead."

"Good," he heard Jimmy Ezell mutter from two seats down. "I hope the nigger-loving son of a bitch is dead."

Somewhere behind Lucky, a girl tittered. A few students softly clapped their hands.

Everyone knew that Mr. Sturdivant was not cut out to be a teacher. He had little patience and a terrible speaking voice. The actual, non-study-hall classes he taught were barely controlled chaos.

But he was a decent man, something that had never occurred to Lucky until that day.

"Ladies and gentlemen," he started again. He always addressed his students thusly, in the same manner you might call a red-haired person "Blue." "The president of the United States has been shot, probably killed. No one but an animal would revel in something such as that."

And he picked up his briefcase and the papers he was grading and left.

Neither Mr. Sturdivant nor Lucky would ever again set foot in Geddie High after that day.

A few of Lucky's classmates went over to the large study hall windows that overlooked the teachers' parking lot.

"Good riddance!" Edward Bates, one of the football team's starting linemen, shouted through the half-opened glass. That gave several of the other students the courage to voice their opinions about Mr. Sturdivant's departure and ancestry.

Lucky, still half-asleep, never moved until he heard Edward Bates's grating bully's voice. Until then, it had seemed like a dream.

He had no memory of going to the window, where he found himself nose to nose with one of Geddie High's larger students.

"Fuck you!" he screamed at Edward Bates, and they began to shove each other. Edward seemed puzzled at first; he and Lucky had always gotten along, and he wasn't used to being assaulted by anyone, no matter what the size or physical ability.

No one backed down from a fight at Geddie High, though, not in 1963.

"I think we better take this outside," Edward said. "You're crazy, man. I'm gonna teach you some manners."

By the time they reached the parking lot, half the school was there. It was the last period of the day, and some teachers had just let class out early and left. Everybody was milling around, many in a holiday mood. The wind had picked up and was blowing wrappers and trash from the Soda Shop across the lot.

Tom Ed was with several other football players when they saw Lucky and Edward Bates getting ready to try to tear each other's heads off.

"What the hell are you all doing?" he asked as he stepped between them. "Are you crazy, Edward? You want to get hurt or kicked out of school right before the biggest game we'll ever play in? Beat up them hillbillies tonight if you want to beat up somebody."

"Ask him what it's all about," he said, pointing over to where Joey Bedsole was trying to hold Lucky back. "Ask your goddamn gimp brother. The son of a bitch is crazy."

Tom Ed got Lucky to their car, leaving behind a disappointed crowd hoping to see blood. But then another fight broke out a few feet away, and Tom Ed took advantage of the distraction and left.

They didn't speak on the way home. A front was bringing in cold weather, and oak leaves blew across the highway in front of them.

They pulled into the driveway, and Tom Ed turned off the ignition. They could see Tommy in the side yard, wrestling with something. They finally realized that he was trying to string a sign between the carport and the chicken house. When he finished tying the side attached to the chicken coop, they could read it: GO REBELS; HOME OF TOM ED SWEATT.

It defused the tension momentarily.

"Oh Jesus," Tom Ed said, putting his head against the steering wheel. "Oh Jesus." And they both burst into laughter.

Tom Ed jumped out and ran toward his father.

"You crazy coot," he yelled. He could get away with saying just about anything to Tommy by then. "What in the hell are you doing?"

"Look out now," the old man said, feigning anger like he always did when Tom Ed talked to him that way. "Don't make me come upside your head."

"What are you doing?" Tom Ed pointed at the sign, flapping in the breeze now. "Do you want to make us the laughingstock of the whole county?"

Tommy looked genuinely hurt.

"A man cain't be proud of his own son?" he asked plaintively.

Tom Ed just looked up, shook his head, and followed Lucky inside.

The old man yelled after them, "Hey, did you all know Kennedy got shot?"

Tom Ed and Lucky were supposed to be back at the gym at four-thirty to dress and then take the bus to Arsenal Hill. The game started at seven-thirty, but Coach Black wanted to have plenty of time to work on his players' mental state.

They heard Tommy crank up the car and leave, probably headed down to the store to bask in the reflected glory of Tom Ed Sweatt. The sportswriter from the *Post* who covered what Geddie games were covered had told Tommy that Carolina, State, and Wake Forest would have scouts at the state championship, and that he'd heard a rumor that there might even be someone there from Alabama. By the time Tommy got through with it, Bear Bryant was going to personally offer Tom Ed a scholarship after the game.

For Lucky, it was still sinking in. They had listened to the radio on the way home and knew JFK was dead. Now, he sank into Tommy's big chair and watched as the TV people tried to make sense out of the senseless.

Tom Ed stood beside him and just listened for a while. He put his hand on Lucky's shoulder and then went off to his room.

Sitting there, listening to the TV commentators choke up as they tried to get a grip on things and figure out what came next, it hit Lucky: There was no way that Geddie High was going to play for the state football championship that night. It would have to be postponed. He was suddenly sure that if he and Tom Ed (particularly Tom Ed) went to Coach Black, he'd understand that. They could play the game next week, after the funeral.

He went to tell his brother.

Tom Ed just stared at first.

"Are you crazy?" he finally said. "Are you trying to mess up my head? Call off the game?"

"Postpone," Lucky said. "They could just postpone it for a week. Till the funeral was over. He was the president, Tom Ed."

"I don't give a shit about any funeral! This is the biggest game of my life, and you want to go messing with it! Maybe we ought to just forfeit, let Santeelah have the championship! Is that what you want? 'Cause them mountain boys sure as hell ain't going to call it off because they're so tore up over Kennedy."

It was dawning on Lucky that he must have been dreaming to think Tom Ed would want any part of this.

"I took your side when they elected that . . . Kennedy," he said. "And look at the thanks we got. They'll have niggers in school with us by year after next, if not sooner. He sold us out.

"I'm glad somebody shot him."

And he began to walk off.

On each end table, there was a baseball sitting on top of a small plaque that told when Tom Ed had used that baseball to pitch a no-hitter. They were from Little League, six years before, but Tommy wouldn't let Genie move them. They were great conversation pieces.

Lucky barely remembered picking up the one nearest him. Or throwing it.

Lucky hadn't played baseball since he was eight years old, but he caught his brother squarely in the back of his head, pitching the ball as hard as he could, and Tom Ed went down as if he were shot.

In the corner, there was a trophy case that Tommy had built to hold Tom Ed's many honors. Leaning against the case was a thirty-four-ounce Louisville Slugger bat that Tom Ed had used to hit the winning home run in the regional baseball championships the year before.

Lucky grabbed the bat and began hitting his prone, almost-unconscious brother with it, blindly flailing away at his back and head. He didn't stop until he saw Tom Ed's blood running away from his right ear in a thin line where the linoleum floor wasn't quite level.

Tom Ed didn't move; Lucky shook him gently with an unsteady hand and said his name twice, but Tom Ed remained curled fetally on the reddening floor.

They'd had their boyhood fights, before the polio. After that, though, until November 22, 1963, they had never hit one another in anger beyond an irritated shove, Tom Ed because he didn't think it would be fair, Lucky because he knew who would win.

So neither of them was prepared for that sneak attack, and neither knew what to do next. Tom Ed just lay there, his moaning a sign that at least he wasn't dead. Lucky left.

Tommy was pulling into the driveway as Lucky opened the front door. Each boy had a set of keys, although Lucky seldom used his. When Tommy got out of the car, Lucky got in, without saying a word, started the engine, and drove off.

He could hear his father yelling something about hurrying on back because Tom Ed had to leave for the gym in half an hour.

Lucky turned left on Mingo Road and then left on Route 47 at Geddie. There was three quarters of a tank of gas; he had no planned destination.

He guessed, later, that he would have eventually gotten to White Oak Beach and then turned around and gone home to face the music if the state troopers hadn't stopped him ten miles east of Geddie.

He saw the red light behind him. Before he could pull over, there was another one coming toward him. As soon as he stopped, highway patrolmen were jumping behind car doors, guns drawn, yelling for him to come out with his hands over his head.

He came close to getting killed right there on a sandy spot on the side of Route 47, with no one to witness it except several jumpy men wearing pointed hats, when he popped out of the car and reached back for his wallet. He heard a chorus of clicks and froze just in time.

He knew right away that Tommy had called the police, but he didn't expect what happened next.

They handcuffed him and threw him into the back of one of the four state troopers' cars that had effectively blocked off that part of Route 47. They weren't answering questions, and they seemed not to care that the handcuffs were drawing blood.

They passed Mingo Road, and when Lucky pointed this out, one of the two state troopers sitting up front said, without turning around, "We goin' to Port Campbell, boy. That's where the jail's at."

Within an hour, he was in jail, charged with auto theft and felony assault. His one phone call was to his home.

Genie answered. Lucky could hear her say hello, but before he could get out more than a couple of words, someone else took the phone, listened for a second, and then hung up.

It occurred to Lucky that his father wanted to teach him a lesson, and the enormity of what he'd done to Tom Ed was starting to sink in. He was sure he hadn't killed his brother, but he almost welcomed a chance to do a few hours silent penance among strangers before he had to face his family.

But nothing happened all Friday night, or all day Saturday, except for a meal every few hours and a chance to walk around in the yard outside about fifteen minutes on Saturday with his fellow prisoners.

Sunday, he felt that someone, probably Genie, would at least visit him if not have the charges dropped. He knew that he hadn't wounded Tom Ed as seriously as he'd feared, because he'd heard enough of a sports report on a radio playing in some cell at the other end of the hall to know that Tom Ed Sweatt started as quarterback in the championship game.

But no one came. By Sunday night, Lucky had gone past denial and accepted that, for better or worse, life as he knew it was over. He wasn't surprised that Tommy would leave him in jail over the weekend. It was Genie that hurt.

Just past nine o'clock on Sunday night, Lucky was watching a cockroach work its way toward his bunk when he heard a familiar voice down the hall, hectoring one of the guards who kept saying, "Yes, ma'm. Yes, ma'm, Miz Balcom."

His grandmother gave him her best cold-fish look as the guard unlocked the door.

"You'll have to pay me back for this, you know," she said, and Lucky promised that he would.

They walked out the door to a waiting taxi.

"Do you want him to take you home?" she asked him, nodding toward the driver when they reached her home on Arsenal Hill.

Lucky told her he didn't have a home.

"Hush," she said. "You always have a home. Even if you never go back to it, you always have a home. Even Genie has a home." Her voice drifted off on that last part.

Lucky thanked his grandmother and asked her if she could just have the taxi driver drop him on the Raleigh Road, that he thought he could get a construction job in Chapel Hill.

She looked as concerned for another human being as she ever had in Lucky's presence. She was quiet for a few seconds, then she sighed and wished him good luck. She shook his hand, the most physical he had ever seen Dorothy Canfield Balcom.

Later, standing on the edge of the Raleigh Road with his thumb out, he wondered how his grandmother had known he was in jail.

It was several days before he heard the entire story. Other than to discover that Tom Ed was not dead or critically injured, it had not occurred to him to care one way or the other how Geddie had done in the state championship game.

But after he reached Chapel Hill and contacted Eugene Solomon's cousin Tony, who ran a construction crew building another wing on the hospital there, Tony filled him in.

Tom Ed Sweatt did indeed start for the Geddie Rebels. Eugene told Tony that they had a moment of silence for Kennedy that lasted about ten seconds and was punctuated with cheers. Tom Ed had a bandage over his head, a couple of chipped teeth, and a badly bruised face.

The whole story might never have come out if a reporter from the *Port Campbell Post* hadn't struck up a conversation with one of the state troopers handling crowd control at the game, which was sold out. The trooper told him what had really happened, not realizing that he might actually be quoted.

So, by Saturday morning, most of Scots County knew that Geddie High's star quarterback had not been himself the night before because he was severely beaten by his twin brother, who then stole the family car and was apprehended and arrested.

Tommy, when he found out that Grandmother Balcom had paid his bail, dropped the charges, and Genie eventually started speaking to him again.

The Geddie Rebels lost, 59–0. The newspaper account of the game said that the Rebels just didn't seem to have their hearts in it.

Over the years, Lucky often asked himself why he did it, why he didn't just hold everything in for a few more months until he left for college. He had assaulted his brother and best friend, costing him a college football scholarship, and he had created a break in his family that he feared would never be repaired.

The years and the pain had blocked much of his memory of what he felt like just before he picked up the baseball and threw it at Tom Ed. Looking back, it didn't even seem like free will, more like one last stone on ten years of weight, the one that collapsed everything. It wasn't just the assassination, and it wasn't just Tom Ed.

If that baseball was meant for one particular person, Lucky knew whom it was, and it wasn't Tom Ed.

Time smoothed him, though, like water dripping on a rock, and by the time he left Virginia to work on Tom Ed's campaign, he felt that he could carry this ancient grudge no further. Barbara taught him that. Lucky knew she had been beaten and generally mistreated by her own father when she was small. He eventually left, to everybody's relief, but he had come back into her life in recent years, and they seemed to get along. There was a boulder there that couldn't ever be moved, but they could talk and exchange Christmas presents and laugh together.

Tommy could still make Lucky laugh once in a while, and when he looked at Tommy's weathered face, he could still see Daddy in there, the same man who took them to the fair and pitched baseballs to them, and wanted them to be better than he was.

In the first decade after Lucky left home, he fantasized about somehow coming back in triumph one day, of being like Joseph in Egypt, suddenly revealing himself, after he'd been sold away, as a near-god to his father and brothers.

But even Joseph forgave, Lucky came to realize. And probably slept better for doing it.

★★★ **17** ★★★

**S**am Bender and Lucky are waiting for room-service breakfast at the Holiday Inn near the interstate in Greensboro. It's a quarter to six on Friday, and the campaign is supposed to be at a Young Republicans meeting in Reidsville by eight-thirty, so there's little time for the morning briefing.

Lucky answers the phone. It's Barry Maxwell telling them that Tom Ed is sick. When they get to his room, Lucky can't believe that Susannah is already there. She can't avoid blushing when she says, in lieu of hello, "I came over as soon as Tom Ed called."

Tom Ed looks like hell. Barry is telling him that he'll have to skip the Reidsville meeting.

"Damn, I ain't even been to Reidsville yet," Tom Ed moans. He's trying to sit up, a little at a time. He's drinking Pepto-Bismol out of the bottle. Every time he opens his mouth, all Lucky can see is bright medicine pink.

Harry Mavredes reminds him that he has, indeed, been to Reidsville, back in August, but that doesn't seem to make Tom Ed feel much better.

"How many votes are you going to get if you pull a George Bush and throw up all over the mayor?" Barry asks him, and the mere mention of vomiting is enough to send Tom Ed running for the bathroom. He slams the door, and they can hear him heaving violently.

Harry looks at Susannah and over at the half-gallon bottle of Early Times that is almost empty on the bedside table.

"Damn, did you all try to drink all the bourbon in Guilford County?" he asks her.

"Fuck you," Susannah explains. "Did you ever know liquor to make Tom Ed Sweatt sick, you bonehead? Why don't you go blow some uncommitted state senator or whatever it is you do and let me take care of Tom Ed?" She gives him a look that promises him he's toast no matter what happens on election day, then goes into the bathroom. If Lucky didn't know Harry, he might have felt a little sorry for him. He's sure, though, that Harry and Barry will be scrapping for every vote right up until the polls close on Tuesday, and that it will have little to do with Tom Ed Sweatt or postelection jobs. To Harry and Barry, the thrill of the chase is everything.

Harry, Barry, and Sam finally leave. Lucky knocks on the bathroom door, and Susannah opens it. Tom Ed is sitting on the edge of the bathtub, with her beside him, her arm around his waist.

"Bo," he says, "we ain't going to make it. Of all the unholy days for me to get sick . . ."

Later, Lucky realizes that it would have been better to have just told him to stay low and rest on his laurels, that no one was going to change his vote that last weekend anyhow. Skip Friday. Skip that damn mess in Charlotte on Saturday. He might even gain some votes by missing the Reverend Gary Thorne Memorial Right to Life Celebration due to illness.

But Lucky doesn't do that. Instead, he takes his text directly from the Book of Tommy Sweatt, Chapter 1. Tommy always told them, when they were small, that you had to fight whatever ailed you, whether it was polio or a cold. Get up and walk it off, whether it was a baseball to your ribs or cancer. Lucky didn't hear it much after Tommy saw that you didn't walk off some things, but he was sure that Tom Ed must have heard that speech five hundred times.

"You've got to walk it off, Tom Ed," Lucky says. "Get mad at it. Whip it."

Tom Ed looks up through bloodshot, startled eyes.

"Damn," he croaks. "Did the old man send you?" But he nods his head almost imperceptibly, and then he stands up.

"You know, Bo," he says, "the old man wasn't always full of shit."

"Just most of the time."

They both laugh at an old routine.

"Give me thirty minutes," he says to Susannah. She looks doubtful, and Lucky is, too. He doubts that even Tom Ed can will himself well.

It takes a little more than thirty minutes, but by eight-fifteen, he's dressed, medicated, and as ready as he's likely to be. Harry calls ahead and reschedules him to be in Reidsville at nine-thirty. They only stop once on the way for Tom Ed to throw up.

They spend Friday chasing votes all over the Piedmont. Eden. Burlington. Chapel Hill. Pittsboro. One poll has Tom Ed Sweatt leading by a percentage point, the other has him trailing by that same point. Lucky can tell that he feels he can't afford to leave one hand unshaken or one baby unkissed. Lucky wonders how many potential voters will miss the election on Tuesday because they caught whatever virus Tom Ed is fighting.

On Friday night, Lucky calls Barbara. She's supposed to come down the next day and meet them in Charlotte. Then, the two of them will go to Port Campbell on Sunday and stay until Wednesday morning, his usefulness to the campaign over. Tom Ed will return to his hometown on Monday night and spend Tuesday, as he says, "preparing for a party or a funeral."

He tells her about how out of sorts everyone is, that they already have had to break up two near-fights among some of the over-worked campaign staffers.

"Do you know what Benny asked me tonight?" she says after she's listened for about five minutes.

Lucky says no, he doesn't.

"Well, he'd been kind of a handful today. His teacher called me after school and said he'd gotten in another fight. That's the second one in two weeks."

"I know." Lucky and Barbara disagree on the number of fights that is permissible for boys Benny's age. Barbara is sticking with zero, but Lucky is a little more flexible. "I'll talk to him when I get back."

He can hear what sounds like a snort of disbelief. "Yeah. Your idea of 'having a talk' is to show him how to fight better."

"If he fights better, pretty soon he won't have to fight at all."

A sigh. "Anyhow, we were having a talk about how he shouldn't be beating up his classmates—"

"He beat one up?"

"It was a girl, Lucky. Anyhow, we were having this talk. And he says to me, right out of the blue, 'If I'm good, will Dad come back?' And I had to sit there and explain to him, very patiently, that you'd be coming back, no matter what. But he still thinks like that, Lucky. He still thinks we might get upset with him, or tired of him or something, and just send him to some orphanage or leave him beside the road like a stray dog."

Thinking about Benny lying in bed worrying about his not coming back, Lucky can't talk for a second or two.

"Are you all right?" Barbara asks. Lucky is aware that, unfortunately, his wife and children know what a soft touch he is.

"You know, you could just bring him with you," he says. "It'd probably be a relief to the rest of the first grade if he stayed out for a couple of days."

"No," she says. "First, it's three days. Second, everything's fine now. Kim and Chris are kind of looking forward to running things without us around for a few days. And you know how much Benny worships them."

"God," Lucky says, putting a wet towel over his forehead, "I know why they're so anxious to have the house to themselves. They're going to have the whole junior and senior classes of West Jefferson High School there. Party time. They've probably already sent out invitations and ordered the beer kegs."

"I'm ahead of you. They've already been told that if I find one cigarette butt or one pop-top on the property, if I see one little indentation where the furniture's been moved to make room for a band, that they'll never see the inside of a college. They'll be cleaning toilets for the next four years. The Barbara and Lucky Sweatt Benevolent Scholarship for Former Orphans will be a thing of the past."

"Nah. That won't be enough. They're gonna have a party anyhow."

"Yeah," Barbara sighs. "I know. But I'm pretty sure that we won't be able to tell that they've had a party when we get back. Better not, anyhow."

She's probably right, Lucky knows. Kim and Chris are so much more mature than he or Barbara were at their ages that it's scary. They went through their crazy years in junior high. It seems to Lucky that everyone grows up faster now. By the time they can legally drink, he figures they'll be too upright and responsible to even enjoy it.

They talk for half an hour. Lucky is struck by how much he misses them, what a homebody he has become. Friends are always trying to get him to go deep-sea fishing or to Baltimore for an Orioles game, or just camping, and he usually finds an excuse not to. They kid him about being 'whipped, but he's lost the taste for boys' night out.

He's already missing Kim and Chris, even before they're gone. The way time seems to speed up the older he gets, he knows he'll turn around one day and Benny will be going off to college. He wishes, as he sits on his motel bed, that it was already Tuesday night and he and Barbara were getting ready to go home.

Lucky goes down the hall to Tom Ed's room. His brother is on the phone and Lucky can tell it's Tommy on the other end. Tom Ed motions for him to enter, rolling his eyes and making an up-and-down motion like a fast-moving mouth with his free hand.

"Yeah, you're right . . . Yeah . . . What? No, I don't think you ought to let WPCN interview you. . . . I just don't; there ain't no telling what you're liable to say. . . . Well, all I know is, you just about killed the black vote for me that time, talking about the coloreds this and the coloreds that. . . . Yeah, I'll give you that; you didn't say 'nigger.' "

Lucky is sure that Tommy would kill to get on the local TV station in Port Campbell. It would probably be the high point of his life so far to be standing there wearing a red vest, a red tie, and one of the buttons that reads THE BEST BET IS SWEATT. This, Lucky knows, is his father's shining moment.

"Hey, you want to talk to old Lucky?"

Lucky can tell from Tom Ed's expression that Tommy is about to put their mother on the phone. Tom Ed rolls his eyes again and then is speaking to Genie. They talk for a while, Genie and Lucky talk some, and then they hang up.

"The old man," Tom Ed says, and then just shakes his head and grins.

Tom Ed appears almost recovered. He does seem to have willed himself well. Maybe, Lucky thinks, it's a carryover from all that athletic discipline, although in general Tom Ed doesn't seem disposed to deny himself much. If people can get so depressed that they almost will themselves sick, he wonders if they can't care so much about something, want it so much, that they can will themselves well. The Reverend Gary Thorne probably would have called it a miracle. Lucky thinks it might be Tommy Sweatt whispering in his brother's ear.

They sit and talk a while, about the campaign mostly. This is the only thing Lucky thinks he will take away from this campaign that's worth keeping: the half hours and hours and occasional automobile trip where Tom Ed and he can actually talk. It's impossible to do it on a weekend with family all around; they might get five minutes alone, and it seems to take them a lot longer than that to just figuratively clear their throats.

"Bo," Tom Ed says after he's had two Early Times and waters and Lucky has drunk a beer, "I miss this." He looks wistful.

"Yeah," Lucky says. "Let's don't let it be so long," knowing that Tom Ed will be even harder to reach in the future, if he becomes governor. He thinks it might still have been worth it, though; he feels they've gotten at least some of the old Tom Ed and Lucky back. He knows grown siblings who aren't even on speaking terms, some holding grudges over an argument or a will, some of whom just never liked each other much.

He knows Tom Ed and he aren't like that, much as he thought they were at one time. They've shared more than he knew. Lucky is sorely tempted, out of the blue, to have matching T-shirts made up that say I SURVIVED TOMMY SWEATT.

With Tom Ed it was the storm, Tommy maintaining a constant turmoil, always railing for more, bigger, better.

What Lucky weathered was drought. While his brother was just happy when an occasional lull would let things dry out and settle down for a while, Lucky was dying of thirst.

Tom Ed mixes himself another drink. He lifts the bathroom glass in a toast. Lucky holds up his lukewarm beer can.

"To the Sweatts," Tom Ed says.

They both smile, pleased to be sitting on a king-sized bed in the Greensboro Holiday Inn with the whole state outside knowing just how high a Sweatt can rise.

## ★★★ 18 ★★★

It is not the possibility of pain, or of poverty or other forms of loss, that makes Horace Morgan cautious. What he fears is humiliation, the laughter of his peers and lessers. He doesn't know why it should be so, but it always has been, and he has watched himself, over the years, save face and lose much else.

In high school, he only tried out for the teams and clubs he was sure wouldn't reject him. He was terrified of public speaking. In college, he only dated girls he was relatively certain wouldn't go back to their dorms and disparage the shy, rather frail boy who blushed so easily. Following his father into the law was the hardest thing he'd ever had to do in his life, but defying his father would have been harder than that.

He married his first wife partly because she was as capable as he of self-sustenance; the two of them could live in the same house for a weekend and never speak.

When, at midlife, he fell like a schoolboy for Susannah, and it became public knowledge, he could hardly bear it. His wife left him without a word. He knew that she was aware of the affair when he came home from work one day and found all her clothes, her BMW, and most of the photographs of the children gone.

There was a note: "I'll be back for the rest tomorrow. Don't be here. Luanne." It was the last time she had tried to communicate with him without the aid of other lawyers.

He didn't wait for her the next day. He didn't talk about his fall from grace with his children, whom he seldom saw. One of his few true friends took him out for lunch one day and tried to advise him to make some kind of peace with them, but Horace cut him off in mid-sentence, telling him to mind his own business.

It soon became clear to him that Susannah was only there for as long as it pleased her; Tom Ed was not the first evidence of this.

So Horace Morgan saw that his world had truly ended, that he was standing there in his underwear, egg on his face, while half of Raleigh and Durham enjoyed his pain.

The only thing that he had left was his dignity. He never showed anyone outside, and rarely ever Susannah, his pain. He adopted the manner of the thoroughly modern man. He was fond of saying that a wife must be wonderful indeed to be better than no wife at all. He went to fewer dinner parties, but not that many fewer, for he was witty and sophisticated.

Horace Morgan, they said, could certainly take a joke.

He has breakfast with Little Sonny Lineberger at a pancake house outside Durham. Little Sonny is wearing sunglasses indoors and is dressed better than Horace. It is hard to tell which is the lawyer and which is the manager of a cheap apartment complex.

They are at a back booth, and Horace stops talking whenever a waitress comes by to refill their coffee.

He is explaining all he cares to explain to Little Sonny, who nods occasionally, eager to do something really important for his mentor instead of breaking up parties and evicting college kids.

"A lot is riding on this," Horace tells him. "What you do might well determine who is the next governor of our state."

Little Sonny wants to ask him why he doesn't deliver this information himself, but he hesitates. He believes he can go far with Horace Morgan, and he doesn't want to screw things up.

Horace saves him the trouble of asking, though.

"Why don't I do this myself?" He says it almost as Little Sonny is thinking it. "Well, that wouldn't do, would it? I mean, we can do a lot more good, or damage, down the road, if nobody knows who we are, can't we?"

Little Sonny nods almost too enthusiastically, thrilled that Horace is using the first-person plural.

"When you contact this person, he's not to know who either one of us is. What you tell him can stand on its own. If he's who I think he is, he'll take it from there."

"Can do," Little Sonny says, regaining a grip on his professionalism. "He'll never know where it came from."

To himself, he's thinking, Mickey Dole. Jesus Christ.

Despite the fact that he has "no fixed network address," Mickey Dole is probably the best-known media personality in the Carolinas.

He lives in a condominium north of Raleigh, but he is seldom at home. It takes Little Sonny two days to reach him and several minutes to convince him that he isn't wasting his time.

Mickey started as a newspaperman. He won several state awards and a couple of national ones working for the *Winston-Salem Tribune* before one of his better stories, a gauzy feature on the town of Cold Harbor, turned out to have one fatal flaw: Mickey Dole had never seen the town before he wrote his story.

He told his editor that he figured if you'd seen one eastern North Carolina town, you'd seen them all. If Mickey hadn't done a few other things almost as dicey before that, he might have kept his job. He was that good.

He had a dark, handsome face full of surface integrity; people wanted to tell him things. He had little trouble catching on at one of the TV stations in Raleigh, then moved on to Charlotte, seemingly destined for a major market. But he kept taking chances, and a cocaine possession charge was, as the station manager indelicately put it, the last straw.

So Mickey went freelance. Any station in the area was glad to buy his exposés, even the ones who didn't want him on their payrolls full time. He could produce.

You might see Dole on the air in Greensboro on Tuesday night, uncovering a county commissioner's secret deal to get a new roof in exchange for a lucrative contract. Then, you might catch him on TV in Durham two nights later doing a story on a girl who had pitched two no-hitters for her Little League team. His showcase, though, was his syndicated weekly show that had been referred to as a regional "60 Minutes."

He was making more money than he'd ever made working for somebody else, as he told anyone who would listen.

Mickey Dole had his own stable from which to pull a freelance crew on the spur of the moment. He had a couple of freelance reporters working for him on a semi-regular basis. He had such high visibility that people often called him with "hot tips" that sometimes actually panned out.

Mickey gets Little Sonny's call at 9 A.M. He got back from a trip to Jacksonville at 1 A.M., one that had yielded some promising footage related to a gay-bashing incident, and he hasn't had anywhere close to his required eight hours of sleep. He does not immediately offer Little Sonny his full attention.

He listens, yawning, as Little Sonny lays it out for him just as Horace Morgan instructed him to.

"Why the fuck don't you or somebody just go to the papers? Why can't you tell me who you are?"

"The person I am representing," Little Sonny says patiently, "does not want his name involved in this."

Mickey Dole is used to calls from people with hot tips who don't want their names used, and he knows how worthless they can be. But he has learned that, for every twenty dead-end leads, one will strike pay dirt.

"Well, how do I fit into all this?"

"The person I am representing believes that, if anyone in North Carolina can get this person to talk, on the air, it would be you."

"Well," Mickey says, stopping to light his first Camel of the day with his free hand, "you're right about that.

"Now, tell me one more time, really slow, how it is I'm supposed to change the course of North Carolina history."

Mickey doesn't really believe this is going to work. If the upside hadn't been so high, he would have blown off Little Sonny Lineberger two minutes into the conversation.

But, while Mickey Dole has broken many rules, he obeys one religiously: If he gets a whiff of a story hot enough to get him to Atlanta or Detroit or, dear God, Washington or New York, he'll give it everything he has, no matter how hopeless it seems.

One day, they'll all regret blackballing him. One day, he'll show all these cracker station managers how you do journalism in the 1990s.

And there is that one in twenty chance that he's just found the accomplice who can make it happen.

"Yeah," Mickey Dole says, "I'll take a crack at that."

## 19

**S**aturday morning, as they're leaving to go to the briefing, Sam Bender tells Lucky that Susannah stayed with Tom Ed the night before. Lucky tells him that's impossible, that it was almost midnight when he left Tom Ed's room, and his brother was still recuperating from the virus he'd fought the day before. You didn't stay late enough, Sam says.

Lucky has learned that Sam usually knows what he's talking about. Harry and Barry are too busy trying to win the election by sheer energy and gall to pick up on some of the subtleties. Sam, though, who sometimes appears too fastidious for politics, is the one who always seems to hear through walls, to catch a glimpse of who's slipping through which door.

The good thing about Sam, though, is that no one else, not even the M&M twins, will know.

Everyone is grouchy and out of sync on the way down to Charlotte. The caravan now has eight cars and vans in it. Lucky is driving the second one from the front, and they all have banners draped around them. The driver in front almost has a wreck when some of the bunting gets loose and wraps itself around the windshield.

There are plastic pumpkins and ghosts and goblins in the scrubby front yards they pass. It's Halloween, and Lucky regrets that neither he nor Barbara will be there to take Benny trick or treating, although he knows the child will be more thrilled to have Kim and Chris take him, anyhow. There's a perfectly good interstate highway running from Greensboro to Charlotte, but Tom Ed insists on taking U.S. 29 because he'll pass more people who might vote for him just because they saw him, thought he waved at them.

"Hell, two thirds of the people on I-85 are Yankees going from New York City to Atlanta," he says when Harry points out the forty-five minutes they will lose. "They ain't likely to come back here Tuesday and vote for me, do you think?"

They reach the Adam's Mark in Charlotte at ten forty-five, feeling the accumulated effects of the campaign. In one of the vans toward the rear, Johnny Ray Roberts and another student volunteer get in as much of a fight as is possible in a moving vehicle. The problem is a mutual interest in Cody Barrett, but Lucky thinks the real problem is that this is no way for civilized people to live, or even politicians.

Barbara is in the crowd waiting near the hotel entrance. As soon as Lucky parks and can wade through the reporters and well-wishers, he greets her with a hug and a kiss, pleased not to have to spend another night without her for a while.

He has forgotten that Tommy and Genie are going to be there, that Tom Ed has reserved them a room as part of the entourage, until Tommy comes running out the front door wearing a red-white-and-blue straw hat. He has at least two dozen campaign buttons on his coat. He's always seemed like a big man to Lucky, perhaps because of the bluster, but here, in this larger world, he seems rather small and second-rate, and Lucky feels slightly sorry for him. He can see that Tom Ed doesn't quite know what to do with the man who has, more than anyone else, brought him to this point, the man he wishes would disappear for a little while.

But Lucky can also see that Tommy is in his element. He has spent much of his life grinding his teeth because somebody was always looking down his nose at him, but Tommy Sweatt never let on, in Lucky's presence at least, that he ever thought anybody was better than he was. You had to give him that.

"This is the big day," he half whispers to Tom Ed when he grabs him with his right arm. He puts the other one around Lucky. "They say there's going to be twenty thousand people out there today."

"I know," Tom Ed says, quieter and more patient than he usually is around their father. "I know. Well, I'm going to give them something to remember."

Lucinda, of course, is absent. Genie says she has some kind of virus. Lucky gives Lucinda credit, though. She must know something about Tom Ed and his women, probably suspects that she shouldn't get too comfortable in the governor's mansion if Tom Ed wins. But even though she and Tom Ed have seen each other once since Lucky joined the campaign, she has been going to women's club meetings and ribbon cuttings and numerous other thankless tasks on Tom Ed's behalf. Maybe she just likes the attention, Lucky thinks, but maybe Tom Ed could do worse than to stay with her.

Genie hugs everyone as the cameras whir in the background. Tom Ed manages to get his arms around Lucky and his parents. In the photo Lucky sees later in the Sunday morning *Charlotte Observer* at the hospital, Tommy and Genie are flanking Tom Ed, his father grinning like a possum, his mother looking happy but uneasy. Lucky is on Genie's other side, just barely touched by Tom Ed's long arm reaching out. He can just make out Barbara's arm in the background.

It's a clear, biting, late-October day with a bright blue sky, the kind of day best spent at a college football game or up on the Blue Ridge Parkway. A lot of people won't know what happens that afternoon until they turn on the eleven o'clock news.

Sam and a couple of other aides get everyone checked in. There are newspaper reporters and TV people throughout the lobby, but the Sweatts finally get on the elevator and up to the eighth floor. Tommy is declaring loudly that this is the fanciest hotel and the nicest room he's ever been in. Finally, Tom Ed asks Lucky if he and Barbara will please take Tommy and Genie downstairs for lunch "or anywhere." He and the M&M twins have some work to do.

Even now, Lucky can't figure out exactly how Tom Ed's speeches get to the point where they're coming out of his mouth at some stadium or auditorium or banquet. Harry does write speeches for him, and they do go over them beforehand, as they do this Saturday morning, and Tom Ed does carry those speeches up to the rostrum with him.

But that's where something happens. Lucky took an extra copy off Harry's bed one time and sat there, backstage, while Tom Ed charmed a room of Rotarians in Sanford. The speech Harry wrote and the one Tom Ed gave didn't have much to do with one another, just barely crossing on some intractable issue like federal meddling or abortion.

A couple of days afterward, he asked Tom Ed why he didn't read the speech Harry had sat up all night writing for him.

"Read?" he looked at Lucky as if he'd asked him why he didn't take his pants off in front of the audience. "Hell, Bo, that's what Knox Cameron does. That's the only reason I'm in this damn thing: I don't read speeches. I read audiences."

Then he gave Lucky a quick lesson in speechmaking, Tom Ed Sweatt–style.

"Do you remember the part in the script where I was supposed to have come out against the busybodies trying to kill the tobacco industry?"

Lucky says yes, that it seemed as if he soft-pedaled that issue.

"Damn right I did," he said. "I start getting into all this stuff with both feet, like Harry wanted me to, 'cause there's lots of tobacco farms around here, when I notice that there ain't a soul in that room smoking. There's damn near a hundred people in there, right after their little prayer breakfast, and *nobody's* smoking. Son, if there ain't nobody smoking at a Rotary Club meeting in Sanford, you don't come out and start kissing a tobacco leaf. I give that same speech over in Belwood two weeks before, and the smoke was so thick you couldn't see the back of the room. I was scared the smoke alarm was going to come on. I give 'em both barrels over there."

He pointed out to Lucky how he'd cut his opponent some slack, too.

"Knox Cameron's daddy grew up outside Sanford," he said.

"Now, everybody around there probably knows somebody that knows Knox Cameron's daddy or uncle or granddaddy's second cousin or something, and they might take it personal when I call him a Communist and a baby killer."

He went down the printed text like that, line by line, and it occurred to Lucky that there were all kinds of genius that he'd never even considered as such.

Barbara and Lucky take his parents down to the coffee shop, hoping to kill a little time. Lucky can tell that Barbara would rather be almost anywhere else. They won't leave for the Church of the Rock until one-thirty; Tom Ed wants to make a grand entrance.

Genie asks if they have child's portions, as Lucky knew she would, and Tommy complains, as predictable as sunrise, that he could have bought a whole cow back in the depression for what a steak costs here.

Tommy has a steak anyhow, using what appears to be about half a bottle of ketchup on his french fries. Genie orders the smallest thing she can find on the menu, a chicken salad sandwich. It makes Lucky want to cry. She has one of those rare chances ordinary working people have to be a big shot, the sky's the limit, name your poison, and she goes for the chicken salad. At least, Lucky concedes to himself, the old man knows how to handle a little prosperity.

They talk about Tom Ed and the campaign. Genie asks Barbara about "the children." Lucky is aware that it is at least partly his fault for not visiting enough, but he doubts that either of his parents could name Kim, Chris, and Benny if you held a gun to their heads.

"That, uh . . . Kim, she's a bright one," Tommy says, his mouth full of steak. "They'll be runnin' this country 'fore you know it." Lucky hopes he means this new, bright-as-a-penny generation, these young-folks-who-are-smarter-than-we-ever-were, but he knows his father probably just means Orientals or women. He squeezes Barbara's hand under the table, hoping she won't say what she's thinking.

"We just think you all are wonderful to take in all those poor children," Genie says and puts her hand on Lucky's free one.

They all have apple pie with previously frozen crust for dessert, and then they do the dance they've done every time they've been in a restaurant since Lucky has been able to afford his part of the tab. He can't believe it has sneaked up on him again.

He produces the gold card to lay on top of the check, but Tommy has already snatched it away.

Lucky tells his father that the campaign will pay for their lunch, that there is no way Tom Ed can spend all the money that's been raised between now and Tuesday, which is true. But it doesn't make any difference.

Lucky seizes the slip of paper from Tommy, telling him that Tom Ed will be mad if he doesn't let the campaign pay their bill. Lucky gives the waitress the gold card. She brings it back presently and he signs, honestly believing it's settled. Then, as they're leaving, he feels a hand reach into his pocket. Before he can react, Tommy has inserted two twenty-dollar bills.

"You give that to Tom Ed," he says. "He don't need to be paying for no dinner for us. He's done enough."

Lucky fights the urge to wrestle his father to the ground, right there in the atrium, and stuff the forty dollars in his mouth, but it's getting late, and he knows that he means no harm.

As they wait for the elevator, Susannah comes up. Lucky feels obliged to introduce everyone. Susannah seems to be sizing Tommy and Genie up as prospective in-laws, although they don't have a clue. Barbara knows what's going on, just from the little Lucky has told her, and she stands back a step.

They all get on the elevator. Lucky is standing between Tommy and Susannah, with Barbara and Genie in front of them, when Susannah reaches over and squeezes his rear end. Lucky jumps slightly, but no one else in the elevator seems to notice. Susannah looks primly straight ahead, the slightest glint of amusement in her eye.

On the way to the Church of the Rock, everyone gets separated. Lucky is driving the van with Tom Ed, the M&M twins, and

Sam Bender aboard. He has no idea where his wife and parents are, just trusts that someone put them in one of the trailing cars; he heard Tom Ed tell one of the volunteers working for the campaign to look out for them or he'd jerk a knot in his ass. Lucky hopes that Susannah and his parents don't wind up in the same car. He's fairly certain that Susannah won't turn to them and say, "Oh, by the way, your son and I are screwing like rabbits," but he dreads the idea of someone like Susannah judging them, focusing on their warts. Hell, he thinks to himself, that's my job, being judgmental.

The Church of the Rock is east of Charlotte, and Lucky can see that Tom Ed is not going to get there by two o'clock. It seems to him that half of Charlotte must be either headed for the rally or driving around aimlessly.

But Tom Ed, who is usually as jumpy as a cat when everything doesn't work out the way he planned it, is sitting calmly in his front passenger's seat. He waves and smiles at people with signs alongside the road as the van gets closer to the church. It occurs to Lucky that Tom Ed knew exactly how long the trip would take, and that he also knew that this rally would not start without him.

They arrive at the church at 2:15, and it's 2:25 by Lucky's watch before Tom Ed makes his way up to the head table.

The rally has grown so that it can only be held outside. The Church of the Rock does not look like Lucky's idea of a church. It is all sharp angles and glass, its modern architecture a contradiction to its traditional tenets. It's set a quarter of a mile off the state high-way, and most of that quarter mile seems to be covered with fold-ing chairs. Where the chairs run out, people are standing or they're sitting on blankets. The sanctuary, which everybody is facing, is flanked by two equally modern buildings set at ninety-degree angles to it, so that much of the crowd is enveloped inside a U, which helps cut off some of the late-October wind.

There are signs everywhere, some of them homemade and some of them obviously done by professionals. Lucky can see the Sweatt for Governor campaign's handiwork in some of the more promi-nent ones.

Every North Carolina state trooper who isn't at a college foot-ball game seems to be here, too, mixed in with sheriff's deputies and members of the church's youth group. With their clean-scrubbed faces and creased uniforms, the kids appear to Lucky like something between Boy Scouts and Hitler Youth. They're selling T-shirts with likenesses of the late Reverend Gary Thorne on them. Many people in the crowd have signs with the same picture on them. Underneath, on the T-shirts and the signs, the lettering reads CALLED UP TO JESUS.

"I wonder who they had to send down when they called him up," Barry says and gets a sharp look from a deputy sheriff nearby.

Tom Ed shakes hands with everyone at the head table. Jesse Helms was supposed to attend, but he had to cancel, making Tom Ed the main attraction. There are scores of ministers, a few county commissioners, and two state senators. There are two long rows reserved for and filled by members of the news media.

Harry Mavredes says he thinks there may be twenty-five thousand people here.

Lucky sits through approximately forty-five verses of "When the Saints Go Marching In" and another thirty or so of "When the Roll Is Called Up Yonder," and by three, the crowd is rocking. Lucky, the M&M twins, Sam, Susannah, and three or four others are standing to one side of the main table. From here, they are looking directly into the sun, which is fast approaching the treetops to the west. Lucky locates his parents and Barbara in the third row of the reserved seats, just as the speeches start.

A man in a red robe prays for fifteen minutes, asking God to for-give all the poor sinners who allow innocent babies to be murdered. From his tone, Lucky wonders if the only forgiveness he wants for Nate Crowell and "the others who blaspheme Your word" isn't per-haps a spot in hell where it's only 900 degrees instead of 1,000.

For the next hour, every politician and minister there says more or less the same thing. And then it's Tom Ed's turn.

He steps up just as the sun is about to disappear behind the educational building that is the west wing. His gray hair is blowing slightly in the chilling late-afternoon breeze, and Lucky can see the wrinkles, mostly smile wrinkles that make his face an inviting one even when he's as somber as a judge.

He doesn't say anything for perhaps thirty seconds, which seems much longer with the large crowd holding its collective breath and waiting for something to justify the day.

Finally, he starts, saying it one word at a time:

"The Lord giveth . . . and the Lord taketh away. . . ." And he's quiet for another thirty seconds. Lucky can see that Harry and Barry are getting uneasy.

"But who are we," he starts out, "but who are *we* to decide we'll take away what the Lord gave? Who made us God? Who gave us the right to take the most precious gift of our heavenly father and . . ." Here, he walks back to where there are several candles burning, protected from the wind on three sides by glass. He has one hand on his tiny lapel microphone, and with the other he reaches inside and pinches the flame to snuff it out, ". . . ext*in*guish it, crush that bright flame before it even has a chance to shine?"

A few people in the crowd murmur amens, and there's a general nodding of heads.

Tom Ed has a way of slowly picking up volume and momentum in his speeches, and Lucky knows he has them going now. In another couple of minutes, they're on their feet, most of them, cheering. With a little help from some of the campaign volunteers, a chant begins: "Tom Ed! Tom Ed! Tom Ed!" It gets louder, its rhythm quickening. Inside that peninsula, the sound echoes around so that it overlaps like ocean waves.

Tom Ed is forced to stop for a few seconds. Several people try to rush the stage, and the police move in to keep them back. Tom Ed holds his hands up as if to calm the multitudes, and they are stilled enough for him to finish his speech.

The choir begins to play "Amazing Grace." Tom Ed stays on stage, leading the singing. It is getting close to sunset, and some of the crowd has lighted candles. Many of them are crying.

When Tom Ed departs, he has to walk through a part of the crowd. Instead of rushing him to shake hands or seek his autograph, the faithful step back, clearing a path. A couple of children reach out and touch him, trying not to be noticed, as he walks by.

When he finally slips into the van, Tom Ed sags into his seat, closes his eyes for a moment, and says, "Well, Bo, if the Democrats can top that, they can have the damn governor's mansion."

Back at the hotel, everyone in the Sweatt for Governor party is trying hard not to jump into each other's arms and start the victory celebration. It would be bad luck, and they've all, individually and as a group, been upbraided by Tom Ed on occasion for overconfidence. Barry Maxwell passes Lucky and Barbara in the hall and, holding his right hand belt high, clenches his fist triumphantly. Barbara whispers, as he walks past, that he looks like he's swallowed the canary.

Barbara and Lucky go to the suite where Tom Ed, Tommy, Genie, and several workers are toasting everything in sight and watching the news on TV. Two of the three network stations have their local news on at six o'clock on Saturdays, and they both seem to spend about half their reports on the rally. At the end of the segment, the anchor on one of the stations says, "I don't have access to any instant political polls, but it says here that this just about wraps it up for Tom Ed Sweatt." A cheer emerges from the suite.

Tommy starts regaling a couple of the younger volunteers with stories about Tom Ed as a boy. They're humoring him, and Tom Ed looks over once in a while, trying to control his father with his eyes.

Tommy has had a couple of plastic cups full of champagne. He's not a drinker anymore, and it's gone to his head.

"What you looking over here at me for?" he asks Tom Ed as Genie tries to shush him. "You act like I'm a young-un or somethin'. You think you can even tell me when I can be on TV and when I can't."

Tom Ed gives his father a quizzical look and is about to ask him something when Harry Mavredes bursts into the room. He looks at the TV, then switches channels. It's just past six-thirty, and WCHA's news has just started.

"Yeah, let's see if they love us, too," Tom Ed says, then starts to get the gist of what the serious-looking reporter is saying. He's seen the man before. Mickey something.

## 20

Tommy was on the couch, watching a World War II movie with Audie Murphy in it, when the doorbell rang.

Genie was in the kitchen, making sandwiches for their lunch, and when the bell rang a second time, Tommy realized that he'd have to answer it himself.

He rose from the couch, steadying himself for a couple of seconds where he stood, then ambled toward the front door, ready to run off another salesman or charm another schoolkid selling raffle tickets or candy.

The man standing on his front deck was handsome, and familiar from somewhere. Two other men stood on the walkway, a few steps back. One of them was holding a camera.

"Mr. Sweatt? I'm Mickey Dole."

"Oh, sure." Tommy made the connection. "The TV fella." He wished that some of his old cronies from Mingo Road could see this.

"Mr. Sweatt," Mickey said, pinning Tommy with his most earnest look, "I'll cut right to the chase. I don't want to waste your time. I'm not a reporter here looking for some story for tomorrow's news. But I've worked a deal with one of the big stations (although Mickey didn't know exactly which one yet) to do a documentary on the people behind the governor, the people who made him what he is. His family."

Mickey Dole had done his homework. He'd read the features that everybody from the *Port Campbell Post* to *The Washington Post* had done on Tom Ed Sweatt. He'd read about how Tommy put a ball in the twins' crib when they were infants, pitched overhand to them when they weren't even school age. He'd read the stories about the daily lectures Tommy gave Tom Ed about succeeding, the ones where Tom Ed said he'd never have made it without his parents, and most of the specific stories were about Tommy rather than Genie. Mickey was surprised to learn that the other twin was driving his brother around North Carolina during the campaign, and he logged that one away for possible future use.

As Mickey recounted some of the old stories now, as if they'd always been part of his memory bank rather than the result of some last-minute cramming, Tommy's eyes grew noticeably brighter. He was sure he'd been right: The old man loved the limelight at least as much as that fathead son of his.

"Mr. Sweatt," he went on, "what we're looking at here is something that would run after the election, which we know Tom Ed's going to win, something that would be a testament to Tom Ed Sweatt and the stock he came from. It would be on the American Dream."

"Have you cleared this with Tom Ed?"

The voice came from behind Tommy, who turned around to face Genie. Mickey Dole introduced himself to the pleasant-looking woman who stepped out of Tommy's shadow to repeat the question.

"We've had a problem with that," Dole said, shaking his head. He paused. "Look, I know how it is with fathers and sons. My father, there's more to him than there will ever be to me, and it's just gotten so recently that I don't treat him like he's going to break something or say something wrong when we're in public together."

Actually, Mickey Dole hadn't seen his father in fifteen years, wasn't even sure that he was still alive.

Tommy nodded his head, sadly. "He don't want me to be on TV. Says I'll embarrass him."

Mickey Dole nodded with equal sadness. "He says he's afraid you'll mess things up. Wouldn't even agree to it when I told him it would be after the election. I guess everybody does things to their parents that they look back on later and regret. I know I did."

"Well, young people can be thoughtless," Tommy said.

"If Tom Ed doesn't want us to be interviewed," Genie said, final as a period, "then we won't be interviewed."

"Yes, ma'am," Mickey Dole said, and the door closed on a sad-looking Tommy Sweatt.

Mickey even knew what time Tommy took his daily walk.

He and his crew had lunch, then parked two blocks away. When Tommy came striding along, Mickey got out by himself.

"Mr. Sweatt," he said.

Tommy stopped.

Mickey handed him a sheet of paper with the name and address of the local Holiday Inn on it and a room number written in pencil.

"I don't want to come between fathers and sons, or cross you and Mrs. Sweatt, but we've got to do this story, and we think it'd be a lot better with you in it. It can't hurt Tom Ed, because it's going to come after the election. And it can be just you if you want; Mrs. Sweatt doesn't have to come."

Tommy looked at the card, started to say something.

"What time does your wife expect you back, Mr. Sweatt?"

Tommy thought about it.

"She's taking a nap. . . . But I could go back, take the car like I was going back out to visit at the store . . ."

"Well," said Mickey, "I don't want you to do something that'll make folks mad at you."

"Hell," Tommy said, "I'm always doing that anyhow. Everybody treats me like I'm some kind of baby or something, got to be watched all the time."

"If you'll meet me at, say, three o'clock at that room, I promise you we'll have you out of there by five."

"Hell, yeah," Tommy said. "I'll be there."

Back in the truck, the fatter of the two assistants glumly handed Mickey a twenty-dollar bill.

"Sucker bet," Dole said.

Tommy left Genie a note, the way she always asked him to: Gone to the store. Which meant gone to gas with his old cronies.

He drove to the Holiday Inn and found the room without much trouble. Mickey Dole was waiting for him and led him to a conference room where they'd set up a makeshift studio.

"Of course," Mickey said, "it'd be much better if we could do this in your home, but . . ."

"Yeah," Tommy said and shook his head. Why wouldn't anyone want to be on television?

They started out just talking. It took Dole a few minutes to loosen Tommy up, to persuade him to look at him and just "be yourself."

When the old man seemed relaxed enough, Dole gave the cameraman the signal to start recording.

They talked about Tom Ed's young life, and about Tommy's life, even back in Purcells. It's a shame, Mickey thought to himself at one point. This actually would have made a good interview, anyhow.

Tommy was careful to say "blacks" instead of "coloreds," he tried to keep from telling any embarrassing stories about Tom Ed's childhood, he was vague but not too vague when it came to Lucky.

"Okay," Mickey Dole said after more than an hour, "that ought to do it." He and the cameraman exchanged glances.

He unbuttoned his shirt and undid his tie, and he could see Tommy relax noticeably.

"You know," Mickey said, lighting a cigarette, "just between you and me, I really, really want to see Tom Ed Sweatt elected governor. Even if we weren't doing this documentary, I'd want it. My people sweated blood for generations, working in mills and on tobacco farms, watching the fat cats stay fat."

Actually, Mickey Dole's father had run a rather successful insurance agency before he disappeared one day with his secretary.

Tommy nodded enthusiastically.

"Yeah, it's time to throw the rats out of the damn barn."

Mickey let out a line of blue smoke.

"Yeah," he said, "we were all sweating bullets when this abortion stuff came out. We were scared to death it would fall in the wrong hands. Even if she was just two months along, it would've been trouble."

Tommy sat back up in his seat.

"Abortion? I don't know what you're talkin' about. Tom Ed ain't paid for no abortion."

Mickey waved his hands dismissively.

"We're not on the air now. Isn't anything to it, anyhow. Pennyante stuff like that. Hell, even JFK dropped his pants once in a while. How about Bill Clinton? You get a good-looking guy, powerful like Tom Ed; hey, it's gonna happen."

"It was probably some secretary or something," Tommy muttered. He hadn't asked Lucinda who it was; he'd been too shocked at the time.

"Well, I reckon we'll all be glad when the election is over and it won't matter anymore."

Tommy looks over at the camera. The cameraman has moved away from it, but Tommy isn't sure.

"That thing's off, right? This is just us?"

Mickey Dole and his two assistants both nod.

Tommy hesitates, then sits back and swings his arm over the back of the chair.

"I tell you," he says, "when I first heard that Tom Ed had knocked up some girl and paid to have it took care of, I like to of died."

He leans forward, motions for Mickey to come closer.

"Do you know who told me about it? His wife! Can you imagine how happy she was?"

Mickey laughs appreciatively. Out of the corner of his eye, he sees the cameraman surreptitiously move the camera a little to frame the subject better.

"Good lord," he says, "you mean that Lucinda Sweatt told you about the abortion Tom Ed paid for?"

"I swear it's the truth."

"I reckon ol' Tom Ed was pretty worried about the Church of the Rock finding out about that. That'd just about do him in, wouldn't it?"

Tommy nods. "Yeah, I reckon there'll be hell to pay if it finally does come out.

"You know, though, I don't think Tom Ed really believes all that crap, about abortions and all. It's just people tryin' to tell other people what to do. But you know what it takes to get elected in this state."

Mickey Dole nods sympathetically. Thank you, God, he says silently.

They talk for a while longer. Dole has to point out the time to Tommy, who has fifteen minutes to get home.

"When will this be on?" he asks on the way out.

"Soon as the election is over, we'll let you know," Mickey says, shaking his hand and winking. "Then you can surprise Tom Ed."

"Damn right."

When Tommy leaves, Mickey Dole and the two assistants exchange high fives.

"You can cut that thing off for real now, Bubba," Mickey says. "Let's go sell somebody some videotape."

## 21

Lucky often has dreams in which he's sure what he's experiencing isn't real but he can't wake himself up. He has that feeling now, and for what seems several minutes, he tries to regain reality.

He sees Tommy on television, chatting as casually with Mickey Dole as he might with his family, telling a mid-major television market about how Tom Ed Sweatt, darling of the religious right, paid for an abortion.

No one speaks until after they see Tommy say, "You know what it takes to get elected in this state," and wink toward Dole.

Lucky hears a low moan from behind him. He turns to see a real-life Tommy rocking backward and forward on the edge of one of the double beds.

"He said they wouldn't . . ." Tommy starts. "Not 'til after the election. . . . I was misquoted."

Tom Ed laughs a dry, hard laugh.

"Misquoted. That's good, old man. Misquoted. I reckon they must have gotten an actor to dress up like you, too, 'cause I know that can't be you I just saw on my television screen, 'cause even *you* ain't stupid enough to say what that ignorant son of a bitch on TV just said. Are you? ARE YOU?!"

Tom Ed moves for his father, who falls to the floor at Genie's feet as if in supplication.

"Leave him alone!" Genie shouts. It's the first time Lucky has heard her raise her voice in a long time. "He couldn't help it. They tricked him."

Tom Ed stares down at his father, his face purple with rage. Finally, he does something that gives Lucky one last hope that what he's seeing isn't real: He spits on Tommy, who flinches as if he's been struck. Then, while Harry tries to ask him if what Tommy said could possibly be true, Tom Ed takes two quick steps and swings his right hand as hard as he can at the door frame.

They can hear the bones crack. Tom Ed crumples a bit, his breath taken away by the pain. For several seconds, no one dares come near him. Finally, Lucky is convinced that this nightmare is for real. He walks over to his brother, puts his arm around him, and leads him out the door. Harry, Barry, and Sam Bender follow.

"Don't let anybody see me," Tom Ed whispers when he gets his breath at last. They're on the third floor, and Sam is able to find a staircase that leads out to a side entrance, one the news media isn't likely to notice.

Barry Maxwell gets the van and meets them outside within ten minutes. They help Tom Ed into the front passenger's seat; Harry and Sam get in as well, and Lucky starts to, but he notices the ambulance that's been by the front entrance of the hotel, the one he first thought someone had called for Tom Ed.

Lucky is standing by the door next to Tom Ed. He's ready to close it and get in the back, but something about the ambulance scares him.

He reaches inside and puts his hand on Tom Ed's neck.

"I have to see about Momma and all," he tells his brother. "I'll be at St. Mary's in half an hour, I promise."

Tom Ed moans and lies back in the seat.

As soon as the van has slipped out of the back of the parking lot, Lucky is running toward the front of the building, where a crowd has gathered around the ambulance.

As he gets closer, he can see Barbara standing beside the open back of the ambulance, her arm around Genie. He doesn't see Tommy anywhere, but he's already sure he knows where he is.

He gets there as they're about to close the door, telling the two women that they can follow in their car.

Lucky puts his hand on the back door of the ambulance.

"I'm his son," he tells the attendant. "I'll ride back here with him." It isn't a question, and no one resists him. Lucky isn't sure if his father is alive, but it hardly seems to matter.

Later, Barbara tells Lucky that Tommy never got off the floor, finally lying down between the two beds. Everyone left the room except her and Genie, and it took them a couple of minutes to realize that Tommy's pain was more than mental. By the time they called the ambulance, they were pretty sure it was a heart attack.

The ambulance is impeded at first by gawkers near the entrance. Some newspaper and television reporters, dispatched even before the WCHA newscast was finished, have arrived, and two photographers have their cameras pressed against the side of the ambulance, snapping pictures of Tommy, who seems barely conscious. When Lucky sees them, he slaps violently against the glass. They jump back for a second, then continue shooting. Lucky tries to memorize their faces so he can kill them when he has time.

They finally escape, also headed for St. Mary's, less than two miles away.

Tommy is silent except for occasional groans. Once, though, when the pain seems to ease, he looks up at Lucky.

"Is Tom Ed okay?" he says weakly. Lucky tells him that he only has a broken hand, that he'll be fine.

"They lied to me," Tommy says. "They said the camera wasn't on."

Lucky tells him that it's okay, hoping his father will be quiet until they get to the hospital, because he doesn't know what to say back to him.

Tommy, though, seems determined to speak.

"Lucky," he says, and it seems to his son that it's been years since he's actually said his name. "Old Lucky." He pats Lucky on his arm. His hand is shaking. "I was just as proud of you as I was of Tom Ed. You couldn't help it. I couldn't neither."

Lucky tells him again that everything's okay, but he can't be sure, then or ever, what is meant by the uncustomarily Delphic words of Tommy Sweatt.

When he said "I was just as proud of you" did he mean before Lucky got sick, or was he already thinking of himself in the past tense? When he said Lucky couldn't help it, was he absolving his son from the guilt of contracting polio, or was he telling him he was forgiven for not sending a Father's Day card for the previous twenty-nine years? When he said he couldn't help it, either, did he mean he couldn't keep his son from getting polio, or did he mean he couldn't help treating Lucky like the distant runner-up in a two-person popularity contest?

Barbara has told Lucky for years that he thinks too much, that some things are better forgotten, but he might as easily forget his name.

Lucky walks beside the stretcher into the hospital, then waits for Genie and Barbara. They go to cardiac care; when they seem to have Tommy stabilized, Lucky goes in search of Tom Ed.

He hasn't been admitted under his name, but Lucky spots Sam coming out of the coffee shop, and he takes him to a corner of the emergency room area, to a small room manned by one of the campaign's bodyguards.

Inside, a doctor is setting Tom Ed's hand, which he's broken in several places. They won't have to keep him overnight, but they want to observe him for a couple of hours because he seems disoriented, almost in shock. Most of the talk among the M&M twins and Sam is about how to get him past the news media and out of town.

Lucky goes over to his brother, who is lying down on a cot, barely conscious from the painkillers they've given him.

Lucky pulls up the only chair in the room and puts his right hand on Tom Ed's left one.

"Where you been, Bo?" Tom Ed croaks. "Where's Momma?"

Lucky tries to give his brother a hint that there might be more bad news.

"Well," he says, as casually as he can say it, "the old man got a little overexcited, I guess, and they took him here, too, just to be on the safe side."

"The old man," Tom Ed says, and he looks as if he wants to strike out at something with his good hand. Lucky keeps a firm grip on it. "The goddamn old man. I don't reckon he could have screwed things up any worse if he had sat down and planned it."

Tom Ed laughs, startling Lucky.

"Bo," he says, "do you think this means I won't be getting most of the Church of the Rock vote?"

Lucky stifles a laugh, and his brother drops into sleep with a slight smile.

The day catches up with Lucky and he dozes off, still holding on to Tom Ed's hand. When the phone wakes him, he realizes that he must have been asleep for almost an hour. Tom Ed is knocked out from the painkillers and doesn't stir.

It's Barbara. He doesn't even know how she got the room number.

"You'd better get down here, honey," she says, and Lucky is immediately awake. It isn't the slightly strange tone so much as the "honey" that scares him. He and Barbara love each other deeply, but they aren't given to endearments except in cases of emergency.

Lucky is already out the door when he realizes that his bad leg has fallen asleep; he has to catch himself on the door frame to keep from falling. Barry is standing outside talking to the guard. He looks as if he hasn't yet run out of ideas.

"When are they going to release him?" Lucky asks.

"Soon as he wakes up, I guess. Look, do you know anything about what that . . . about what he was saying?"

Lucky just stares at him, saying nothing. As soon as his leg regains some feeling, he limps off down the hall.

A couple of turns take him back toward the nurses' station, where he left Tommy, Genie, and Barbara. The hairs are standing up on the back of his neck.

He's three doors down from Tommy's room when he sees that it is as bad as it could be. In the hall, Genie is crying into Barbara's arms. Barbara sees him and gets ready to pass his mother to him, but Lucky goes right past her into the room.

Somebody has already come and put Tommy in what looks like a very large Ziplock bag. He's lying under plastic, looking as peaceful as Lucky has ever seen him. He knows that the only other time he will be able to touch his father again will be after Tommy has been drained and waxed by some undertaker, and it suddenly seems very important to make contact one last time.

Lucky unzips the bag far enough to expose Tommy's face. His eyes are closed, and he already doesn't look like himself. It takes Lucky a few seconds to understand why. It isn't the pallor, and death itself hasn't twisted his expression.

It's the complete letting go. In life, neither of his sons recalled ever seeing Tommy Sweatt truly relax. His jaw was always out, his teeth were always clenched, his brow had creases that now seem to have all but disappeared.

Lucky touches his father's already-cooled cheek. His hand runs over a ridge, right over his cheekbone, where one of Lucky's last line drives leveled him. He bled like a stuck pig, his son remembers, but he seemed as proud as either of the twins had ever seen him.

"Rest in peace, old man," Lucky mutters, stroking him one more time before closing the bag. But that won't really do it, he knows. He wonders if anything will, but he feels he has to make the effort. He leans close to the dead man's face and whispers to it:

"Rest in peace, Daddy."

Lucky spends a mostly useless hour trying to comfort Genie. Sam has somehow heard the news and comes by to offer his sympathy.

"Does Tom Ed know?" Lucky asks him.

"No. They got him out of here before we found out."

He tells Lucky that his brother has been taken to another hotel, across town, until they can figure out what to do next. Lucky gets directions, kisses his mother and Barbara, and leaves them to sign all the papers and start making funeral plans.

The Ramada room is in Harry Mavredes's name. When Lucky reaches it, it is unlocked and cracked. Inside, Harry is on the phone to someone else within the campaign, talking as quietly as he can but with great intensity.

To Lucky, Harry looks much as he did eleven days ago, the first time he saw him, except with the volume turned down.

Eleven days, Lucky thinks to himself, and shakes his head.

Tom Ed is stretched out on one of the two beds, lying on his back and staring at the ceiling. His right hand is wrapped in an enormous cast.

He sees his brother and stirs slightly.

"Well, Bo, you think Knox Cameron has started the victory party yet?"

Lucky says he doesn't know. Then he blurts it out, wanting to just get past this somehow.

"Tom Ed, there's some bad news, and I don't know how to tell it except just to be done with it."

To Lucky, his brother resembles a dog that has been hit by a car, and someone has to put it out of its misery.

"It's Daddy," Lucky says, plowing on. "It's Daddy, Tom Ed," and Tom Ed seems to know immediately what it is, as surely as Lucky did when Barbara called him honey.

"Oh my God," he says, turning back to stare at the ceiling. "Oh my God oh my God oh my God . . ." and on and on, louder and louder, until Harry Mavredes has to put down the phone and close the door.

Lucky motions for Harry to leave, which he reluctantly does, and Tom Ed finally calms down.

"Where's Momma?" he says. The way he says it, Lucky feels he is looking to be comforted as much as he is to comfort.

"They're still at the hospital, probably, signing papers and things."

"Did he say anything?"

Lucky tells Tom Ed that he asked if he was all right.

"You know he loved you," Lucky adds, because he can't think of anything else. "You know he thought the sun rose and set on you."

"He drove me crazy," Tom Ed says. "I reckon he drove us all crazy, including himself. But you know, he did it because he loved us. He wanted us to be something."

Lucky feels he has to say it:

"You can't blame yourself, Tom Ed. He did this to himself. You know that."

Tom Ed smiles slightly, staring straight ahead.

"I know that, Bo. In my mind, I know that. But in my heart, I'd give every cent I've got to have about two minutes with him."

He breaks down, and so does Lucky.

In about five minutes, Harry is back, sticking his head in tentatively.

Tom Ed looks up.

"Get the van," he says to Harry. "We're going back to Port Campbell."

"We can't do that," Harry protests. "We can still pull this thing out, Tom Ed. You can convince them that he wasn't in his right mind . . ."

Lucky moves as quickly as he's moved in years. He puts his right hand over Harry's mouth and pushes him against the door.

"Don't say anything else," he says, his voice tight and strangled. "Please, don't say anything else. Give me the keys to the van and don't let me hear one more word from you. Please."

Harry gives up the keys and leaves quickly.

"Well, Bo," Tom Ed says, rousing himself slowly off the bed, "let's go home."

## 22

**H**orace Morgan heard about it at his club Saturday evening. The condolences for his candidate were given nervously, if at all, because just about everyone assumed there was a good chance the abortion was Susannah's. By Sunday morning, it would be confirmed.

Horace went home early and alone. There, he opened the bottle of Dom Perignon he'd been chilling, just in case, since Little Sonny told him that Mickey Dole had taken their bait. Horace opened the last tin of goose foie gras with truffles he'd had shipped down from New York and found some appropriate crackers, wishing you could find a good baguette in Durham on a Saturday night.

Sunday, he woke up with a mild hangover and only left his house to retrieve the newspaper. He read every word about Tom Ed Sweatt. He kept the TV on CNN most of the day; the news channel seemed to have invested most of its resources in the pursuit of what one somber commentator called "a story as real and earthy as America itself." Where, Horace Morgan wondered, do they get this shit?

Mickey Dole was interviewed at length. He'd heard of the abortion from a hospital employee, he said, just as Little Sonny Lineberger had instructed him to say, and he had felt compelled to ask Tom Ed's father about it, never imagining that he would reveal all.

Horace took three phone calls and thanked God for an unlisted number and an eight-foot fence with a gate that locked. Two of the calls were from members of the Sweatt for Governor campaign. He made it quite clear to them that he was no longer affiliated in any way with the candidate.

The third call was from Little Sonny Lineberger. Horace had been halfway expecting it.

"We have to talk," Little Sonny said. There was iron and certainty in his voice.

"We're talking right now."

"About Mickey Dole, I mean, and not on the telephone."

Horace reached over to his desk drawer, and he proceeded to explain to Little Sonny, line by line, why they didn't "have" to talk, then or ever. He explained about the two witnesses he'd found while researching Little Sonny's case, ones he didn't use and was thankful the police didn't find. He explained that, just because he got Little Sonny out of one scrape, didn't mean there weren't people out there who knew too much.

"It would be tragic," Horace said, "if those two persons with whom I talked were to fall into the hands of the police. You might not have as good a lawyer next time."

There was a silence on the other end of the line.

Horace's voice came back, hard and pitiless.

"Leave me alone, you little cracker, and I might not send you to prison."

Little Sonny sputtered something about not trying to blackmail him, for God's sake, just wanted to talk, but Horace cut him off.

"If you ever call here again, you will go to prison." He said each word slowly, forcefully. He didn't even have to hang up on Little Sonny.

It was late afternoon when the electronic gate opened and Susannah's car passed through. A reporter outside on foot almost followed it in, then apparently thought twice about the NO TRESPASSING sign.

He waited for her to unlock the front door and come to him, in the study. He had just switched to the local news.

He looked her over. She had no makeup on, and she looked as if she had slept in her clothes. She seemed as close to helpless as Horace had ever seen her.

He motioned for her to come to him, and she came. She sat on his lap, her head on his shoulder, like a little girl who's dropped her candy, he thought. She was crying softly.

She turned slightly toward the TV, where an image of an ashen-faced Tom Ed Sweatt emerging from a van illuminated the room.

"Can you turn that thing off?" she asked, and he did.

They sat there in the fast-closing dark. Horace Morgan knew he would do this. He knew the humiliation that would follow, as long as they were together, and he knew that even this would not give him Susannah for all time. Horace thought to himself what a terrible thing it was, after all these years, to be vulnerable.

## ★★★ 23 ★★★

Genie has insisted on going back to their old home on Mingo Road to receive mourners. All Sunday afternoon, Monday, and Tuesday, people stream by, mostly the old people who knew the Sweatts when they lived there. Lucky realizes that Genie and Tommy never really had that many friends in their new home by the lake.

Felton is the only one of Tommy's siblings still living, and his brother's death hits him hard. Lucky finds him in a corner, wringing his leathery, shaking hands.

"Lord have mercy," he says when Lucky brings him a ham sandwich and some tea, "he wanted so much for you boys. He wanted so much."

Tom Ed stays at the old house until the funeral but avoids most of the mourners. Lucky and Barbara let their children, who hardly knew Tommy, stay in Willow Cove, but Tom Ed's sons are at the service. No one expects Lucinda to come, especially with all the TV and newspaper journalists lurking around, and she doesn't.

Tom Ed wants the minister of the First Baptist Church in Raleigh, a supporter of his, to conduct the sermon, but Genie insists that they use the Reverend Boyle, their old pastor at Mingo Road Baptist Church.

Reverend Boyle is almost eighty years old, but he knew Tommy, and Genie declares that she isn't going to let some hypocrite who never even met him preach over him. These are strong words for her, and Tom Ed seems to have lost the will to resist.

Wednesday is a cold, gray day. The church is full, but Lucky sees no one from the campaign, not even Susannah. All that seems a million miles away. The only outsiders appear to be reporters; Lucky has to pull Felton off one of them at the cemetery.

The Sweatts aren't buried in the large Glen Allen Memorial Park in Port Campbell, where just about everyone in Scots County seems to be buying plots. They still have their old graveyard on a low hill overlooking the river near Purcells, and that's where Tommy always declared he wanted to be buried. Genie tells her sons now to be sure she is buried here, too, with her husband.

It seems appropriate to Lucky that they are driving by Tommy's boyhood home on the way to the burial. The old house is in a field off from the main road; none of the children or grandchildren wanted any part of it. The ones who made it in the world moved as far away as they could, and the ones who didn't decided they'd rather be poor somewhere else, even if it was in a house trailer.

Tom Ed and Lucky used to hit fly balls to each other in the field between the house and the road, now consumed by broom straw and thistles. Sometimes, if enough cousins were around, they'd play a real game.

Lucky asks Tom Ed if he remembers the time they got into a fight with some of the cousins and he knocked two of Pervis Cope's teeth out with a rock. Tom Ed looks out across the field and says nothing.

Later, they return to Mingo Road. Tom Ed tells Kevin and Kyle that they can go on home, and they seem relieved.

Lucky and Barbara also sleep over that night, on sheets Genie stored away in the closets before she and Tommy moved to Westlake. Barbara and Lucky get his old room; Tom Ed has appropriated his. Lucky awakens at 3 A.M. to the sound of ice being forced out of an old metal tray. He follows the light to the kitchen.

"Can't sleep?" he asks Tom Ed, who is making a rather large mess trying to serve himself with one hand.

His brother silently shakes his head, and it seems for a minute that he forgets what he's doing. He shakes his head again, harder, as if he's trying to free it of cobwebs.

"Bo, I keep hoping I'm going to wake up and find out this ain't real. Find out that somebody knocked me out right after we got back to that hotel room Saturday afternoon and I'm just coming to . . ."

He's drifting again. Lucky sees that he's drinking a Pepsi to chase some Pepto-Bismol.

Lucky suggests that if Tom Ed can hang on a while, things are bound to improve. How, he's thinking to himself, can they do otherwise?

"Hang on," Tom Ed repeats, softly. "Hang on to what, Bo? Hang on to the memory of the old man the last time we were together? Hang on to the belief that I probably killed him? I tell you what: I ain't in the hanging-on mode right now. I'm in the letting-go mode."

Lucky tells him that Tommy brought it on himself, but Tom Ed isn't listening anymore.

It hadn't been pretty. By Sunday night, CNN was broadcasting the whole morbid story to a rapt nation: Antiabortion candidate pays for his mistress's abortion and is exposed, on television, by his own father; father has heart attack and dies; mistress turns out to be the wife of one of his chief supporters.

The M&M twins try to set up a last-hope press conference, on Monday afternoon from Port Campbell, but Tom Ed won't even talk to them, tells them he'll sic the dogs on them if they come anywhere near him.

He tries to stay out of sight as much as possible, and a sympathetic sheriff's deputy helps as much as he can.

Tom Ed is finally persuaded to vote on Tuesday. He is in and out in less than five minutes. He exits the polling station warily to a long *zzzinnnggg* of cameras. He makes no pretense at bearing up: no broad smile, no victory sign, no thumbs-up. He holds his hand in front of his face as the cameras all flash at once, and when someone asks him for whom he voted, hoping for a brief return of the

Yosemite Sam bravado, he gives them a weak smile and hurries as fast as he can to the waiting car.

Lucky, helping Tom Ed into the car that will take them back to Mingo Road, hears a reporter say something just out of earshot, and several of his colleagues break into hearty laughter.

Tom Ed is sunk wearily into the passenger's seat, and Lucky thinks he's nodding off, when suddenly his brother's eyes shoot open.

"Bo," he says, "they love to see a poor boy screw up. Nothing makes 'em feel more superior than seeing us whipped."

The old place is one of the few homes in Scots County where the election results are not followed; there isn't a TV there anymore, even if they wanted to watch it. The mourners whisper among themselves, though, that it doesn't look good.

By nine o'clock, it's obvious that Tom Ed Sweatt is going to get something less than 35 percent of the vote, and that Knox Cameron is going to be the next governor of North Carolina. In the Democratic deluge, even Axel Sprague is defeated, by a black attorney from Southern Pines. Harry Mavredes, speaking for "Tom Ed Sweatt, whose great humanity made it impossible for him to put his political fortune before his family in this hour of loss," makes the concession speech he wrote himself. For once, his words get read exactly as he has written them.

Lucky, standing on the cold linoleum floor, tells Tom Ed that he can still be many things: rich, famous, happy. All he's really trying to do, though, is stall until the sun comes up again.

They talk awhile longer, and Lucky persuades his brother to do something made possible by disaster. Tom Ed seems devoid of will, open to any suggestion.

"Hell, Bo," he says finally with a shrug, "it can't hurt."

On Thursday morning, Barbara and Lucky's car resembles one of those luckless vehicles driven from Oklahoma to California during the Great Depression. The trunk and luggage rack are full of suitcases and bags, and what's left over is stuffed around and behind Barbara and Genie in the backseat.

Lucky actually had a harder time talking Genie into it than he did Tom Ed.

She kept saying that she'd be all right, that she just wanted to stay there on Mingo Road by herself for a few days, and who was going to take care of the ironing, and what about the senior citizens' meeting, and how was she going to be able to take care of all the paperwork about the will and all from somewhere up in Virginia?

Finally, Barbara takes her by the arm and tells her that she is going, that she and Lucky plan to take care of her for a while. Lucky thinks that it probably means more to Genie, coming from her daughter-in-law, that maybe she really won't be in the way. This time of year, the inn has many more rooms than customers, but Lucky figures Genie just needed someone to tell her: This is what you're going to do.

Tom Ed seems happy to be leaving the state of North Carolina for at least the immediate future. He makes one call at the pay phone at the Hit 'N' Run in Geddie as they're leaving. He stays on the phone for less than five minutes, and when he returns, he says he guesses that he's put gasoline and a match to all his bridges now.

Lucky tells Tom Ed that, unless Chris has pulled an upset of monumental proportions, the inn is about two weeks behind in wood chopping for the winter, and that he intends to put his new guest to work.

Tom Ed waves his cast at Lucky and says he'd better let him off right there. Lucky tells him that, until his hand heals, he can stack while Lucky splits. For a few seconds, Tom Ed thinks he's serious, and then everyone laughs, something the Sweatts hadn't done together in a long time.

They stay until Christmas. Kim and Chris are so good to Genie that Barbara asks them why they don't treat all adults, even their parents, with such respect and consideration, and Benny loves having a grandmother. They're all crazy about Tom Ed, who soon enough starts to regain his old spirit. Lucky finds himself getting a little jealous. He knows that, if he ever had Tom Ed's ability to make a room light up just by entering it, polio took that, too. Having that thought is worrisome, because he believed he had left self-pity in the dust years ago.

Then, one night right after Thanksgiving, Kim comes up to him while he's washing dishes and puts her arms around him from behind.

"Dad," she says, "do you know why I'm glad you're not like Uncle Tom Ed?"

He's so glad to be preferred that he hardly cares why, but he asks her anyhow.

"Because you're a gardener, and he's a flower."

Lucky has no clue as to where she picked that up. Kids, he thinks to himself. You think you're educating them, and the first thing you know, they're educating you.

In bed that night, he tells Barbara what Kim said. She laughs quietly and rolls over so that her head is on his chest.

"We're both gardeners," she says, "maybe because we never had any practice being flowers. I heard once that two gardeners could get along, and a gardener and a flower could get along, because the gardener could take care of the flower, but that two flowers didn't have a chance in hell."

Lucky tells her that he's too ugly to be a flower, anyhow, but that she will always be the prettiest rose in the garden.

This appears to be the right thing to say.


Tom Ed loses twenty pounds by Christmas. He does do a lot of work around Willow Inn as his hand heals, helping with repairs and raking. He comes to be a minor celebrity at the store in Willow Cove, and once in a while a reporter calls or comes by. When Dr. Nate Crowell gets a five-year sentence, with three suspended, after plea-bargaining the charges down to vehicular homicide, Tom Ed is in great demand, but he refuses to comment. Lucky and Barbara buy an answering machine, and the dogs take care of the drive-up interlopers.

But no matter how rosy-cheeked Tom Ed gets, no matter how much he declares that this is the life for him, no matter how much pain he might have taken on for life that Saturday in Charlotte, Lucky knows in the back of his mind that Tom Ed is still Tom Ed.

They have a good Christmas, under the circumstances. Genie cries some, and so do Lucky and Tom Ed, on Christmas Eve, but at least they're crying together. Genie and Tom Ed seem to have made their peace. Kevin and Kyle come up for a couple of days, and, sitting in the living room with a fire going and several Sweatts of different generations and ethnic backgrounds talking, playing computer games, or snoring within earshot, Lucky has more of a feel of family than he can ever remember.

The day after Christmas, Tom Ed and Lucky go for a walk up the side of Turkeycock Mountain, behind the inn. It's a forty-five-minute climb to the top, although it took Tom Ed an hour and a half the first time Lucky brought him along, while he was still sweating out barbecue and bourbon.

But now the twins are in step, on the same pace. They reach the top, from which they can look down on the inn and out to the interstate, where even on the day after Christmas the big trucks are grumbling up the grade.

They sit on the rough bench someone fashioned decades ago, and they don't speak for a while.

Finally, Tom Ed clears his throat.

"Bo," he says, "I been thinking. This might not be the end after all."

Lucky knows he means the end of politics, or at least ambition.

"I mean, we got more than a third of the vote, in spite of everything. Do you know what I'm thinking, Bo? I'm thinking the people of North Carolina haven't given up on old Tom Ed Sweatt. And I'm thinking I owe it to Daddy not to give up."

Tom Ed has taken to calling their late father "Daddy" after referring to him as Tommy for most of his life.

"What you think about that?" he asks, looking expectantly at Lucky.

This is what Lucky has been telling him off and on since the funeral, but he knows that Tom Ed has to figure it out himself, say it himself, before it's real. And if he's referring to himself in the third person again, Lucky knows it's real. Part of him wants his brother to do what he's been talking about doing for weeks and move to Willow Cove, even if Lucky does get uneasy when Tom Ed starts talking about development and golf courses and friends with big money.

But Lucky knows the one great immutable fact: Tom Ed is Tom Ed. Lucky can sit through a nine-inning baseball game and see something different every inning. Tom Ed's the type, even though he played the game, who's looking for a telephone by the fourth inning. As much as Lucky has enjoyed having him around, Tom Ed's restlessness makes him uncomfortable sometimes. Lucky sees how still he has become compared with his brother.

Lucky knows Tom Ed needs some action.

He has seen enough of the campaign to know that people don't want Integrity and Commitment. People want the room to light up. He even believes Tom Ed might have won the election if he could have somehow brazened it out, if he hadn't looked so whipped. That was what cost Tom Ed Sweatt the governorship of North Carolina, Lucky believes: a starch shortage.

They will forgive Tom Ed, a truth that galled Lucky to no end when they were teenagers and his brother could get away with anything by flashing a winning smile. Now, though, it seems a blessing to them both. And Lucky harbors the hope that a different Tom Ed Sweatt will come roaring back down there to seek the forgiveness they've been dying to smother him with since the election.

On the long November and December nights, the twins have talked and sometimes argued until well past midnight about poverty and justice and even the dreaded "A" word. Sometimes, Lucky thinks he's making progress.

But Lucky will wait and see. He knows you could put Tom Ed in a room between a holy roller and an atheist, and the holy roller and the atheist would both leave that room thinking Tom Ed agreed with them. It is his sustaining gift.

The parting comes soon enough. Genie thinks the senior citizens have gone on without her as long as they can. She plans to go back to the old place on Mingo Road as soon as she can get everything moved from Westlake.

Tom Ed, curiously, is renting, with an option to buy, one of the homes in Westlake that has been on the market for two years because of a cracked foundation.

"Hell, Bo," he says to Lucky, "if we dig the footings out and reinforce 'em, I think we can still save it. And if we can't, I'll get used to walking uphill to get to the living room."

Everyone kisses and hugs everyone else good-bye. Lucky walks around to the driver's side of the rental car and leans down to the open window. Tom Ed looks him in the eye, and Lucky sees, perhaps because he wants to, something new there, something deeper than what Tommy Sweatt had in mind.

"Bo," he says, "it isn't over yet. I'm fixing to turn words like Democrat and Republican upside-down. They're going to see a Tom Ed Sweatt that'll knock the old one right on his butt."

Lucky squeezes his arm, Tom Ed turns the ignition, and in a few seconds, he and Genie are gone, followed by a preternatural quiet.

They stand there, like someone's personalized family Christmas card, Lucky's arm around Barbara, with Kim and Chris on either side.

Lucky feels a tug on his trousers and looks straight down into the impatient face of Benny.

"Are you *ever* going to put up my basketball goal?" he asks, as exasperated as any six-year-old in the commonwealth of Virginia.

Lucky stifles a laugh and turns slowly toward the house, happy and thankful to be a gardener.